Bill & Tracie!
Follow your dream!
Alicia Stephens

MW00633952

SPURRED

to

JUMP

YEAR
of the
BOOK

ALICIA STEPHENS MARTIN

Copyright © 2022 Alicia Stephens Martin
All Rights Reserved.

Year of the Book
135 Glen Avenue
Glen Rock, PA 17327

ISBN: 978-1-64649-233-6 (paperback)
ISBN: 978-1-64649-234-3 (ebook)

Cover design: Pixelstudio

This is a work of fiction. Names, characters, businesses, places, events, locales, and incidents are either the products of the author's imagination or used in a fictitious manner. Any resemblance to actual persons, living or dead, or actual events is purely coincidental.

DEDICATION

To J.J., my forever daughter!

CHAPTER 1

"Wyatt Evans! When I get my hands on you, I'm going to ring your puny neck."

Wyatt squeezed the syringe in his palm. The boy and the man focused on catching him were the only two people left in the barn, home to several valuable thoroughbreds and high-priced show jumpers. Everyone else was outside on the platform waiting.

Wyatt could picture the scene as he'd witnessed it a hundred times. The stuttering ticket master, hardly able to announce, "*All a-ab-aboard,*" was most likely checking his stopwatch, the one with a gold dangling chain he kept tucked in his vest pocket to verify the train's arrival time. Various riders would be congregating on the makeshift wooden platform, gripping empty green and red velvet pouches. And the dark-haired lady would faint because her billowing breast puffed out the white ruffles of a corset tied too tight… or so that was her excuse. All of them were waiting, as Wyatt was supposed to be, for the train to thunder to a stop in less than five minutes.

"Do you know what it's like not to catch a breath?" Wyatt heard the man who was chasing him flip the light switch several times.

The boy couldn't run anymore. His boots were two sizes too big, and Wyatt almost tumbled as he dodged into a stall without checking, followed the wall, and crouched in the corner below the feed bucket.

The electricity had been cut off to prevent a power surge, and the barn was pitch black except for outside light streaming in through the sliding doors. The man hunting him had splayed them wide open upon entering. He slid the doors almost shut with a clang, leaving only a ruler of light slicing through the edges.

1

Trapped in the corner, the boy had never dreamt of being trampled to death at the ripe age of twelve by an angry horse. He'd clearly chosen the wrong stall—a temperamental stallion, and not just any stallion. Perhaps, this was a better fate than at the hands of Mr. Michael Prickler, "Sir Prick" for short, as everyone hissed behind his back. Sir Prick was rumored to have whipped the last boy to smithereens, and then like that he disappeared. Prick would surely savor squeezing Wyatt's neck to his suffocation.

Wyatt imagined the call to his mother as he held his breath hovering in the straw bedding he now shared with an agitated steed. "Mrs. Evans… we're sorry to inform you… your son is dead… a strike to the head by a hoof. Stupid boy entered a stallion's stall… he couldn't follow directions."

His mother, Wyatt hoped, would cry at least a little, knowing she was the guilty one who insisted he take the job. Afterward she would be ticked off, reminding herself Wyatt was the mirror image of the man she'd tagged as his loser father. Then she would worry how to pay for her daily habits now.

A hoof soaring above the boy's head, parting his red curls, almost splitting his skull like a watermelon, brought Wyatt to reality. He curled into his knobby knees, fisted the syringe tighter, and cradled his head in his arms—skeleton arms like the rest of his body that provided no protection against the mighty beast.

The horse snorted and stamped at him as if a snake were coiling in the corner about to strike.

"Please, buddy. Please, shhh. I mean you no harm," Wyatt pleaded in an anxious whisper to the horse.

The avenger neared. "I'm coming for you, boy. I know you dodged into a stall. Your fate is going to be just like your predecessor!"

Wyatt clasped his mouth to mask his heavy panting.

The ebony horse froze, then perked his ears in the direction of Prick's voice and the man's uneven gait, scuffling closer. Prick had one leg that dangled, so he was unable to lift and walk in a normal strut. As he approached, the left boot clawed the cement with an increasingly annoying scrape. There was another sound, too. A rumble. Wyatt could feel the straw quiver and the ground beneath him quake.

The train.

Wyatt eyed the steed and realized it was the Australian's horse—the black stallion, the one called Dundee. The boy had only ever dreamt of witnessing Dundee in the flesh. A poster of this horse and his famous Australian owner hung above his bed in the subsidized apartment on Fifth Street. Here Wyatt was balled in the corner under the stallion's powerful legs.

The horse's massive neck arched forward and rummaged his muzzle into the boy's red tufted curls. Then he powered his head straight up in one motion and flared his nostrils as if swirling Wyatt's aroma into the air. He inhaled again for a better sense of the intruder who'd invaded his stall.

Suddenly, Prick's thick fingers gripped the bar above Wyatt's head. "You little toad, can't follow directions. Now hand it over."

Perhaps it was the odor of Prick's cigarette—a permanent appendage to his lip—that irritated the steed, causing the horse to press his muzzle to the iron bars. Or perhaps it was the deafening whistle, announcing the train.

Wyatt attempted to stand, to reveal himself, but the horse stepped forward and planted a hoof, snagging the edge of his borrowed, oversized boots. The boy clutched his mouth tighter, digging his nails into his cheeks to prevent a leaking scream. Dundee's hoof was the size of his thigh. Wyatt was imprisoned, unable to move.

The horse exchanged a glance with the boy, and for an instant Wyatt thought, *Are you trying to protect me?*

The horse pinned his ears as the man faced him dead on through the iron bars. Sir Prick blew a cloud of smoke directly up Dundee's muzzle. The stallion snorted and Wyatt felt the spray of wetness shower over him.

"Get back, beast. That'll teach ya... you only demonstrated how stupid you are... like the boy." Prick swirled the cigarette in a circle at the horse as a form of defense. "Damn failures, including the ticket master. Now, Wyatt Evans, you will pay." Prick hooked the stall door, then edged it open.

Unexpectedly, Wyatt spied movement on the barn wall as the twelve inches of light radiating from the main door expanded out in a V. The entry to the aisleway was opening again. Like the eclipse of the sun, a shadow of a man emerged. Prick stopped, then flicked his head in that direction.

Dundee broke the silence with an ear-piercing scream, proceeding to prance in a circle. Wyatt, now freed, slithered up the wall to peer over the edge between the bars. An immense shadow lurched across the doorway. Muscular legs slightly bowed proceeded toward them in a steady rhythmic jingle of spurs.

He knew it was the Australian, Jaxson Bay. Wyatt's heart raced faster. Jaxson's kangaroo hat tipped, shadowing his face except for stern lips. Dressed in khaki pants, his off-white shirt was partially unbuttoned, revealing powerful chest muscles and a whip curled on his belt. In his hand, he clenched a rope halter.

"Well, Jaxson Bay." Prick cleared his throat and pointed his finger in the air.

Wyatt eyed the older man's leathered face, wrinkled from repetitive visits to the Caribbean on his private island. Prick was quite a hideous man inside and out, and Wyatt ducked in fear.

Prick continued, "I hear the train approaching the depot... Isn't that where you're supposed to be?"

The Australian didn't utter a word.

Prick made the throaty noise again. "Do you hear me? You have one more chance."

Wyatt ascended the wall for another peek in time to see the Australian angle his hat to the left and cock an ear toward the outside.

Something was wrong, and he could see the Australian sensed the same. Wyatt thought the engine's steam should be releasing by now, with screeching of the metal wheels as the engineer cranked the brakes to a stop. Instead, the thundering energy of the train seemed to be building momentum, rumbling stronger.

The Australian stepped toward Prick.

Prick sent his arm into the stall like a rocket in search of Wyatt's neck. "Boy, you are mine, including the contents in your hand."

Another man spanned the doorway behind Jax.

"The tr-tr-train… it's not st-stoppp-stopping. S-something is wrong!" It was the stuttering ticket master. His blundering didn't stop the claw-like hand which surrounded Wyatt's neck.

"Boy, you are no good, not to mention this freaking horse."

Wyatt, paralyzed from horror, could only watch as the jaws of the black stallion chomped closed on the man's forearm. Dundee had intercepted.

Prick echoed a scream that melded with the roaring train. His cheeks flushed with fury, madder than a hornet. He raised a fist to swing at the jaw biting down on his arm.

Wyatt could only think to fall back, gliding his shoulder along the powerful horse's body. When he reached the rounded rump of shining black fur, Wyatt lifted his hand. With a simultaneous whisper, "Sorry, boy," Wyatt slapped Dundee with every muscle of sixty pounds. "Ya, boy. Ya!"

Dundee powered out of the stall, plowing into Prick who tumbled to the ground, struggling to regain his balance like a turtle on its back.

The Australian, instantly prepared for the galloping stallion, noosed its neck with the rope halter, latched his one hand onto the mane and mounted bareback. The duo raced past the stuttering ticket master, out the barn doors onto the platform.

Wyatt shoved the syringe deep in his pocket. He would take the evidence to his death. Carefully he scooted by Prick, almost falling on top, but somehow adrenaline kept him afoot.

The platform was a frenzy of satchels flying open, people darting in every direction, papers flying amidst bloodcurdling screams. The train appeared to be a mere fifty feet from its destination and had not slowed. Its metal wheels against the tracks screeched and sparked as the whistle sounded, scattering the awaiting crowd like a colony of angry ants. People criss-crossed in front of Wyatt's view as his eyes bounced in search of Jax and Dundee.

Subsequently the ticket master bellowed, "Thereeeee there." He was pointing at a dark-haired lady sprawled out on the tracks ahead.

Wyatt's eyes captured Jax and Dundee leaping along the edge of the rail like a balancing act. One misstep and they both would fall several feet onto the track's steel and gravel.

The maneuvering was precise until Jax reached the lady hollering in panic because her shoe was imprisoned in the rails. Jax cued Dundee to jump, wrapping his legs tighter.

The black balked, sucking back as he had many times before, leaving Jax no choice. Jaxson did what any brave man could... there was no refusal. He added a pressure with a slight spur this time.

"Come on, boy. Come on," Wyatt muttered under his breath as a man bulldozed Wyatt, almost pushing him to his knees.

"Hey, get out of the way, boy. Is that where you're supposed to be?" the man grumbled.

Wyatt ignored him, gathered his spindly limbs and rushed the tracks in time to see the engine mere feet away from the rear of Dundee. The stallion soared mid-air, but late on take-off. Dundee's back legs streamlined over the tracks as Jax curled a free arm around the woman who looked up and met his velvet brown eyes.

The lady bent her head and arched her back, her arms dangling like a dead dog. Upon seeing Jax soar in the air, she convulsed and blacked out. Jax lost his grip on her limp body which slipped like molasses onto the tracks, about to become nothing more than minced meat from the massive locomotive.

Wyatt slapped a hand to shield his eyes, afraid to steal another look at the train plowing over the lady.

CHAPTER 2

Jessica McCoy was hiding in the horse trailer, her pen resting on the edge of her upper lip. She was reviewing a text she had forwarded to her cell phone... a message she had been secretly scrutinizing on Sam Quaid's phone earlier. It was the same sender. Someone named Lola.

> Hey sweets, can we meet at Ginger Jake's. I would love to meet you face to face. Our texting has taken this relationship about as far as we can. We can do more than exchange numbers at Jake's and finally see the man behind that captivating voice.

Jess cringed, twirling the engagement ring Sam had given her the prior Christmas. This past month, her heart felt splayed open, and each text was another splinter wedged dead center, piercing deeper every time.

Sam had one response.

> Okay, baby.

Baby? That was what he called Jess, baby! Her heart slipped out of place for the first time in two years, her unblemished feelings now marred about the man she thought was her life and future. She had so hoped Quaid would become her new last name.

Jess never considered inspecting his phone, until Sam had been drifting away in the last months, and after she found Lola's name repeatedly popping up. The love of her life, the man who claimed he would never let her go again, was conversing with another woman in some inappropriate text she could not help but follow.

Jess laid her phone down. She was confined in her usual sanctuary at horse shows. There was no need to babysit Anna now that her twelve-year-old daughter had become quite a proficient rider. At least that was how determined Anna viewed herself.

Besides having a cell phone, every regular spectator on the show grounds knew where to find Jess. She would be in the trailer, writing. If she didn't hear the show announcer call Anna's number, someone else would alert her.

Independent Anna loathed when her mother hovered like a nervous lunatic. So, at best, Jess calmed herself by doing what she loved, writing articles. Plus, since she had taken a job as contributor with the local paper, *The Seven Springs Chronicle*, she had to meet deadlines.

Jess was executing what Jaxson Bay, the Australian horse whisperer, suggested over two years prior. Her latest article had evolved into an informative piece on drugs in the horse world until Jess and her cameraman Buddy stumbled into some serious allegations. After hearing a recent claim, she chased a lead that horses at well-to-do Show Jumping barns were indeed subject to illegal performance injections.

Jess expressed to the paper's owner, Ben Donahue, a horseman himself, the possibility of featuring the expensive and sometimes shady culture of Show Jumping. He reluctantly agreed. His adamant last words were, "Keep me abreast of every development before you go to print. I don't need the *Chronicle* to develop the reputation as a troublemaker. Sporting rumors and such."

Jess's vet had verified her suspicions and reluctantly claimed to be able to connect her to an inside source. The day after their conversation, this insider was supposed to reach out to Jess, but that was a week ago. Now it appeared the lead was nothing more than a dead end. Considering Jess was unfamiliar on that level of show venue, her article would not even have enough credentials to appear in the classified ads.

Jaxson Bay had been right, two years back, when he stood in Jess's home office bare-chested, drying off after she'd rescued him from a horrific rainstorm. Jess often reminisced about that first meeting, remembering how he had gazed at her writing awards on the office wall. Jax questioned why she no longer worked at her passion. Although, as she pondered alone in her horse trailer, what she recounted most about him was his shirtless chest. The torso and biceps of a man she had only met an hour before that day in her office, a man who transformed into the hero that rescued her entire family and life. A man she had not heard from since.

Jess suddenly realized her lips were pressed tight onto her pen as the muffled announcer's voice captured her attention.

Number 222? That's Anna.

The broadcaster's voice echoed quite clearly the second time because the trailer door had been inched open by a slight tap. She recognized Tina, a fellow show mom.

"Jess, you better come out. Anna's being called to the ring... called twice... and... well... you better come out." Tina cleared her throat, but not her condescending tone. She pivoted out, muttering under her breath, "If you ask me, the horse looks like an out-of-control barrel racer, not a quality show jumper. Dumb luck for a novice. But who am I... Simply the daughter-in-law to one of the wealthiest and most knowledgeable owners around. So much for the *Australian-trained horse* your daughter brags about."

Jess ignored the woman's back-ended slur and dropped her pen.

"Number... 222."

Tina's daughter Maria was a top contender in the jumping circuit. Although divorced, Tina was supposedly the ex-daughter-in-law of a famous director who had provided the pre-teen with the finest horses and mounds of money to compete. Tina could buy their way into the winner's circle. Rumor had it she was concerned that Anna was a threat in the national jumping circuit. Apparently only the fear had brought them to such a nominal schooling event that day.

Jess shoved her folding chair away from a makeshift desk in the tack dressing room and stormed toward the door. Tina had let the screen clang against the metal trailer, although Jess instinctively knew the woman would be waiting on the other side.

Jess was right and almost landed on Tina, scrambling to maintain her balance.

"Oh my, Jess. Really, you should be out here."

Jess tucked her brunette hair behind her ear, ignoring Tina. The last day of August air was warm against her skin. She visually combed the show grounds in search of Anna somewhere on her mount Belle.

The venue consisted of three riding rings—Ring A for English and Western Pleasure classes, Ring B for events like jumping, and Ring C for barrel racing and pole bending. Anna and her mount Belle seemed to be naturals at jumping without one intention to do so. Anna loved barrel racing and the horse community assumed that was the division in which she would compete. But the duo shocked everyone, from the pony club where she was a member, to anyone who was anything in the jumping circle. Belle, a roan quarter horse, was undersized for a typical jumper, and Anna never jumped formally in a show ring until late the prior year. Yet by mid-year, they were climbing into a rhythm, and her dollar winnings accumulated.

Suddenly Belle and Anna were in the running for a prestigious top five national award with equestrians like Tina's daughter and Ben Donahue's granddaughter. Now she was vying for the youth title of the Alliance Championship. The two synced with speed and heart until the recent July break. On return, all hell broke loose.

Jess swiped a glimpse of a roan neck trimmed in a black mane that waved as it surged above the crowd. A chill embraced Jess. *Not again.*

The second pop was like a rocket blasting off. She caught Anna's zebra striped helmet cover, which she was notorious for wearing at schooling shows. Jess watched as Anna commanded the audience to stay clear. The crowd widened.

Anna side-passed and checked Belle up the aisleway toward the gate in a dust of clouding dirt, a scene that escalated at every passing show. Then circling outside the gate, Belle once again refused to enter.

"Number 222, that's a scratch," the announcer called with no remorse. The crowd moaned.

Jess witnessed Anna spring from Belle and whip off her helmet as a group of girls from Anna's pony club in English riding attire snickered and whispered.

Anna led Belle with seemingly no mercy past the group until the mare's hoof accidently stepped on Anna's English spur, causing her to fall, face planting into the dirt directly in front of her rival Maria.

"So much for the Australian-trained horse!" the girl's insult mimicked what had come from the mother moments earlier.

"Should've sold that horse when you had all the offers," Tina murmured as she passed Jess. "Your daughter just isn't ready for real show jumping."

Jess dashed to aid Anna, taking the reins when Belle nudged her pal in the dirt as if nothing was wrong.

Anna rejected them both and surged to her feet, dirt crusting her face and attire. "Dumb horse! I told you, Mom, she's not the same horse! It's not my Belle!" Anna stomped to the trailer leaving Jess holding the reins.

Jess didn't realize Tina was stationed an inch behind her until the woman said, "Another trainer maybe? There is always a cocktail of legal sedatives."

Jess exchanged a glare. "What are you even suggesting?"

The woman's daughter giggled with the group of whispering girls, then said, "Mom, maybe Anna should join another pony club. Like a Western club. They use those cumbersome saddles like olden days, with horns to hold on to. Who allowed her in our club, anyway?"

"Yes, honey. After watching this escapade, you see why the Western riders need horns on their saddles. Our English discipline is so refined." Tina clapped her hands to the Tri-County Pony Club, herding them together except for Anna. "Come on, ladies. Lesson for the day... how *not* to enter a gate."

CHAPTER 3

𝒥ess momentarily watched Anna rush to the trailer while Tina verged off to join the pony club. Her heart was broken for her daughter. The roan mare dropped her head and shifted weight into Jess, waiting for a rub. Jess touched her neck which was drenched with sweat.

"End of August already, girl. The summer has gone so fast. Maybe you're just tired." Jess gave her a final pat. "You can get a good bath at home." The mare stretched her neck, turning slightly, and chomped on the bit. Jess released the bridle. "There, girl." Then she led her by only the reins noosed around her lightly.

The roan mare and Anna had become an amazing team, attracting more spectators than any rival. Show jumping was a timed event, and speed was of the essence. But so were clean jumps. Recently Belle had turned into a version of Anna's old reluctant pony Charlie. At home, the once gentle mare never balked about carrying Anna over the hills of their farm near Seven Springs in Lancaster County. Jumping logs and floating in swimming holes, no obstacle was a hinderance. Almost babysitting Anna. Now it was quite the opposite. Belle had become an out-of-control monster.

As Anna and Belle climbed the ranks, their nerves quivered, so Jess had hired a private instructor for weekly lessons at their farm. After only two sessions, Jess fired the woman after she suggested a pre-show cocktail of drugs to calm the horse. Clearly the trainer was mistaken, because looking at the horse right now, Belle seemed completely compliant.

Jess's thoughts were interrupted by her phone. It was Doc Hammond returning her call. "Jess?" the long, time veterinarian asked.

"Doc, hey that informant you promised never reached out to me. Did you give them a call as you said?"

Doc Hammond cleared his throat. "I hate to let you in on a little secret. I know it upset you when that trainer you hired suggested drugs. But, in some barns... well... there are more horses on than off the drugs."

Jess hated his implications. "I am attempting to write an important article to bring this drugging out in the open."

"I wish I could do something, Jess. But there's no law about certain drugs, and for the ones that are illegal, it's a catch-me-if-you-can attitude," the vet confessed. "Plus, there is enormous money involved that half my clientele might snub me."

"Oh, I get it. So, money talks?" Jess was convinced he was part of the crime. She began to remove Belle's saddle with one hand, the horse standing quietly untethered.

"No, I don't condone drug use, nor do I supply it."

"So, you just turn a blind eye if you aren't involved in the actual crime." Jess wasn't taking that defense for his argument. "We've been friends for a long time. I know you don't approve, Doc. So why stand by and do nothing?"

There was a lull, and she thought he'd hung up.

"Damn it, Jess. The Alliance show is coming up. I don't want to make trouble or—"

She interrupted, "Perfect timing." She massaged Belle. "So did you call that contact you were talking about or not?"

He paused again, then conceded. "Diaz. The informant's name is Diaz. And I will see what happened if I get a chance."

"Diaz? Where have I seen that name before?" But the doctor had hung up.

Jess shook her head. *Well this so-called lead, Mr. Diaz, appears to have mutated into a dead end.*

She could hear Anna trying to place the saddle back in the trailer tack area when another trainer approached. "Looks like your girls are having trouble," he said.

Jess shook her head as she touched Belle's forelock, quiet as a mouse at present.

"Maybe she's trying to tell you all something."

"She isn't the same Belle," Anna curtly intercepted as she snatched the mare and placed her zebra halter on.

"Anna! You say hello to Mr...." Jess tried to correct, but the girl ignored her and proceeded to load Belle onto the trailer.

Jess frowned. "I am sorry. Belle has transformed from two summers ago, from the sweet-natured mare I traded Jax for the unbroken black stallion I couldn't handle."

He touched her shoulder. "Maybe you need that Australian back here, huh?"

"Haven't heard from him since he left," Jess responded almost whispering, distraught to think about Jaxson Bay.

"I thought you two might've had a fling. Make that the *entire town of Seven Springs* thought the two of you..."

Jess's eyes opened wide.

"Well, but then Sam stole your heart." He must have seen her mood transform at the mention of Jax. "You are still planning that wedding this fall with Sam?"

It took every effort for Jess to nod, then quickly pivot before heading to the trailer.

Driving home, Jess tugged at threads to console Anna who hid her face under a Western hat, her boots crisscrossed on the dash. Jess could hear the girl's sniffles and caught the glimpse of an occasional tear which cut a path through the grime on her face, although the girl uttered no words.

"Anna, Belle is a good horse. Look how nice she walked back on the trailer. She hung her head like a doll."

Anna erupted from under her hat. "Mom, really. I've been telling you she's not the same Belle! We never win anymore! And I hate the Tri-County Pony Club. Why did you make me join?" The young girl slumped deeper into her seat.

"Anna..."

Jess hugged a tight turn, handling the trailer like a pro, something she'd only mastered in recent years, weaving on the country roads trying to concentrate and console Anna at the same time. The silence was suffocating.

"You cannot run from problems like this and say she's not your horse." Jess glanced over, but Anna remained hidden. Anna had

15

insisted after the summer break that Belle was a different horse. The more Anna tried, the more the roan refused to cooperate. Jess even had Doc Hammond explain that sometimes horses are in pain, or just need to change up their schooling, but Anna refused to listen. Just like she was doing right now.

That was the last shutout before Jess's surrender. Anna plastered herself against the truck door as if ready to fall out onto the road.

Everything had been so perfect before. The love of her life came back to Seven Springs and took a job as a small-town police chief. Anna finally started speaking for the first time in two years after her vocal cords had become paralyzed, and Sam's daughter Sela was doing great at college for nursing.

Suddenly, it was all shifting. Sam had started spending more time at work—too much time. Conversely, so was Jess. She had been enthralled in her own new career. However, inappropriate messages and hang-ups on Sam's phone from someone named Lola were increasingly disturbing. Then there was Anna. The horse Jax had left for Anna struggled to even enter the ring. And Anna certainly was not the nice little girl lately. She combated everyone including fellow equestrians. Jess's fall wedding appeared to be nothing more than a forgotten promise.

"I hate that horse," Anna whined. "I don't even know what Jax saw in her. She refuses everything. I'm telling you she's possessed. I didn't even get to practice the Oxer. How could we ever compete in the championship show if I can't practice?" Anna raised the hat above her forehead. "I'm done with pony club, too. They'll never respect me. I quit." The young girl kicked the dash. "And I miss Sela."

"Anna!" Jess hollered. "You loved that horse when you were winning. What you and Belle need to work on is nerves. That Oxer is a piece of cake. I think what this is really about is Sela…"

"Then there's the Triple Bar!" Anna swiped the hat over her face again.

Jess shook her head. She had reached the lane to Tunnel Hill and wanted nothing more than to wrap Anna in her arms.

The ring of her cell interrupted, and Anna curled back in the corner against the door.

Jess lifted the phone, hesitating, not recognizing the number.

"Is this Jessica McCoy?" a woman's voice inquired.

Jess waited.

The woman repeated, "Jess McCoy?"

Determined not to respond, positive the call was spam, she slipped the cell lower, prepared to turn it off.

"Please, I don't have much time. It's Lola, Lola Diaz," a muffled voice cried.

Jess whipped the phone back to her ear. "Did you say Diaz? *Lola Diaz?*"

"They said you needed information. I tried to reach your husband, but he won't answer."

"My husband?" Jess said. "My husband has been dead for almost five years..." Then she sighed. "Do you mean Sam? Diaz, are you the person the vet told me about?"

She wanted to say, *Aren't you supposed to be meeting Sam at Ginger Jake's?*

"Meet me tonight," the voice ordered. "I'll tell you everything."

"What's everything? Tonight? I can't..." Jess negotiated the last turn to her farm then idled, waiting to park the trailer after the phone call.

"Okay, forget it..."

"No! Lola, wait."

But the woman on the other end was silent. Jess heard her breathing, as if she was running or lifting something very heavy.

"Lola, I'm sorry?" Jess had to keep her on the phone.

"Meet me in the west barns. East is busy with some sort of production. Barn eight, Stall 23 in thirty minutes. Come alone."

"Thirty minutes, are you kidding?"

"No joke."

Jess started to plead, "I can't be there in thirty," but the woman was already gone.

CHAPTER 4

Sam Quaid waited before shutting off the ignition at Ginger Jake's. He wasn't about to make the cat and mouse game difficult for the person who had been following him. He eyed the grey sedan in his rearview mirror, windows tinted too dark to recognize any driver, as it veered to the lower level and parked.

Sam shoved away a manila envelope lying on the passenger seat in search of his phone. He had avoided looking inside at its contents about a case for which he had been sequestered as an expert witness. He had no time for that business at present, which involved a horse escaping after a storm and someone filing an insurance claim. He scrolled back through his phone for the text from Lola Diaz.

She had sent him on another wild goose chase. Tonight it was to the infamous bar Ginger Jake's nestled on the cliffs overlooking the Susquehanna River. The establishment was known for two reasons—its picturesque setting and its reputation.

Sam was well known at the century-old institution after growing up in Seven Springs. He had frequented the bar with his pals... until he joined the FBI. Twenty years later, he'd returned as police chief and maintained good terms with the new owner, Jake's son, Sam's high school friend J.R., otherwise known as Jake Junior.

He massaged the dash of his Mustang. "We're going to stay out of trouble tonight. Right, girl?" Sam loved to drive his favorite horse-powered machine instead of the typical police vehicle. The Mustang was his undercover partner, secretly souped up with police upgrades and a potent motor. Besides, his police cruiser was still in the shop at Red's for at least another week.

Sam proceeded past a line of half drunks waiting to pay the cover charge to the bouncer, Vince. About 250 pounds of muscle,

Vince was encased in another hundred pounds of overlaying fat. At 6'4", he towered over Sam's lean frame by a few inches.

"Hey, back of the line, pal." Some thug hung over his lady, locking a hand on Sam's forearm.

"Yeah, back up, or we'll take you back," another threatened.

Vince had been about to stamp a patron's wrist. His bulbous bottom hugged the stool and he didn't flinch except his eyes. "Not a good idea, Merv," Vince said to the man.

Sam knew his badge held clout. After twenty years as a federal agent, he possessed multiple skills from sharp-shooting to combat. Sam stared at the thick fingers pasted onto his forearm.

"Merv, is it?" Sam eyed the brute. "I'm going to give you a chance to remove your hand from my arm."

Merv's girlfriend rocked from one foot to the other and whispered, "Honey, I think you should listen."

Perhaps the stout man read the spark of enjoyment in Sam's lone dimple from his curled lip, cemented from an arduous four months working this case… a case that was tearing his life apart.

After a silence, Merv inched his hand loose.

"Good move." Vince proceeded to stamp the patron's wrist.

Sam winked at the man. "Good move, indeed."

Sam approached Vince who reached his hand out and fisted Sam on the bicep. "Uh-oh, feeling a little loose."

Sam flicked a smile.

"Why are we graced by your presence tonight? Should I expect trouble?"

"No promises. I have company." Sam motioned toward the sedan in the bottom lot. "Do me a favor. If the driver comes in, give me a heads up."

Vince combed the parking lot as he opened the door. "*Comprende.*"

Sam entered the vestibule and then the double oak doors to the watering hole. He stood three steps above the main floor which provided an ample view of the room. A band was setting up for a six o'clock performance and the dance floor was already crowded. Sam scanned the pool room in the back, alive with patrons laughing, shooting darts, and clanging bottles.

He raked his fingers through his brown hair tinged with flecks of grey as a woman in a low-cut blouse and high-heeled cowgirl boots gifted him a smile. She winked and pointed to a table. Fortunately, he was saved by a gesture from the bartender. Sam shot her a smile and politely turned down the invitation. Then he stepped down to bump and shove bodies to get to the bar, an ornate masterpiece chiseled from the early 1900s.

The bartender chased a patron to slide over and patted the counter, instructing Sam to take the corner seat. "Business or pleasure?" J.R. held up the bottle of Jack.

Sam raised a hand. "I'm good with a shot of plain seltzer."

The owner frowned. "Business." He set the bottle back and poured a seltzer with a lime. "Try not to cause too much damage."

"Come on, J.R.," Sam teased. "Just a brief stop to meet someone. Any of the grooms here tonight?"

Ginger Jake's was a hangout for off-duty grooms and barn help at the elite facilities, especially the white stucco cottages in the back. They often rented rooms until they secured somewhere to live. Wages for barn help were incredibly low unless you were that one lucky jockey.

"I'm looking for a Lola Diaz. Know her? She has a reputation as a trusted groom," Sam asked.

"Lola, you say?" J.R. cocked his head. "Oh, I do have something for you, but it's not from a Lola. More like a Leroy."

Sam scrunched his forehead. "You sure?"

"Look, Sam. I know my Leroys from my Lolas."

A bottle crashed to the floor, and the bar hushed. Sam vaulted forward, clutching the side arm under his jacket.

"Relax," J.R. coached. "A common occurrence here."

A waitress scurried to the scene, broom and bucket in tow, while the laughter restored. Sam eased back on his barstool.

"You're a little edgy, my man."

Sam returned his attention to J.R. who was slipping an envelope across the bar. "Leroy seemed nervous. Little guy, like most of the grooms." J.R. tapped the envelope. "For you."

Sam reached out, disappointed not to meet Lola. He scanned the room and the double entrance doors, happening to catch sight of the bouncer at the top of the steps. Vince messaged Sam with a sharp head jab toward the crowd.

Suddenly another clatter echoed, followed by a yell, "Watch it!"

Sam's fingers touched the corner of the white letter-sized envelope, simultaneously eyeing the commotion.

J.R.'s bellow caught Sam's attention. "Hey! That's not yours!"

Sam pivoted his concentration back to the envelope which had disappeared off the bar, snatched up in a flash, and in the hands of a dark hooded thief darting through the crowd.

Sam gulped down the water.

He cast a gaze to Vince who was still barricading the front entrance, bobbing to see the crowd from a better vantage point. The thief dodged low, tunneling through the patrons. Vince pointed toward the restroom. The scoundrel swerved in a new direction after seeing Vince as a roadblock.

Sam winked. "Gotta roll."

J.R. sighed. "Oh well, bathroom needs remodeling anyway."

"Have faith." Sam slid his hand under his coat, gripping the pistol as he bulldozed through the crowd.

He examined the hallway leading to the restroom where a couple were necking voraciously against the wall. The girl eyed Sam first, her arms noosed around her partner's neck.

Sam flashed his badge and the two scurried. He slammed open the men's room door and cautiously entered. He boxed open both stall doors. Then it hit him; he'd made a poor decision. It was not a Leroy, but a Lola after all.

He pivoted to the hall and pushed opened the ladies' room door. A full-bodied woman soared out, leveling Sam's body. She let out a scream, and his only thought was to protect an innocent by shielding her fall. He landed with the larger woman on top. The force blasted the breath from Sam's lungs.

The robust woman lay entwined with him on the floor. Sam attempted to lift her, but she eyed the pistol, stirring her hysteria. He tried to shift her back, but her weight made it difficult. Sam placed a finger to his lips. She clasped her own mouth to be quiet, and he was eventually able to help them both stand.

Sam charged into the ladies' room. The elevated window was slanted open, barely wide enough for a small-framed body. Two black boots with metal roweled spurs were squirming for freedom. An envelope drooped out of her back pocket as her legs scissored back and forth.

Her kicking stopped for a brief second, and the culprit looked back, shielded under a dark hoodie.

Sam heard her panic for air, followed by spinning legs to wiggle further out the six-foot high window. A metal trashcan was lying on its side, clearly the prop used to climb up.

Sam bolted past the stalls and kicked the can with a clang to close in on the escapee. Jamming his gun in the holster, he nabbed a boot with his free hand just above the steel spur. Once his other hand was free of his gun, he clamped the slanted window tight, compressing the person, trying to force her retaliation.

The unrestricted boot recoiled, then kicked. The pointed English spur nailed Sam's lip, exactly when a pistol was aimed at his head. He arched, to avoid being shot, losing his grip on the slant window, allowing freedom for the body. Instantly, Sam seized the boot with both hands.

The culprit kicked again, pirouetting at his face. Sam flew backwards, slamming into the broken tiled floor.

He raised his head in a crunch, a high black leather riding boot clutched in his hands dead center on his chest. No leg connected. The taste of blood curdled in his mouth.

Sam scampered to his feet, out of the lavatory. He raced across the dance floor, reaching Vince on the steps. Still clutching the boot, Sam stopped to take a breath. Vince held the door open and eyed the footwear.

The boot, cradled in Sam's arm, was black, trimmed in a band of tan with a metal spur attached. Vince squished his shoulders into a hunch. "The little person do that much damage?" He pointed to Sam's lip. "Ouch, pal. That's gonna leave a mark."

"You forgot to mention to check the woman's stall first," Sam remarked.

"Didn't look like a woman to me."

Sam quirked. "Let me guess. You know a man when you see one."

"Sure do. He was little, but he was a man." Vince's voice followed Sam's back as he raced out.

"Thanks, man."

The bouncer acknowledged in a boisterous tone, "Don't mention it."

"And, Vince, you look a little flabby yourself."

Sam halted once on the macadam, as he eyed the sedan ripping rubber from the space below.

CHAPTER 5

Jess glanced at her phone—7:00 P.M. She brought the trailer to a halt in front of their barn on Tunnel Hill Farm.

"Mom, go. I'm fine. I am twelve years old."

Clearly, Anna had heard the entire conversation.

"I'm not about to leave you alone..."

"Well, would you look at that?" Anna tipped her hat above her forehead. "Aunt Becky is pulling in, right behind us. Did you forget it's movie night? You're in luck. You can miss it. Again." Anna opened the door with a swift click of the handle. "She'll watch me. We have so much fun! As usual, I'm on my own because everyone works around here."

"Anna, we just spent the day..." Jess stopped, reluctant to edge further into a confrontation. Plus, she did not want to admit the truth. Becky, her sister, would most likely consent to stay with Anna alone for movie night. And Jess was compelled to pursue Lola Diaz.

Becky waved as she exited her car, then headed toward the log cabin with the wraparound porch.

"Oh hell, I can unhitch the trailer when I get back," Jess goaded herself. "I have to follow this lead."

She scurried into the house, zipping past Becky in the kitchen to the office to gather a few items. Her sister immediately followed. Jess informed Becky about her plans as she searched Sam's desk. She noticed the article with a highlighted name—Lola Diaz, a groom at the West Diamond Park Equestrian facility. Jess touched the picture on the paper. She traced the petite woman standing with a horse in the winner's circle. At least the body appeared to be that of a woman. Her head was shrouded behind the horse's neck. Why was Sam interested in her? Perhaps she was helping him uncover something? Perhaps they were falling in love after working together? She certainly had called and hung up when Jess picked up his phone or the land line in the past. But today, this Lola spoke, requesting to meet her?

Jess was determined to go.

Becky started chattering, "Don't worry... it's movie night and Anna and I will be fine. What does this person you're meeting want, anyway? Please be safe. Should I call Sam or maybe Martin because I'm sensing some bad vibes?"

Typical, Becky was rambling on, Jess taking in bits and pieces like when they were kids. Then she made a sharp 180-degree turn to face her. "Becky, take a breath!"

Her sister practically plowed into Jess because she was tailing too close. Jess sliced her hand in the air and rerouted toward the front door. "Enough. I don't want Anna to worry."

Becky hesitated before trailing her out the screen door. Jess skipped a step, practically leaping off the porch. Becky froze at the top.

Anna was staring at her mom from her position beside the porch rocker, hands on her small hips wearing an oversized Western belt buckle, the attire she preferred to English. The glare alone said that her mother was overreacting.

"Look, you two. I'll call on my way back. I'll be home by the second half, promise. Save me some popcorn!"

The black and white border collie, Bandit, plopped at Anna's feet. Jess held the Jeep door open and continued, "After you do the barn chores, you lock the doors. I'll call Uncle Martin to check on you both."

"Uncle? Mom, why do you call him that?" Anna cocked a leg. "Officer Martin works with Sam. He's not my uncle, and really, Mom, he is a little goofy. I could take him down in one punch."

Becky nudged the girl. "No punching, Anna. Maybe we'll take him down with a warm chocolate cookie instead." The two giggled.

Jess swirled her eyes as she watched Anna take Becky's hand. The pair headed to the barn to feed and bed the horses. A jealous pang sliced her heart in half.

Jess climbed into the Jeep and pressed the ignition. She thought of slowing down after this article, spending time with Anna. But at this moment, she was driven by a passion.

Jess flicked her wrist—7:15. She dialed the previous number on her cell, hoping Lola Diaz would answer. At least if there was voicemail, she could leave a message to say she was on her way.

Jess sped out the driveway toward the highway. She knew the equestrian center and didn't need a map. There were two elite training facilities a few miles on either side of the State Show Arena, both called Diamond Park Equestrian Center—one termed West and the other East. Horses came from all over the world to train and school for the different venues. Unfortunately, West Diamond Park was ten minutes farther.

"Lola, I'm on my way. Please wait. I'm coming, but it will be closer to 7:55."

Within seconds Jess felt the vibration of a text. When she reached a stop sign she glanced down. One word flashed on the screen.

HURRY

Jess floored the pedal to merge onto the highway, almost sideswiping a vehicle whose driver laid on the horn.

Distracted, she placed a Bluetooth call at the same time. Again, she had to leave a message. "Martin, it's Jessica McCoy. I'm not sure where Sam is. He hasn't been home much the last couple days... well, weeks for that matter." She mumbled the latter, then cleared her throat. "Letting you know that Anna and Becky are at the house, alone, and maybe you could check on them. You know my sis, Becky. I'm headed to do a story at Diamond Equestrian Park, West Barn. I'll be fine. Talk soon. And, hey ah, there might be a cookie or two in it, thanks."

She made one more call to her friend and partner on every story—Buddy, a retired Marine in his early seventies who snapped footage for the paper. "Listen, I don't have time to talk, but the informant on the drugging finally reached out to me. I'm meeting her at West Diamond Equestrian Center. She says it's urgent."

"Jess, wait. I don't think this is a good idea. It's late and you need to call Sam. We really don't know anything about the source, and there's something I have to tell—"

"Look. Definitely no to Sam." Jess inhaled. "This is what it's all about, uncovering something newsworthy. That's how your article gets national attention, Buddy. The past two years we've stuck together like glue..."

"Almost," he interrupted. "There's something I have to..."

He sounded determined. Jess imagined Buddy twirling his dog tags, a habit he did every time he got serious.

"Buddy, I'll go it alone, but I hope you'll consider meeting me there." Jess was too consumed to inquire.

"Did I ever tell you my favorite book was Jillian Javett's *The Child Spy*?"

"No, Buddy. Can't you tell me about it later?"

Buddy conceded and promised he would be at the Equestrian Center's main entrance, geared with his camera.

Jess scanned the horizon, the pinkish-orange edge cupping the earth. The sun was setting, and by the time she would arrive at the west barn it would be dark.

Anna led her aunt to the great room. "I'll make the popcorn, Aunt Becky. You go and pick a movie."

Anna backed away until no longer visible, then darted into the kitchen. Becky began rearranging the coffee table and pillows on the couch, conversing to herself with every move. "Anna, you can sit here, and me here, and where are the movies? There they are... and to the TV I go..." Then she started fiddling with the remote while chatting to herself.

Anna pretended to concentrate on pouring the popcorn into the air popper until Aunt Becky sounded completely immersed. She mocked her aunt by flipping her head back and forth, her lips pretending to speak. She had a mission to complete at the round oak table. Earlier, Anna had thought about switching the breaker box to *off*. That would set her aunt in a panic and buy Anna some time. However, then she wouldn't have electric or light either. And it was critical that Anna could see to operate the blender.

She had an ingenious idea—disconnecting the cable box, knowing it would take her aunt time to investigate before realizing what happened, hopefully ensuring enough time for Anna to complete her concoction.

"What in the world is wrong with the TV?" Aunt Becky asked from the great room.

"Well, I don't know," Anna answered in a deliberate voice. "The cable man was here this week. He worked on the box, but I'm not sure. You'll figure it out." Anna rolled her eyes. Good thing Aunt Becky was as ditzy as Officer Martin sometimes.

Anna was already spinning the Lazy Susan. Hopefully the air popper would mask the sound of the blender when it was time to mix all the ingredients.

Anna pulled a piece of tattered paper from her pocket and tried to read the scribbles. Sam's daughter Sela and Anna had concocted a potion two years prior calling on magic—magic that brought them the Australian named Jaxson Bay—and now she needed him again.

Anna squinted to read Sela's handwriting. But the scribbled notes were not legible. How could she mix the same concoction if she couldn't read the ingredients? Anna crumpled the paper and tossed it to the floor. She could never repeat the mixture!

Her hand spun the magical Lazy Susan that fulfilled her wish for help in the past. The same Lazy Susan she'd spun on a rainy thunderous night with Sela, the girl she missed and the girl she wished would become her sister. But that didn't look like it was going to happen. At this point nothing was falling into place the way Anna imagined. Not the wedding between her mom and Sam, nor Belle's demeanor. When Jax was here before he sparked only good magic and everything had been perfect. Now, life was falling apart.

Anna spun the Lazy Susan again, trying to remember. She pictured Sela that night two years ago when they made the first potion. And the Australian appeared like a mystical cowboy.

"Was it bananas?" The bananas flew past. Anna spun them back. "Yes, I remember she said bananas and salt and..." Anna collapsed in the chair and spun the Lazy Susan so hard that some of the contents flew onto the table with a crash.

Sam and Mom were always fighting these days, Sela was away at college, Jax probably didn't even remember her, and Belle was a laughingstock to Maria and the whole pony club. Tears mounted and slid down Anna's flushed cheeks as she cradled her head in her folded arms on the table.

She never heard Becky sneak up from behind. "How's that popcorn coming, little lady?"

Anna stiffened and wiped her face. "Nothing, nothing's wrong."

"I didn't ask if something was wrong."

Aunt Becky came closer and stopped the whirling Lazy Susan. "Hmmm, seems you are mixing something. You have the blender and several ingredients." She began placing items back on the Lazy Susan. "Maybe, since I reconnected the TV..." she cleared her throat "...which I might ask Miss Anna about..."

"I don't know anything," Anna tried to deny.

"Later, squirt. I don't think you intend to watch a movie at this moment, do you?" She held a finger in the air to silence Anna. Aunt Becky was almost completely opposite her mother—blonde and plump except she shared the same hazel eyes. "Maybe, would you like to make a potion? A magical potion?" She bent into Anna's face with a Cheshire cat smile.

"You know about magic potions?" Anna's eyes widened.

"How do you think *you* acquired the power? It's in the genes."

"I'm adopted." Anna wiped her face. "As if you haven't noticed." Anna pointed to her darker complexion, adding a tumble of her eyes, unmistakably annoyed.

Aunt Becky shrugged. "Horsehair! That's a minor detail. Let's do this."

After an hour, the kitchen was a littered mess of sugar, bananas, water, and milk just to mention a few ingredients. Anna said she didn't remember quite this much mess with Sela. Aunt Becky said it was vital to call on the most powerful magic for the mixture to be potent. Anna could barely recall when she'd laughed as hearty as when Aunt Becky brushed her nose with flour.

"Anna, make the last wish. Then the potion needs to be chilled in the fridge! Oh, and a dash of salt over our shoulders. Did you memorize the chant?"

Anna nodded. She picked up the saltshaker for a dusting over her shoulder onto the floor. Bandit barked.

"Come back to us, Cowboy. Come back to us, please. Boots and spurs, saddles and whips, man of our dreams, to touch our lips."

They giggled. Anna and her aunt both swallowed a sip. Aunt Becky shivered and garnished the swallow with an *ugh.* Anna snickered again. Then they rested the mixture in the bottom corner of the fridge to brew in hopes the magic would age to perfection.

When the door shut, Anna closed her eyes with an added silent prayer. *Wherever my mom is, please, God, keep her safe.*

CHAPTER 6

Jess was right. When her Jeep drove into the elite West Diamond Park Equestrian Center, night had set in. She checked her phone—7:52 P.M. She'd made record time, but not in the requested thirty minutes.

She attempted to call Lola, but no answer. Jess again left a message. "I'm here, at the barn."

She waited. Maybe Lola would send a text. Nothing. Then she slipped the phone into her pocket.

Before opening the door, Jess looked around. Most all the tiered parking lots were empty. Only a few cars, trucks and stored horse trailers were tucked in dark corners, uninhabited, locked up until morning.

She scanned the parking lot for Buddy's red van which she eyed at the corner of the second barn. A sense of ease rushed her, knowing he was on the premises. Somewhere.

The late summer night sang with a harmony of crickets and katydids as Jess inspected the grounds and stepped out of the vehicle. The clear evening was heavy with an array of stars and a full moon on the rise. This was good, providing some visibility since most of the lights above each long rectangular barn were blown out. There was a long grassy walkway lined with twenty barns, ten on each side, housing horses. At the beginning was a small building labeled "Office." In the distance she could see the outline of a large facility, most likely an indoor arena.

The office next to the barn was locked and completely dark inside, a plastic CLOSED sign hanging crooked across its window. To the right of the office, protected under the eave, was a square map describing the layout of the facility. The map was bolted under plexiglass to the siding. Jess scanned it, stealing a double glance at a flyer taped to the side of the clear plastic.

Shining her phone for light, she touched the paper announcement with her index finger. Jess traced the face of the man on the horse—the same man who'd stood in her home after that horrid storm rescue. The advertisement was for an afternoon riding clinic—$500 for a session with the famous Australian. Jess blinked. Had she read it correctly? Sunday, this Sunday. She had not heard from Jax in almost two years, and he would be here in the area? Never notifying her, or especially Anna?

Disappointed, Jess sighed. Since they'd last met, Jax sure had made a name for himself, along with fame and fortune.

She aimed her cell phone light back to the map, searching for the location of Barn 8. She took a deep breath and glanced at her phone again, praying for a text from Lola.

Nothing.

She texted Buddy. Nothing.

Jess prayed her plan was a good idea because she didn't particularly like that not a single soul seemed to be rousing around a facility that probably stalled over a couple hundred animals.

She located her flashlight and headed to the walkway between the barns. In the daytime, she imagined a traffic jam of horses, riders and grooms collecting on the grounds, a circus of activity. It was odd that everyone would be tucked in for the night, not even a groom overseeing horses or preparing for the next day's training or events. An eerie feeling encompassed her.

Jess walked at a fast pace. Perhaps she wasn't too late. The odor of hay, straw and horses filled her head as she passed the first barn.

Barn 8, of course, was near the end. What she had not noticed was on each side of the numbered barns was a letter.

A or B? Lola hadn't mentioned Barn A or B? The map didn't say A or B.

Jess hit redial as she paced. "Lola, come on and answer. It's Jess McCoy, are you still here? Are you in 8A or 8B?"

As Jess passed Barn 4A, the light over the double doors flickered on and off several times. She hesitated. Drawing her fleece tighter as if to protect her, she scurried forward. Turning over her shoulder, she glanced back at the presence of a shadow behind her. But it must have been her imagination from the Barn 4 light flickering again.

"Buddy, where the hell are you?" Jess whispered.

She should have been relieved when she reached Barn 8, but neither 8, 9 or 10 had lights at side A or B. She timidly chose A.

A before B, she thought.

She wanted to dart inside for safety but glanced back while clinging to the door. Jess slid it open deliberately. A funny feeling seared her bones again. She stepped inside as if touching a tub of scalding water.

"Hello, Lola... Lola Diaz? It's me, Jess. Are you in here? Buddy?" Jess's voice echoed as she stood firm, ready to bolt if she had to.

She scanned the outside around to barn 8B, shocked when she eyed a figure in the double doorway, a black shadow, waving her across. As with most of the barns, no light beamed above the door, so Jess only saw the outline of a small-framed person waving vigorously in quick strokes. She could not tell if it was a male or female. Subsequently, the shadow disappeared inside.

"Lola? Is that you?" On faith, Jess raced across the pathway to the barn. The door was ajar enough for her slender body to enter. "Ms. Lola Diaz, please answer. It's Jess McCoy."

Her voice echoed.

Silence.

She caught sight of the shadow seemingly dodging into a stall at the very end. Jess fanned her flashlight into the pitch blackness of the barn. She scanned both side walls for a light switch, oddly finding none. Her thin frame froze, assessing the situation until a horse released an abrupt shriek, causing her to shiver.

Each stall was labeled with a brass number above the door. *Of course, it had to be Stall 23,* Jess thought as she shined the flashlight and skimmed the brick pathway down the barn's center. Just her luck, at the end. She figured the barn would be of top-notch architecture, stalls lined in iron rails, brick floor and oak boards. Oddly, none of the black iron ornate lights that lined the ceiling were lit. The screaming horse paced a circle in Stall 1 as she passed—odd numbers to the left, even to the right.

Jess skimmed to Stall 24 with her eyes. Lola, or the shadowy figure, had darted in right about there. What the hell kind of game was this? Jess checked her phone one more time. Nothing.

"Lola," Jess called again. "I can't do this... I'm calling for help..."

A hand appeared, reaching from the end stall, then cut the air hard, waving her to follow, urging her to hurry, but no one voiced a word. Only another whinny from a stall made Jess clutch her heart.

She pocketed her cell phone and wrapped a free hand securely around her other to steady the flashlight. She trailed the quivering glow as it shed a pathway on the brick aisle, wondering what had possessed her to agree to meet Lola alone.

I must be a lunatic.

She cautiously trod, examining each stall as she passed.

About halfway down the barn, Jess heard a click. She glanced back and shone the light. *I swear*, she thought, *I left the stable door ajar. My mind must be playing tricks because now it's shut.*

None of the high-priced jumpers, mostly thoroughbred crosses, munching on hay or rustling in their stall, seemed alarmed as she passed.

As she neared Stall 23, she thought of Sam who would be furious she made such an arrangement.

Too late to turn back. "Lola?" Even the grip of her two hands could not prevent the trembling that bounced the light from left stalls to right. In a murmur, Jess repeated, "It's going to be all right." She was stiff with anxiety.

A horse to her left grunted. The sound spooked her, and she stopped in front of Stall 21, her heart racing.

Jess peered in. Two puffs of foggy air snorted at her. She jumped and then released a slight smirk.

"Okay, what's this all about? Where are you?"

Jess edged in the corner of Stall 23. She directed her flashlight in a search before entering.

A body lay face down in the dirt, a petite lifeless frame. Jess shuddered and fell to her knees in the straw, shuffling for the cell phone in her pocket. But it slipped from her hand into the thick bedding.

Jess gasped, then froze. "Lola?" The body was lifeless.

She edged her hand out and wiggled the shoulder. No movement. The figure had long black hair covered in a matted goo. Jess shook the shoulder again, and some of the thick wet matter brushed her hand. She attempted to turn the body over, flipping it like a rag doll. Jess instantly plummeted back, barely seeing the face.

"Lola? Are you Lola?"

Jess fingered the straw, still searching frantically for her phone. Catching the edge of a buried piece of wood, deliberately she inched it toward her. Her other hand discovered the flashlight and directed the beam on the victim's bludgeoned face.

Jess tumbled back again, overwhelmed with nausea. Then she studied the wooden item with the light. A hammer. She raised the tool. Palming its handle, she swirled it around. The steel head was covered in the same red matter that matted the woman's hair, covered her face, and stained her hand. Blood.

Then Jess felt an excruciating force slam the back of her own head, before all went black.

CHAPTER 7

"Damn it!" Sam cussed as the sedan ripped out of Ginger Jake's lot.

He sprinted for a few steps, then realized he was too late to catch the apprehender of the envelope meant for him. He scanned the line of dense pines at the bottom edge of the parking lot. The sound of the rushing Susquehanna River below the rocky cliffs could be heard over the chattering crowd gathered to enter the bar.

He proceeded to the side of the building where the bathroom window jutted out. The drop was more than ten feet. He scanned a thick pyracantha bush with two-inch thorns, contemplating what had spurred the person to jump, let alone steal an envelope they had supposedly just dropped off.

"What the—" Sam tightened his jaw and the riding boot at the same time when he eyeballed something white.

An envelope.

Half of an envelope, pierced by thorns, tattered in two, hung by sheer luck right before his eyes.

He snatched up the shreds and checked his phone. He was late for his second meeting. No time to examine it now.

In the car, Sam tossed the envelope and the riding boot on the seat atop the other papers, then angled the rearview mirror to examine his bleeding lip. Vince had been right. The swollen slit appeared to need a stitch or two. Nothing Sam couldn't tolerate after his FBI days. He struggled across to the glove box in search of a butterfly bandage. One-handedly plastering it on the cut, he glanced at the tall but tiny riding boot on the passenger seat. *It was supposed to be a simple meeting with Lola...* the secret informant.

Sam floored the Mustang, and she responded immediately as he advanced onto the highway. He had met Lola through a simple call. And that was as far as it went. At least for Sam. A covert message from Dr. Hammond had slipped Sam's name to her. She had evidence that illegal drugs were being supplied at the upscale barns. The usage was becoming so widespread, Lola suggested, that now blatant selling of drugs laced with romifidine hydrochloride and dormosedan were almost under neon lights at the front entrance. These were drugs that required prescriptions from a vet. Lola claimed the safety of riders, horses and the reputation of the sport were at stake.

At first, Sam was compelled to believe her pleas, her undercover language dotted seemingly with clues. The performance like she was his lover seemed sincere, the kind of mole every detective needs. But Lola continually led him on, not showing up. He began to question her authenticity. When he ignored her, she started reaching out to Jess, asking for Sam and then hanging up as if threatening him.

But Sam wasn't willing to risk the love of his life or put his family in jeopardy for some wacko informant. He'd decided the matter was out of his jurisdiction. He suggested P.E.T.A.—People for the Ethical Treatment of Animals—to Lola, but she insisted, "You have no idea the money involved and well-known names caught in this web. Their reach is extensive. I need someone to trust." After that conversation a week prior, so-called Lola never reached out again.

Until this morning.

Her frantic message claimed she had been threatened. She was adamant. If Sam showed up at the equestrian center, the lives of her family would be in danger. Lola begged for direction, a trusted meeting place. They settled on Ginger Jake's, where she would reveal the evidence of suspected crimes and culprits.

Sam veered into the East Equestrian Center and stopped at the vast barricade of the entrance gate. As he waited to be acknowledged, he was curious about the contents in the shredded envelope and decided to check the torn evidence. He reached for it, then cautiously handled the fragile pictures that dropped to his lap.

Simultaneously his phone rang. He pressed the steering wheel Bluetooth button. "Sam? Doug Kinard, the Humane Officer. You called me?"

"Doug, yes, I need some information. I've been investigating a lead as to the possible use of illegal substances—"

The voice on the other side interrupted. "Let me guess, Sam, at Diamond Equestrian?"

Sam hesitated.

"Drugging is not uncommon in the world of high-performance horses, just like at a competitive gym. Horses are given performance drugs and steroids to fly high or keep them focused. Some are legal, some are not. Not a big deal for a so-called investigation. My department can handle it. That's what we do."

"No one said you couldn't. I don't even—"

"Look, if you're wondering how I guessed... there's a groom shooting off his mouth... making a little trouble. A Diaz, I believe. But regardless, it's out of your hands now. I'll take it from here."

"Take what?" Sam thought the conversation was evolving with a strange twist.

"The investigation, so you can hand over the envelope to me at—"

"I didn't say I had an envelope," Sam interjected. "What envelope?"

There was silence.

"You know the saying... like passing the torch." Doug's voice weakened. "Concentrate on your sleepy little town, Quaid. Cats in trees and candy bar thefts at the local Dollar General."

Sam didn't like the condescension. "Well, this so-called groom..." He had noticed Doug tagged Diaz as a man, so he remained tight lipped on any first name. "This Diaz person seems pretty shaken. Do you have a full name?"

"No clue. A shady source, if you ask me. Anyhow, give me anything you acquire in the future. It's my case now."

Sam fingered the torn bits on his lap. Unfortunately, none of the pictures or notes were clear or complete. There was also an illegible invoice. He remembered Lola's words: *This will be the proof of a corrupt world surrounded in a web of secrecy and lies.*

Crimes you cannot imagine." Sam decided now was not the time to interrogate the Humane Officer with a barrage of questions.

"I have nothing. It's all yours, Doug."

"Good to hear. And one more thing."

"What might that be?" Sam stiffened his jaw.

"I was at a party with Donahue, the owner of the *Chronicle...* the paper your wife works for."

Sam raised an eyebrow as to what was coming. "Jess and I aren't married, but you were saying about the party?"

"Donahue said you were having a surprise guest at Tunnel Hill Farm in the next week. That true?"

Sam bit his cheek. "Look, Doug, that's a surprise for my family. Not one bit of your business. I needed to be sure Jess could be off the week, Ja..." Sam almost slipped a name in his angst. "Off the week the guest is to arrive. This is confidential, and we don't want added media attention. Frankly, it's none of your business."

"All I wanted to know," Doug snapped in haste and was instantly off the cell, leaving Sam burning. He had every intention of phoning Ben Donahue to discuss his conversation with Doug when Sam was being paged again.

"Sam?" He recognized the voice of his too-trusting young deputy.

"Martin? What's up?" Sam was toying with the papers, collecting and organizing them like a puzzle neatly on the seat.

"Sir, I received a call from Jess earlier. Said she was headed out to the Equestrian Park West, and I should check on Anna at the farm."

"What would she be doing at this hour on a Saturday night?" Sam's voice elevated.

"No clue, sir. Anna is here with Jess's sister Becky. They are all safe, and by the way, watching a movie and making the best chocolate chip cookies..."

"Martin..." Sam pressed.

"Anna seemed a little concerned. Said your wife, I mean Jess, got a call from a Lolly or—"

"Lola?" Sam shuddered. Sure enough, Jess was stepping into trouble as usual with that *Seven Springs Chronicle.*

"That's it."

Sam checked his phone—7:55. "Look, I have a quick meeting here at the East Barn. Can you pursue her? I'll call in back-up, other security staff, to help you."

"Yes, sir. On it. If it's any consolation, Anna said Jess was meeting Buddy, the cameraman, at the location."

Sam hesitated.

"He's retired military, sir."

"All right. Keep me informed, Martin."

Sam could hardly believe he was wrapped up in something this bizarre for a second time. He'd thought taking the job as head honcho at the local police station would keep him free from human trafficking and drug dealing. Doug Kinard was not far from the truth. He had envisioned working on simple cases—missing bikes, cats in trees, wallet theft at the fairgrounds or insurance claims like the one on his passenger seat.

His main reason for taking the job was Jessica McCoy. Her eyes, that muted from olive to brown, had captured his the moment they met twenty years prior. Coming home to Jess, he had every intention to marry her and be the father he'd missed being to Sela and Jess's adopted daughter Anna. But in the last few months work consumed him.

Sam started the Mustang, heading to the gate. The entire center was barricaded off by patrol cars from private detective agencies.

He flashed his badge at the gate attendant who radioed the security guard ahead. The man waved Sam through with a hand and pointed. "Stay to the left, away from filming. Security personnel will direct you to a parking space, and the person you are looking for." The man shook his head and scoffed. "But good luck. You might have trouble wading through his fan club. Been battling fanatic devotees all week."

As Sam circled for a space, his phone rang.

"Buddy?" Sam leaned forward, his eyes weaving in and out of aisles of parked vehicles.

"Hey, Sam, I need to make you aware that Jess phoned me. Said she received a call about drugging horses and meeting an informant. I'm here waiting for her, but—"

Suddenly a car beeped at Sam who was about to turn in the wrong direction. "What the hell! What's she up to?" He arced in the correct direction, attempting to stay focused, still searching for a space. "Okay, Buddy. I have to take care of something first. I should be there in about thirty minutes to an hour. Martin's already on his way. I hope that's not enough time for her to get into trouble."

"You know Jess. But no worries. I'm packing."

Sam hit his flashers to double park in front of the arena. He wasn't going to be long, especially now.

CHAPTER 8

"Cut." Wyatt heard the order by Mr. Prickler, the famous director, or so he seemed to revere himself as such. The twelve-year-old opened one eye at a time. The entire set was in disarray like his curly top of red hair.

The grooms were gathering loose horses, as many as they could tether in one hand. Stage crew members were helping actors gather their props of suitcases, hats and bags that had fallen and spread across the 1880s reproduction set. Others stood stiff like corpses, waiting for another command, as onlookers attempted to enter the area in hopes of a glimpse of the infamous Jaxson Bay, while security thwarted them back.

"Cut, cut…" the ticket master echoed Prick's commands as he stumbled to the platform from the barn.

The train's halogen switched off after Prick yelled, "Shut it down," three times and threw his director crop on the ground. Someone was already fanning the dark-haired actress on the tracks, but not because any real train rumbled over her. Although the locomotive had appeared so authentic every time the cast acted the scene, it was only a simulated halogen that Wyatt thought probably cost millions.

The woman was slowly waking, wrapped in one arm of the Australian, Jaxson Bay. A band of male stagehands surrounded them. Always an entourage of men running to her defense because, Wyatt was positive, they liked to help her resituate her ruffle and eye her bulging breasts. Maybe they even hoped for a little mouth to mouth.

The Australian had slid off the black horse Dundee to see if she was okay, and when she gazed up and eyed him, she passed out again... or at least pretended.

Prick was hollering orders in Wyatt's direction. Wyatt hurdled down off the stage onto the makeshift tracks and dodged under the shoulder of a crewman to stand between Dundee and Jax. The dark-haired lady was comatose, spilling over his arm like a rag doll, her breast bubbling, all but exposed. Wyatt thought for a moment that he saw her open one eye to confirm the Australian was focused on her, then shut it when she noticed Wyatt.

Actors scurried like ants to their mound as Prick yelled more obscenities in every direction. "Clean this shit up. Goddamn it, what number take is this? People, why the hell can't you idiots get it right? And someone call maintenance. That halogen is not working properly!" Prick kicked a dropped satchel out of the way, perusing closer. Wyatt knew he was searching for him.

One of the stage crew standing with Jax cleared his throat and hollered out of fear. "The boy wasn't in his place." He pointed to Wyatt. Wyatt slid further behind Dundee's shoulder to gain safety.

"Sir, the Australian didn't jump the horse at the right time. It's not our fault."

Wyatt studied Jax, awaiting a response. The Australian was magnified, towering over the crowd while ignoring the remark. He appeared engrossed in the woman, worried that another human might be hurt. Jax laid her body into the arms of two anxious crewmen.

Jax, Wyatt and Dundee stood in the gully on the rails as the lady was carried off. Then the Australian turned his attention to Dundee and slid his hand down the horse's shaking legs.

"Sorry, boy. Time for a break. I pushed you too hard." He stroked the horse in a gentle touch, the black steed bowing his head as if in forgiveness.

Prick reached the edge of the platform, clearly contemplating a jump to the tracks below. But unstable from his bad leg, he curled his bottom onto the ledge. He stumbled, almost falling flat on his face. Tossing his smoking cigarette in the air, he tripped over the train rails. Even though the tracks were staged, they were hard as steel and as authentic as possible. Wyatt shuddered for wishing Sir Prick would fall and smash his head. The movie would be cancelled, and he could tell his mom working for the mad director was over.

Prick reached them and immediately lunged a hand forward to grasp Wyatt's shoulder. "I have had enough of you. You have something I want. Good for nothing boy! Hand it over."

This time it wasn't the jaws of the powerful steed that immobilized Prick. The director's knees buckled under Jax's strength. The horse jolted in reverse along with Wyatt as if sheltering the boy yet again.

Wyatt shuffled his fingers deep in the pocket, rotating the needles.

Prick was ranting directions to the cast and crew, all stunned and ogling from the platform.

"You, boy. I'm going to tie those pants legs of yours together and drop a barn rat down if you don't get out of my sight. Now, pull that hand out of your goddamn pocket!"

Jax's stare intensified. "Leave the boy alone."

Prick ignored him. "People, clean this mess up. We'll rerun this scene until 1:00 A.M. if we have to, until I'm satisfied." He cleared his throat. "And you," he glowered at Jax. "This horse is useless... he can't jump. I need a horse that can jump. This one is worthless. The boy is worthless..." He pointed at each iteration, almost stabbing Wyatt with his finger.

The stage was so quiet you could hear a leaf drop until Jax spoke. "The horse is tired. He's young..." Jax's hand stroked the black stallion's neck.

"Do you think I care?" the director ridiculed. "You signed a contract." The older man purposely edged out of Jax's range. "You have five minutes. Saddle up. Spur the beast and force him to jump. That's what you do. I've seen you in a coliseum with thousands of people... tens of thousands of fans. That *is* why you're famous. Do you want me to hire another trainer?"

The actors and crew shuffled to clean the set. Wyatt observed the veins bulging in Jax's hand as he squeezed Dundee's halter. Wyatt slipped his own hand out of his pocket, simultaneously observing the ticket master who had leaped off the platform and appeared to be heading to retrieve Wyatt with two stagehands.

"Force?" Jax's voice was even and calm, demanding attention from Prick. "There will be no forcing. Children are not worthless, nor horses. Only some grown men." The crowd's silence was interrupted by a lone clap, then a few others for Jax's truthful remarks. The ticket master appeared stunned and awaited Prick's comeback.

Wyatt jetted out his arm to Jax, revealing three syringes in his palm. Dundee snorted at the hand, hoping perhaps for a treat. Wyatt shoved the items closer to Jax, who gripped his kangaroo whip in one hand and Dundee in the other.

Jax studied the syringes. "Seems there are some things going on in this barn that better have nothing to do with this movie set." He connected with Prick's stare.

Wyatt could feel the ticket master at his back breathing down his neck. The boy shut his hand as quickly as he could, but the ticket master clasped the needles, snatching them up. A second later, the kangaroo whip snapped in the air and curled around the ticket master's wrist, causing the crowd to shudder in shock.

The ticket master dropped the syringes which, to Prick's sheer luck, all bounced and rolled under the steel tracks. Shrieking in pain, he knelt and grabbed his wrist. Jax fixated on Prick who was cocked on his good leg.

"Oh my, now look at that! The so-called evidence disappeared." Prick slapped his cheek in a sarcastic flip of his hand. "So, there is not one issue on this set."

Wyatt watched as Jax recoiled the whip off the wrist and stepped back. Dundee joined him, almost anchored to his side.

"Whatever fell in the boards—" He angled his body slightly as if peeking under them.

"Whatever fell is no concern of yours," Prick interrupted, "and has nothing to do with me."

The ticket master rose, struggling to catch Wyatt's shoulder. Jax's eyes demanded otherwise.

The ticket master suspended his hand in the air and backed away.

Prick scanned the crowd, ignoring everything that had transpired. "Now, we are going to retake this scene again. And you, boy, are coming with me."

"No," Jax said emphatically.

"Mr. Bay, no need to grow spicy. You and your horse, take five. Cool off. I call the shots here." Prick pivoted. "Now…" His voice shot up like a cannon. "Roll the train scene back to the tunnel and prepare to bring it to the platform again."

Jax stroked Dundee's neck, then smoothly repeated, "No."

"No? Mr. Bay, you do remember the agreement regarding the children's hospital." Prick faced him and the wrinkles in his skinny gizzard neck bulged. He lit another cigarette and set it on the permanent groove in his lip. "You can kiss the donation goodbye, oh so famous horse whisperer."

Jax showed no emotion. The ticket master mumbled in Prick's ear, "Maybe let him go, sir. He's calm as a cucumber."

Wyatt wondered momentarily how a cucumber could be calm.

"No, Mr. Prickler, we are finished." Jax stroked the face of Dundee, skating down between his ebony eyes to his prickly muzzle, then made a 180-degree turn to leave.

"You can't quit, not until we complete this movie. Do you know who I am, the most worshiped director in Hollywood? Why the hell I came here to this pathetic community to do a movie, does anyone know?" His face went beet red. "My blood pressure has to be soaring."

"You… you came here to see… to see your… granddaughter to… to be… be clo-closer to Maria." The ticker master had an odd way of trying to calm Prick down.

"Really, I make a living directing movies to buy her the best horses, of which I am invested in to make money, might I add. This scene must be complete by the Alliance Championship Gala this Saturday night where it will be reviewed. Less than one week. Anyone who's anybody in the industry will be attending! Let's go!"

The ticket master zipped back to the platform. Sir Prickler threw his arms up, again screaming obscenities in the direction of the performers.

Jax extended the tether toward Wyatt and asked in a soft accent, "Would you tend to my horse?"

Wyatt instantly agreed, gathered up the lead and pivoted toward the barn. Glancing out of the corner of his eye at Prick, the boy could only watch as the director snatched a crop from a passing groom's pocket and elevated it. Then, the madman took aim. "Oh no! Not you, boy. You're going with me." Wyatt protected his face with his free hand.

CHAPTER 9

Quaid's police badge glittered in the spots of the camera lights directly in front of the whip aimed for Wyatt. The director's arm suspended mid-air, erected to high heaven about to inject pain on Wyatt's back. Slowly he shifted his arm back and rocked forward to try to slice Sam's wrist. A devilish smile scarred his face.

Sam braced inwardly for the swat, hoping this guy was prepared for the backlash he was about to instigate.

The director swung, but at the last possible second, purposely veered at the point of barely missing the badge.

Sam didn't flinch. He locked a stare on the guy who appeared to be blazing with evil.

Once the crop rested at his side, the director remained frozen, then commanded, "I said cut!" His eyes oscillated to a lone camera that was still rolling—a disobedient crew member attempting to capture him on film. The man fumbled with the machinery to quickly shut the lights off and disappear behind an intentional cough.

"Who the hell are you?" He faced Sam and tapped the whip inside his palm, perhaps hoping to intimidate.

Jax was arched around, ready to assist, while Wyatt peeked out from under his hands.

The director squinted at the badge. "Quaid?"

"Officer Sam Quaid," Sam announced.

"Just who do you think you are? None of this concerns you."

"Well, Mr.... is it Prickler or Prick? I was called upon to meet with... let's say a client, about providing extra security on this movie set that we in this small tri-county pathetic community are blessed to have filmed here," Sam mocked. "However, I might have a new interest now." He continued to hold his badge aloft without falter while his other hand pointed to the spot where the syringes slipped under the tracks.

"What are you insinuating? Do you even know who I am? It's *Sir Prickler* to you." The man slapped the crop in his hand again.

"Appears I need to dissect this set with a fine-tooth comb to discover what disappeared under the railroad ties."

"You touch one splinter of this set, and I will have lawyers on you like a fly on—"

"No need for bad language."

"Shit. A fly on shit, Mr. Quaid. You are way under pay grade here. I have a multitude of friends, including the governor of this damn state and the current appointed Humane Officer Doug... Doug... something. And I might add, if you are suggesting abuse—"

"Sir, I am positive you do have friends, and I didn't insinuate any crime at this point. Although I do suggest placing the whip down. That, now, would be considered an act of violence." Sam waited a mere second then added, *"Now."*

Prickler eyeballed the whip, then tossed it into the air, spinning it like a ceiling fan until it crashed, almost hitting an actor.

Sam turned to Jax. "You look like hell."

Jax's lips went lopsided as he simultaneously tipped his hat. Then a serious demeanor returned when Prickler entered his space.

Sam had not seen Jax in person for more than two years, though he had followed the Australian's career on the internet as recognition and fame flourished. Recently, Jax had appeared as a guest on a Netflix show, and now he'd landed an enormous Hollywood movie deal, donating all his salary to a children's charity. The movie deal was being filmed here in the tri-county area by a well-known director, Sir Prickler. However, Sam surmised by Jax's appearance, notoriety had drained some life from his gentle spirit.

The two men ignored Prickler and shook hands. "Now Wyatt, take Dundee back to Jax's trailer," Sam suggested. "With approval from Jax, of course." Then he pivoted back to see Jax nod and slide a hand down Dundee's neck, ending in a pat. Wyatt, however, paused in fear.

"Who the hell—" Prickler asserted.

"It's fine," Sam reassured Wyatt, then turned to Jax. "Seems I'm a little early. I came to check out the set after a call for extra security. One of the actors was causing a fan frenzy. Any idea who?" Sam curled his lip with a tease. "Plus, I wanted to make sure we're still on for a surprise visit to Tunnel Hill next week after Friday night's Qualifier." Sam's eyes never left Jax, but he could almost feel steam releasing from Prickler's anger.

"What?"

Sam ignored him and continued, "I have an idea. How about you come early for that visit? You look like you need an early vacation, plus Anna could use some instruction and I may need your help."

Sam motioned Wyatt, who remained stationary, to get going with Dundee. "It's fine, son."

"Listen, Officer Stupid. You are out of your jurisdiction." Prickler proceeded to stall Wyatt.

Sam instantly clutched the director. "No sir, Jax has not answered me yet." Sam knew the underweight director was no match for his grip. "I need an expert on a case regarding a runaway horse, and an insurance claim... not to mention, keeping a close friend of his busy and out of trouble."

Prickler ripped his arm away from Sam. "I don't know what is transpiring, but Jaxson Bay has a prior commitment."

"We played in your movie. At this hour, I am done." Jax simply turned and headed off the set behind a backdrop of low chatter from crew.

Sam followed, noticing the camera still rolling to catch Prickler's response.

The director began to chase them, screaming. Sam focused on Jax the entire time. It was evident his friend needed a respite.

"Thanks for the compliment about my appearance," Jax remarked. "Working in Seven Springs suits you well, the big bad FBI detective in a small town."

"Well, it worked until this past summer," Sam mumbled.

Jax cocked his head, lifting his hat inquisitively. "I know that feeling." He pointed to the director who was practically crawling up his shoulder into his ear.

Sam had nerves of steel and discounted Prickler's presence. "You look damn good as a movie star on the big screen. In person, not so much."

"Not all it's cracked up to be."

"I missed having you on the force. It will be good you're in town."

"We did solve that last case, and you got the girl. What happened to the wedding? I was waiting for an invitation."

Sam ignored the question.

Jax tapped his shoulder. "Let me guess. She's the friend I need to keep busy?"

The director was still trailing closely. Then he blew an enormous ring of cigarette smoke between their heads.

"I really have had about enough of this *prick*," Sam remarked to Jax.

The horse whisperer pointed to his left. A huge manure pile was forming from an automatic machine that belted down the tracks.

"Well, would you look at that?" Sam stopped as if in awe of the machinery.

"The bucket goes down a track from the barn. No towing or hauling manure in a wheelbarrow. Easy on the back. Eventually a tractor comes and removes the sizable pile."

"Wow, that is quite the modern piece of equipment. Seems it needs only one more little pile." Sam rubbed the sides of his moustache.

"You, Mr. Bay." Prickler's pointer finger burrowed into Jax's pectoral muscle. "You quit this movie, and you will be nothing but a manure pusher. I will see to it. You'll never have the opportunity to have a lifestyle like this once I'm finished with your reputation."

Jax met Sam's gaze. For the first time that night, Sam witnessed his friend's brown eyes twinkle. In simultaneous motion, each man nabbed a side of Prickler who continued to voice vulgarities.

Sam stole the cigarette from his lips. "You won't be needing this. Too combustible here. Besides, everyone knows not to smoke in a barn."

Sam tossed the cigarette on the cement, crushing it as they carried Prickler in airplane fashion toward the manure. Then on the count of three, the two men released him through the air.

"What the hell do you think you're... you mother—"

Prickler never finished his sentence before his face plastered in the pile.

"I warned you about bad language," Sam said. "What was that you said about a fly on what?"

Both men clapped as if dusting off the dirt while the crew burst into thunderous applause.

"You're a hell of a partner," Sam congratulated. "And my family sure misses you."

"I was waiting for the wedding invite," Jax reasserted.

"Well, the wait is over, at least to come and rest."

Jax raised an eyebrow. "Sure sounds like a nice thought."

"Forty-five minutes and you're home."

Jax confirmed with a tip of his hat. With that, Sam's phone sounded. He glanced at the time... 9:30 P.M. He answered immediately. "Martin?"

"We found the missus, sir."

"Missus?"

"Your wife."

"Oh, you mean Jess. Martin, she is not my wife..."

"And I'm not Anna's uncle either, sir. But they call me that"

"Please, what is she up to? Is she okay?" Sam's frustration was mounting.

"Yes, sir. The missus... I mean Jess, she's refusing to leave the west barn. She has a pretty good bump on the head. Keeps talking about a body, a woman, something about a Lola, a hammer, blood... I can't make any sense out of it. She was just lying here in a stall, passed out. Alone, sir."

CHAPTER 10

Sam could hear Jess's muffled voice in the distance. Her tone was adamant, trying to convince Martin she was telling the truth about a body.

"Martin, move the hell out of the area. I can't hear you with all the background commotion. What is Jessica ranting about?" Sam stopped and pressed a hand over his other ear while clusters of people shouldered past in the aisleway. Prickler was still hollering from behind, horses clopping with grooms to their stalls.

This time Sam heard her clearly. "There was a body right here, Martin. I'm telling you!"

"What's she talking about? Where are you?" Sam could hear her whimpers in the distance, splintering his heart.

Martin evidently cupped the phone, whispering, "I don't think the missus... I mean Jess, sir, has been drinking or anything, but she is certainly delirious. Maybe a concussion, sir?"

"A concussion?"

"She insists on not leaving the site until we find the victim." He lowered his voice again. "Honestly, sir. I don't know how to proceed. She's one stubborn woman. We have no victim, no evidence of a crime."

"Martin..." Sam exhaled, but the officer kept rambling. Jess was babbling. Sam ran his thumb and forefinger down the sides of his greying moustache. "Let me talk to her."

He overheard Martin attempt to hand Jess the cell, then the sound of sirens roared louder in the distance. "Sam wants to talk to you. Here... let's go into this tack room."

Sam raked his hand through his hair. "Martin, is that an ambulance, fire, police? Was Jess bleeding? What the hell is happening?" Sam felt helpless as his agitation mounted.

"Yes, sir. She was out cold. She's shaking her head no, sir."

"Is she bleeding?" Sam heard the creak of a door.

"Let me get her in this tack room and see if she'll calm down."

Sam could picture Martin coaxing Jess gently, calling her "miss." He could hear the quiver in her voice. Then suddenly he heard an earthshaking, pulsating scream so raucous that Sam jerked the phone away from his ear.

"What the— Jessica!"

Martin was puffing in short breaths. "Sir... sir... I renege that last... that last statement."

"What last statement? Where's Jess?"

There was no answer, only heavy breathing.

"Martin, what?" Sam clutched the phone, powerless and stranded twenty minutes away. "Is Jess okay?" He picked up his pace with Jax by his side.

"Sir... we have a... a body, sir."

"A body? Whose body? Where...? A *dead* body? Where's Jess?"

Sam pivoted to see Jax concentrating on his every word. Sam wanted to crawl through the phone.

"Hanging from a... from a... saddle rack," Martin stammered.

"Whose body? A woman? Why don't I hear Jess?" Sam's aching jaw stopped chewing. He'd hoped the gum would've relieved some tension for the last hour, but it wasn't any help. Then he heard Jess crying hysterically. Flooded with relief he whispered her name, "Jessica."

"No, sir... it's not a woman."

Sam breathed, "Jess is okay then?" Relief came until he caught the inside of his cheek instead of the gum.

"Sir, it's a man... it's, oh God...."

"What, Martin?"

"The ex-Marine... the cameraman."

"Buddy?" Sam guessed.

"Yes, sir. Hanging by a leather strap of some sort... round his neck, from a saddle rack on the wall," Martin babbled. "Hung next to rows of saddles... His camera's ripped open. This is so wrong... a camera on the floor... the film's gone, sir. Gone! God, I liked that man."

"Martin, calm down. Don't touch a thing. Nothing," Sam commanded. "I'm on my way. Just keep Jess safe. I'll call for back-up."

Jax eyed Sam as if knowing something was incredibly wrong.

"Every new writing adventure with that newspaper lands her in trouble," Sam complained. "Damn it!"

At that moment an actress passed, ogling Jax. He tried to smile politely, as both men picked up the pace.

"Need my help?" Jax offered.

"I think I can handle her. How about you head straight to the farm? That way, I know Anna and Becky will be all right. They can create enough trouble by themselves—and one woman in trouble is all I can handle at the moment." Sam checked his phone. "You can settle the horses in and find comfort in the springhouse. It's been remodeled since the fire. You remember the way to Tunnel Hill Farm down Dead Man's Hill and across the bridge?"

"Can't forget that memory."

Sam noted that old familiar charm of Jax come alive.

"Be patient with Jess," Jax advised. "Remember, her passion is her writing like mine is my horses. I couldn't live without them."

Sam nodded, then hastened toward his car. There was something about Jax that lured others to him, deep from his soul, an attraction, a gentleness. That was evident from screaming fans Sam had witnessed at the expo, the lineup for autographs, and the sales at his display booth.

But that was not the real Jaxson Bay. Jax was neither an actor nor a fake. His concern for humans and his beloved horse partners was genuine and deep.

Sam floored his black Mustang as she delivered a purr for a second time that night, aimed for the other side of the city and the West Diamond Equestrian Center. Even with sparse traffic and his swirling red light, the drive seemed like hours.

Glancing in the rearview mirror, once again he had company. This time he had every intention to stop the trailing. Traveling at near ninety miles an hour could be dangerous to innocent lives. Sam radioed for a police convoy to help. Upon reaching the next exit ramp, three squad cars were waiting, ready to pull over the pursuer.

Sam's mind drifted to Jess, replaying the insistent voice he'd heard through the phone. She was the one he wanted to spend the rest of his life with. Years of being alone, living on the edge with nothing but his career in the FBI certainly wasn't a fulfilling life. Sam longed to have a family in Seven Springs.

There was no reason for Jess to be pretending to be an investigator. Sam was about to make his point clear to her. He would demand she lay low on the writing career until this investigation was over.

Finally, Sam turned into the west park complex, busy with security and flashing lights as at the east, but for a different reason. That was Hollywood; this was real life drama involving drugs and murder.

Sam had no problem locating Barn 8. The facility was lit up like the Seven Springs fairgrounds for its summer festival. Grooms and riders, some clearly disturbed from sleep, appeared to have rolled out of their beds or a late night at the bar, after being alerted to an incident. Some were wandering around in flannel pajamas. Several were on their phones relaying information to owners of highly valuable horses.

Upon reaching the stable, an arm divided the air in front of Sam, halting him at the sliding doors. Sam peered in at a heavy conglomeration of people and activity convening in the barn aisleway.

"Who do you think you are?"

Sam displayed his identification. The man who stopped him appeared to be a barn manager. Sam's badge roused the man, who immediately permitted Sam to enter. At that moment, a thin, chesty blonde bumped him, taking advantage of an opportunity to sneak past security.

Sam cinched the inside of her elbow to block her. "Whoa, whoa." He clued the barn manager with his eyes, then shook his head. The woman who was talking on her phone grimaced at him with daggers.

"Yes, I will hold for Daddy. It's majorly important. Tell him his daughter-in-law Tina Prickler needs to speak to him, *immediately*. Tell him he is fine... Did you even hear me? The horse, *Ernest Living*, is okay, but there has been a murder over at the west facility in Barn 8." She tilted the phone away from her mouth and cocked her head toward Sam. "Excuse me, we own an expensive horse in this barn. I'm sure it's beyond your means, so you wouldn't understand... but do you mind?"

For the second time that night, Sam's income was cheapened, and he was already in a bad mood. "I do. This is a crime scene. You have to remain outside."

"I need to check on Ernest." The blonde's hair was stretched tight into a ponytail that swung at a ninety-degree angle when she stamped her foot. She appeared to be about his age, around forty, her lips and cheekbones cosmetically enhanced.

The barn manager verified with a gesture to Sam that she was indeed a horse owner. Sam detected intimidation when the man also muttered, "She's the daughter-in-law of that famous director. Well, ex, but still under his thumb. He owns the horse. Come to think of it, he owns several."

"That answers her behavior." Sam had already connected the dots and turned to the blonde. "Did you say your name was Tina?"

"Yes, Tina Prickler. Maybe you know that name? And you are?"

"You've got to be kidding," Sam uttered faintly.

"See, I told you that you would recognize it." She jostled his hand away. Her ponytail flipped again, lips pressed to deliver an over accentuated pout. Then Tina glanced down at the badge in his hand.

"Hey, I know you. You're... Sam, Jess's husband?" Her nail, perfectly manicured in red, tapped his badge.

"We aren't..."

"Your daughter has that horse, Belle. Did you realize she tells the pony club that it was a gift from a famous Australian? You really shouldn't let her concoct such fantasies." Tina only stopped lecturing to suck in a breath before she blurted, "Your wife was involved in a murder."

CHAPTER 11

Sam Quaid touched his forehead. He was in need of aspirin. He wasn't about to gift Tina Prickler an explanation. In fact, she had severed the last nerve left under his skin. He gazed over her and directed his orders to the manager. "I don't care who she is or how much *Ernest the Great* is worth, she doesn't get in."

Tina was scanning the interior, her head stretched out like an ostrich, as the barn manager heeded Sam's command and encased her arm.

"Come on, Ms. Tina. You go and wait outside. I have Ernest on my checklist. He's in Stall 22. I'll keep a special eye on him."

"Oh my God, that's her... your wife!" Tina's arm was aimed directly down the barn aisle. "There on the hay bale. My Lord, Jessica McCoy, what are you involved in?" Tina's voice resounded off the brick floor.

Sam lurched forward at the mention of Jess's name, scanning the barn which was lit up like a circus. Exactly in the middle, Jess was slumped on a hay bale, her face mortared in her hands. An EMT held an ice pack against the back of her head.

She jerked up at the sound of her name. Sam observed her mouth the words, *"Tina Prick. Really, Sam?"*

The EMT asked her to remain still, then gently tried to restrain her.

Jess looked mortified, her eyes puffy from crying. She shook her head as if pleading Sam to remove Tina, then reached back to take the ice pack from the EMT.

"Would you please get her out of here?" Sam propelled Tina into the barn manager's arms.

"Yes, sir."

Sam tweaked a fresh stick of gum from his pocket. In his FBI days it would have been a cigarette or toothpick before he entered a crime scene, but those days had passed. He stepped forward and watched Martin hand Jess more tissues, then wave Sam toward the tack room door. Sam barely eyed the outline of another figure behind the officer.

Like the East Center, the floor was red brick, iron lights decorating between the eaves, lumber walls of the stalls hand-scalloped, and dressed in bars to the ceiling. Sam's instinct was to rush to Jess and wrap her in his arms. He had so missed that with her in the last months. But he knew protocol, especially when he realized the identity of the individual hovering over Jess—Sergeant Ty Burns.

Sam was positive the man was adding to Jess's distress. This locale was his jurisdiction, and he wasn't a fan of Sam. Not since Sam had busted a human trafficking ring two years ago that took down Ty's favorite congressman.

Sam acknowledged Martin and headed down the aisle, horses seemingly uninterested in the commotion as they bedded down in their stalls.

Sam slipped into the tack room without being noticed by the sergeant. Martin tagged in behind. The room was filled to capacity with riding equipment. The smell of leather, saddle pads and daily used tack was overwhelming in the confined space.

"How's Jess?" Sam asked.

"Pretty broken up, sir. Buddy and her... well, they were tight. Not to mention her head must be pretty sore."

Sam immediately observed a man's body hanging from one of the black iron saddle racks, mounted three tiers high on the wall. The feet were a mere five or six inches off the floor. In striking shape for a man of his age, Buddy had been choked by what appeared to be a leather rein twisted around his neck

"Strangled," a voice from behind uttered. "Damn shame. Buddy was a good man. Like you, Sam. And I might add, a fine specimen. He must have enjoyed the gym. Unlike myself."

Sam pivoted to see a stout man, his pants, as usual, held up below a protruding belly by a pair of thick red suspenders. Sam's county coroner was tucked in the corner between rows of saddles, jotting notes in a small composition tablet with a pencil.

"Still doing things the old fashioned way?" Sam reached out for a firm shake.

"This notebook is like my suspenders. Had the same pair since I can remember. And I can't live without 'em. Hell, my pants would be at my knees." Dallas Garver let out a hardy laugh, his belly jiggling like a jolly Santa Claus. "Well, well, it's my lucky night. First Ty and now you."

Sam smiled. "Why are you overseeing a case in Ty Burns's county, Dallas?"

"Good question. I guess business has been slow. Although, when I see you at the crime scenes, I know we're going to be in for an eventful investigation. I'm sure I won't get any sleep this month." The latter statement seemed to have been spoken to himself. "Truth is, my cohort is on vacation. They called me in on this one. Just remember the difference between me and Ty—I like you."

Sam barely had time to respond because another voice confronted him from behind.

"Sam Quaid, you are out of your jurisdiction."

Sam pivoted in the other direction to discover Sergeant Ty Burns looming in the doorway.

"Hell, Ty, aren't you over the human trafficking case? That was over two years ago," the coroner remarked. "Face it, Sam earned his reputation on that one."

Sam chose not to argue. Besides, Dallas would update him later. Sam raised his arms in concession as if in a stagecoach hold up. "It's all yours, Ty."

He scanned the room with an eye for even the slightest detail with his photographic memory. In any case, Sam's main concern was to contend with Jess, and he knew Ty Burns would follow. Ty would be obsessed with Sam's every move, worried he might unearth an overlooked detail.

Sam headed down the aisleway toward Jess, who at that moment was struggling to stand. She wobbled. Then Martin steadied her back to rest on the hay bale.

"Ma'am, you need to have a scan. That's a pretty nice size bump on your head. You may have a concussion," the EMT insisted.

Jess just shook her head, staring at the ground. "I want to see Buddy."

Sam pressed past the onlookers. Jess's head inched up, following his lean stature, her green eyes immediately connecting with his. He read the plea for assistance, and his heart melted. However, Sam had other intentions, and he did not reveal any emotion. What he was about to exhibit was not at all going to help their relationship.

"Jess, what are you doing here?"

Her face washed in a disturbed expression. "I received a call," Jess defended bluntly, cocking her head and refusing the offered ice pack.

"At this time? Here, alone. Jess?"

"I was meeting Buddy. You did see him in there... he's dead." She shoved a finger toward the tack room door. "How can you be so cold and not even ask if I'm all right? Buddy and I didn't just work together. We were *friends*. More than I can say for us right now."

Martin stepped back and arched away. "I'll wait over here, sir, if you need my help."

Sam and Jess both ignored him. "And it's not usually a scary place." Jess rolled her eyes and tried to stand once more.

"Listen, for once. Could you follow some directions? The EMT wants you to get checked out." Sam reached out tentatively.

Jess swiped him away. "Look, let's get right to the point. I was called here by Lola. You know Lola—the woman you've been taking calls from the last month?" Jess's sarcastic tone stormed at him.

"You received calls from someone named Lola?" Ty had appeared like Sam's shadow, almost rubbing shoulders.

Sam disregarded his intervention. "I don't have the slightest clue what you're talking about. Maybe you do have a concussion, and the events are blurred together."

"Sam? Sam, really?" Jess heaved his arm, swaying. She towed him to Stall 23. "There, Sam. I was right there! Kneeling by a body of a woman with long black hair, her face bloody and bludgeoned.

I picked up a hammer from the straw, also covered in blood!" Jess glared at him.

"Jess..." Sam's voice softened, and methodically he touched her shoulder, sliding a smirk toward Ty as if she were crazy.

"Why are you being so damn condescending?" Jess defiantly walked between the two men.

The entire performance was killing Sam inside, but Ty was falling for the concussion presumption. Sam couldn't let Ty know he had made contact with Lola, whoever's side she was on. He started after the woman he couldn't live without even though he was doing a hell of a job pushing her away. "Jess, we need to get you to the hospital to check that head. Martin, you can arrange to have her car taken home."

"Sam, Buddy's dead!" Jess spun to face him. "Dead like your heart! Your job has made you a cold son of a—"

Jess was suddenly cognizant that the entire crowd was gawking in her direction, heads peering out of stalls. She leaned against him, her chest almost pressing him, reducing her voice to a low harsh tone, her eyes no longer pleading.

"What has transpired is this... I was hit over the head, there was a dead woman, and when I awoke, Buddy—who did not show up—was dead and the woman's body had disappeared!"

Sam's heart skipped a beat because she was so close. Her face lifted up toward his, olive eyes penetrating, lips quivering. Then her hand brushed him. Sam flinched. He jerked away, fingered the sides of his moustache, and avoided eye contact. Her aroma was stirring more than his heart.

His eyes tracked Martin, Dallas and Ty. Then he forced a stern tone. "Jess, there's no blood in the stall, no hammer, nothing. Only you, with a bump on your head. You heard Martin." He grasped both her biceps. "You need to simmer down until we figure out what happened here. Your little playing around as a journalist might have caused Buddy's death. Now, let us do our job!"

Tina Pricker let out a slight gasp where she stood at Ernest's stall number next door, absorbing the entire conversation.

Damn barn manager couldn't even do his job, Sam silently conceded, but they all were playing into his hand.

Jess was so stunned that she freed herself from his grip and adrenaline sent her outside. Sam tailed her, concerned she would trip or pass out.

She braked at the tack room, looked past Dallas and caught a vision of Buddy's swollen face transformed to a purplish blue.

She cupped her mouth as Sam egged her forward. "You don't need to witness that." She ripped from him. "Jess, please…"

"Sir, let me tend to her." Martin sped after Jess. "She's perhaps a slight bit delirious."

Sam rocked back and rested his hands on his hips, shaking his head. "Nothing delirious about Jessica McCoy," he whispered to himself.

CHAPTER 12

Anna paused the movie and decided to head back into the kitchen. Officer Martin, as her mom always referred to him, had shown up to check on her and Aunt Becky at Tunnel Hill Farm. His knock on the door fueled Bandit into a barking explosion. Clearly at the request of her mother, Martin was asked to monitor the two. He had Aunt Becky cornered in the kitchen, talking in a whisper. Since her aunt had pretended to gift him a bag of her freshly baked cookies, Anna decided to sneak into the kitchen. *Something's up.*

Anna nonchalantly opened the fridge, pretending to check the magic potion designed to return the Australian to Seven Springs. As soon as the two spied her, they split apart.

Martin cleared his throat and raised his voice. "Wow, Becky, you sure do know how to lure someone in. These cookies are fantastic."

His zealous reaction was a dead giveaway. Anna cupped the container, then carried it to the table like a blessed chalice in church.

"Anna, you have to let the mixture settle. I'll be in for the rest of the movie shortly," Aunt Becky coached.

"I have to stir it once or twice." Anna spun the Lazy Susan and picked up a shaker. She sprinkled the mixture with an overlay of brown sugar to hide the horrid smell she managed to inhale. The room stayed awkwardly silent until she tucked the concoction back into the fridge.

Another call came in for Martin, and he reacted with concern.

After he hung up, a serious expression was locked on his face. "I must head out." With that, both Martin and Aunt Becky took off for the front door. Anna heard him repeat, "Everything is going to be all right," to her aunt three times.

When Becky reentered the kitchen, she scurried to the window above the sink, rammed the curtain to the side and scrutinized the outside. "It's so dark out here in the country. Alone, in the middle of nowhere. How could your mother leave you here alone? No neighbors, no one even living in the springhouse." She thrust the curtain panels closed and ran her fingers along the seams as if pressing every inch tight against the frame. "So remote. Give me neighbors."

"What was Officer Martin telling you? I heard him say it was going to be all right. Was someone following Sam?"

Anna never received an answer. Aunt Becky's cell phone rang with the Sherwood Fox Hunting Bugle sound, and the woman jerked as if shocked by a jolt of electric.

"It's just your phone," Anna disparaged.

But Aunt Becky seemed paralyzed, staring at the phone vibrating a path to the edge of the table. She had become increasingly nervous since Martin left, checking the clock. Bandit didn't help matters as he startled and growled at every whistle of the wind.

"Aunt Becky, aren't you going to answer the phone?" Anna prodded. "I have to go close up the barn for the night."

"No, no!" Becky raised her hand in the air, the washrag swinging like a surrender flag. Bandit rose to attention from his sitting position, alerted by her harsh tone.

Anna was stunned.

Aunt Becky must have recognized the shock on her face. She coughed and softened her voice, "Anna, it's late, not to mention too windy. Your mother or Sam will do that when they get home. You head upstairs and take your bath. It's past your bedtime."

"I always shut the barn, especially when it's cold or windy. I'm not afraid. Besides I need to apologize to Belle." Anna was being honest about the latter remark. She had begun to feel a slight remorse for how totally angry she had been at Belle earlier. If Jax knew, he would not be proud of her in the least.

"Not on my watch," Aunt Becky nipped back.

Anna sighed, then shrugged, as her aunt fiddled with anything she could touch.

"Go back to the living room." She was in the mudroom securing the deadbolt. A gust of wind sent something crashing on the porch against the window, and she released a shrill, "What was that?"

Anna sneered at her with almond shaped ebony eyes. "One of the rockers, most likely. They always blow around. I'll go out and..."

"You most certainly will not, young lady! Up those stairs right now!"

Anna was flabbergasted. Aunt Becky never ever raised her voice. Best not to upset her any more than she already appeared to be.

Her aunt herded Anna on one side, Bandit on her other. Anna sulked into the great room and marched the steps to her bedroom in the loft.

Aunt Becky must have suffered some remorse because as Anna entered the bedroom she called, "After your shower we can watch the rest of the movie."

Anna nabbed a towel from the linen closet, parading to the bathroom and ignoring her aunt who kept rambling, "I know it's late, but we can cuddle up together on the sofa." The woman hesitated. "Okay? Then you won't be scared."

"I'm not the one who's scared," Anna hissed under her breath as she closed the bathroom door.

Anna took her time in the shower, then dressed. Her thoughts were on Belle. She needed to see the roan mare and apologize. Maybe it would make things improve between them.

She could hear Aunt Becky scampering in circles downstairs and talking on the phone. The woman was in her own world, and the probability of escaping was good.

Anna peeked out toward the landing. She could crawl on all fours across the balcony over the catwalk to her mother's side of the loft. She would be able to hear better from that vantage point, plus dip into her mom's room, then onto the terrace, and climb down the lattice work.

Anna wrapped her soaked hair into a ponytail, slipped on her riding fleece and stuffed a small flashlight into her pocket. She stopped at the door and looked back, right before executing her plan.

What if Aunt Becky peeks in?

Anna decided to maneuver the pillows into a tootsie roll, placing them under the covers. That way if her aunt checked her bedroom, it would appear Anna was already asleep.

Everything proceeded as planned. Aunt Becky never detected Anna crouching as she crossed the catwalk, entered her mom's room on the other balcony and softly shut the door.

Anna dodged into the room and opened the sliding glass doors. The chilly late summer air sent goosebumps up her spine causing her to zip the fleece. Luckily a pair of riding gloves were stuffed in the pocket too. Anna would need them to climb down the lattice.

Anna walked to the end of the terrace and scanned the horizon as she slipped the gloves on. It was pitch black. Only the flood light at the barn door was glowing in the distance. Anna scaled her eyes down from the second story, inspecting the lattice. Fortunately, her petite size helped in her flexibility; plus, climbing the lattice was something she had gotten in trouble for more than once. She was an agile tree climber since she could remember.

The twelve-year-old inhaled, then mounted the rail, facing the house. Immediately her foot stepped down in search of the stability of a wooden slat.

The first rung supported her, but when she dropped in pursuit of a second, the wood creaked and cracked, giving way. Her body was hanging, secured by only her own arm strength. Anna swung hard and found another board, then mounted her body on a side angle. The lattice seemed unstable and disconnected in places, leaving Anna with the sense this was a bad idea.

The darkness made it difficult to see. She extended her arm and her hand explored, searching for a stronger support to level herself. To make matters more challenging, she hadn't considered the wind, and a gust almost lifted her from the spot.

Using all her might, she held her position, then decided the best plan. Anna determined that her focus should be to move as quickly as possible to reach the ground. A fall from this height could mean a broken bone or worse. Aunt Becky would certainly have a breakdown.

Anna took another breath as if about to dive underwater. Giving no time for the rickety wood to break, speed was the answer. She spidered down the lattice, leaving only splinters in her path. When her feet safely touched ground, the girl knew slowing down was not an option. Her aunt could discover her missing at any moment.

An enormous gust of wind swayed the double porch swing, rattling the chain which caused Bandit to bark from inside. *I wish you were here with me, but no chance of that. Sorry, Bandit.*

She could hear the piercing clang of the flagpole's metal hook ding against the pole. Both rockers were lying over; one bounced off the porch, rolling toward her like a tumbleweed. Anna concentrated on the light at the barn doors. There was no way she could turn on the flashlight. Aunt Becky was surely investigating out the windows in her nervous routine. Anna beelined for the barn.

When she reached the doors, she had to slide open the barn door a mere six inches so her thin body could slip inside. The barn was only a few degrees warmer, with the chill from the wind whistling between the boards, but the smell of oats, hay and horses automatically heated her soul. Once inside she sighed heavily. "Operation Escape" was complete.

Anna decided not to turn on the barn lights; instead she relied on her flashlight.

"Belle!" Anna called in a low voice. Belle released a whinny recognizing Anna's voice. "Come on, girl. Let's go work this out. We have one more chance to hold our spot in the top five and make the championship this Sunday."

Anna led Belle to the indoor arena. Even in the dark, with only a flashlight, she was not afraid. She flicked on the row of lights down the center, then hoisted her English saddle onto the mare's back. Brushing across her belly, Anna searched for the one white spot the size of a softball on her underbelly. She slipped on the bridle. "Girl, you know I love that spot." They headed toward the arena.

A few stalls were located on the edge of the arena. The pair passed two. The first was normally open for the barn cats to nestle, and she continued without peering in, looking ahead, anxious to ride Belle. The second was Snowball's, a small pony her mom had rescued. Snowball was pure white speckled with black dots. He was beautiful except he only had one eye, one large saucer-shaped black eye. The other had been gouged out by an abusive owner with a metal steer prod. Anna could hear Snowball munching on hay as they approached.

Anna and Belle didn't proceed much farther when a ruckus flared from the open stall, not allotting her a minute to pivot around. A hand cupped her mouth while a forearm grappled her in a headlock.

Belle spun in a half circle, then lunged back. Anna was imprisoned, pressed against a chest, not a large one, but sculpted. She could feel its muscles expand as she squirmed. Her small frame raised off the ground, restricting her from walking. Her feet were airborne. Her legs started spinning like a bicycle, kicking hysterically. Her fingers dug into the back of her captor's hand and forearm to no avail.

"Brat, that is going to leave a scratch," a man's voice grunted. He wrapped her tighter. "Best you simmer down!"

The man was drawing her back, Belle heaving Anna's arm in the other direction. The avenger's constriction prevented Anna from screaming. Her lungs could scarcely manage an inner moan under his callous palm. She experienced the roughness of his hand scraping her lips and cheeks. Anna breathed through the fractions of space between his fingers, telling herself to settle.

Calm yourself. Keep your head.

Anna was a contortionist, and if she concentrated, she could nail him with the heel of her black muck boots. If she could just build enough momentum in her bean pole legs to deliver some pain.

Her kidnapper transported her to the back barn door with Anna entangled in his grip.

"If you don't make this easy, I won't have a choice but to knock you out for the drive! I came for the horse, not you. Your bad luck."

At that moment, Snowball lurched to the edge of the stall and bellowed a murderous cry.

That's it! Knock out his eye!

Anna bent her right arm by the elbow several times. Her hand was free and her arm movable. Then, she exercised her index finger twice. If she raised her arm over her head, perhaps she could poke the man's eye out. But if she missed, her captor would surely rage, and there was a good chance he would follow through on his promise.

Anna prayed her poker aim was dead on. She just had to be patient, like waiting to cue your horse when to jump the Oxer or the Triple Bar... waiting for the perfect moment.

CHAPTER 13

Anna's heart raced. She was in the clutches of a brute who'd intended to kidnap her mare Belle, and she obviously interfered with his plan. The consequence? Now he intended to kidnap her too! Anna had to try anything possible to prevent this.

"Stop squirming!"

She pretended to heed his order, letting her body fall limp. Her captor reeked of sweat as he angled her body sideways, belting her against his abdomen, her long black ponytail scraped the barn floor.

Belle's reins were still secured inside Anna's bent elbow, but barely. The mare danced a weaving pattern to resist tugging on her arm.

The kidnapper's other hand ironed Anna's mouth shut, like sandpaper against her lips. "If you promise to be quiet, I'll let you breathe." He inched his hand away. "You going to behave?" Anna nodded. He freed her mouth and snatched up a rein. He jerked Belle, causing the horse to flare in reverse, projecting her two front legs in the air. This did not intimidate the man, and he firmly ordered, "You too."

Perfect timing, Anna thought.

Gently, she loosened her arm, bending her elbow back. She imagined aiming her pointer finger toward his face exactly at his eye. Hopefully, she would plant it dead center, and with all her might.

One, two, three...

The instant her poker finger made contact, the ogre screamed and all but dropped her. Anna's head practically landed against the cement floor as he flipped her vertically. The hand that had grasped Belle quickly covered his wounded eye.

Anna was in a predicament, dangling from his side like a rag doll, her long black hair dragging on the barn floor, her head a mere inch from being scalped. Belle's hooves were prancing, shooting sparks from her iron shoes as they hit the cement oscillating around Anna's head.

Anna stretched for Belle's reins. Once secured, Anna kicked at the man violently. Her airways freed, she screamed, scaring even her. She prayed Bandit would hear the commotion and alert Aunt Becky.

Upon falling, Anna's metal spur hit the intruder's kneecap. He released his hold and this time he stumbled. No time to evaluate her own wounds, Anna rotated her legs as if she were mountain climbing. Her adrenaline lunged her small frame forward until she tackled Belle's neck, wrapping both arms in a tight hold. Belle stampeded in fear and headed straight for the side barn gate to the outside. Anna's body was suspended horizontally on the mare's side, banging like a stirrup against her girth.

The reins, luckily still in Anna's grip, were drooping too low. She knew she had to reduce the slack before Belle's front leg became entangled. In addition, losing her balance was definitely not part of the plan. Anna knew the best chance to escape was out the gate, but unfortunately the gate was secured shut by a padlocked chain.

"Bandit, please stop that incessant barking. You are driving me crazy." The black and white border collie's barking at every sound was growing annoying to Becky. He spun in circles growling at walls or the ceiling if the porch swing chains jingled or the lights flickered.

Becky peered out the kitchen window again toward the fields, woods, and the stars. The saucer-sized moon was more like a full dinner plate, a grayish white color as the scattered puff ball of clouds shoved by the extreme wind crossed the sky. The wind whistled between the logs, but the gusts were frightful. Fall was moving in.

"Bandit, it's the wind. Just wind." Becky was coaching herself as much as she was the dog. Her nerves were shattered. Frankly, she never had nerves of steel, unlike her younger sister Jessica.

Becky was never much for country life, animals, spooky movies, or darkness... merely the beginning of a list of traits that set her and Jess apart. Becky would rather be called Rebecca. She loved her little suburban neighborhood lined in lights and Tuesday night Bridge. Presently, her gut felt like a ball of electrical cords zapping her with mega shocks.

She roughed up her short, tousled hair and eyed her phone. It was now past eleven. Anna had not returned downstairs from her shower. She was always a strong-willed child, and Becky positively didn't want to reveal she was the one who was afraid. She wished her niece would cuddle on the couch, for Becky's own sanity. Anna must have fallen asleep upstairs. She had been very upset with Becky for not being allowed to go to the barn before being sent right to bed.

Becky returned to the great room, then peered up to the loft. Oddly, the lights were on in Anna's room. Becky sighed, contemplating what to do until Bandit broke into another barking serenade, forcing Becky to almost climb the stairs to the girl's room in practically one leap.

"Bandit, please." Becky held her heart in place as she gazed down to the open great room. She had the lower level lit up like the fairgrounds. Perhaps Anna was scared after all; maybe that was why she left her light on. Becky inched the door open and examined the room. Her aunty instinct was dead on.

Anna was in her bed, curled and nestled in a mound of blankets. Becky turned her smile on and off like the light, then gently pressed the door shut with a quiet click. She was not about to wake the girl even though she would prefer to have her downstairs.

As soon as Becky closed the door, goosebumps pimpled up her arms. "Wow, quite a draft up here," she whispered with a shiver. Becky gazed across the catwalk. Jessica's bedroom door on the other side of the loft was partly open. Maybe Anna had gone there to retrieve something. Becky had been sure the room door was closed when she looked up earlier.

She headed across, Bandit almost clipping her calf as he raced in front of her. The dog shoved the door open with his nose and weaseled into the room, his fluffy tail disappearing as Becky hailed him back in a low husky voice as not to wake Anna.

The door almost shut again as Becky heard a firestorm of barking erupt inside. She reduced her steps like a zombie until reaching the door. Becky touched the knob with apprehension because Bandit's unrelenting barking concerto scaled to a lower octave.

Questioning whether to probe beyond, Becky tapped the door enough for it to span open. The curtain to the balcony was flung wide, and the moonlight shown in the room making Bandit's fur glisten. His head was partially prodding out the open sliding glass doors of the second-story terrace.

The door's open?

Then it struck Becky like a whip. She slammed the door and raced back across the catwalk to Anna's room. Her niece was her first concern. She bulldozed into the bedroom, to the bed and rattled the girl's body rolled in the covers. Only the mound contained no one. The blankets had been spun in a cylinder around pillows.

Flabbergasted, the woman jolted back, gasping, fighting her panic.

No, Anna!

Anna windmilled her body, hoping to build enough momentum to vault onto Belle's back, a talent she had practiced repeatedly after Jaxson Bay had taught her his secret to mounting bareback in one easy swing.

Anna swiveled her hips into the saddle, catching sight of the man chasing her, lunging toward them. He was aiming for her free leg that was searching for a stirrup.

Anna thrust that leg into Belle's flank, offsetting her balance, then flattened over the mare's back. She jiggled the reins. "Girl, we are going to have to head for the gate and jump!"

The gate was fast approaching, feet in front of them, and by this point the Belle she had grown to love would be preparing to go airborne at Anna's request to clear the fence. But this wasn't her Belle—the horse she knew from early summer that cleared every log, fence and Oxer she encountered.

Anna jostled the reins together, then whispered, *"Please Belle, you have to jump!"*

The gate was a height Belle had the ability to conquer. However, the horse visibly had no intention of hurdling over. Instead her head arched like a bull aiming for a red target. The horse was determined on accomplishing one goal—to bulldoze through the gate.

No Belle, please no! Anna squeezed her eyes. *Not good. We're goners.*

Belle, smothered in an uncontrollable frenzy, was unstoppable. Anna could almost feel the metal before impact, the moaning steel and bending bars, Belle entangled, her hooves clashing, legs striking unable to break the steel. Anna had a second to decide to dismount or stay the course. Did she have the stability to launch her body far enough away knowing she would hit the cement and most certainly injure herself? Or stay the course, ending up wrapped in iron bars and thrashing hooves, hoping to survive?

Anna braced herself for impact while the culprit behind them scuffled to follow.

She felt helpless until a man's familiar accent opened her eyes. The voice was not her predator from behind. No, the voice came from the other side of the gate.

"Whoa, girl. Whoa." The low voice was loaded with such command that Anna sensed Belle instantly suck wind and hesitate.

That same tone empowered Anna to raise her head slightly, still unable to steady her body or regain the saddle.

The outline of a man stepped into view, positioning himself dead center in their path to freedom. His hand calmly elevated in the air. His brimmed hat tipped above his forehead, and a concentrated stare aimed directly for Belle.

Jax! Could it be?

Anna closed her eyes. The vision had to be her imagination. She blinked and upon opening she saw Jaxson Bay. He strode forward. His presence overpowered Belle, and the mare's front legs struggled like a baseball player sliding home to a halt. Jax must have realized the horse didn't have the time or space to completely stop. He rotated sideways, reached for the reins, and snatched them up.

"Easy, darling. Whoa."

Belle did her best, pawing at the ground. She hoisted forward several steps as Jax guided the reins so she could pivot on the forehand to face him. Finally, halted, the horse stood trembling.

"Jax!" Anna cried, every inch of her vibrating as much as Belle. Losing her strength she began slipping to the ground.

Jax dove, catching her body with his free arm before she smacked the cement.

Anna's petite hands were like a headband holding back the loose hair from her ponytail, helping her see more clearly. "Jax, it's really you!" She wrapped her arms around him. "The potion worked just in time! It really worked!"

Anna didn't often cry, but tears streamed down her cheeks.

Gazing over his shoulder to Snowball's stall, she vented, "The man... the man!"

"What man?" His accent was soft, his chocolate eyes fully intent on believing her. Jax steadied her on her feet.

"He was right there, I swear. He nabbed me there!" Anna pointed. "He said he was here to... to take Belle, but I couldn't let that happen!" Anna could hardly catch a breath. "In front of Snowball's stall!"

Jax studied the area, tipped his hat more and rubbed his forehead with the side of his index finger.

"I'm sure, darling. But he's gone now. Come on, I'm here. Let's get this girl safely in her stall so we can lock her in tight. I promise no one will take her."

Anna nodded, trusting every word of the magical Australian.

Becky rushed down the stairs, Bandit in front leading right to the double doors. She was yelling Anna's name in rapid fire, but the girl appeared nowhere. When she landed on the first level, something stunned Becky like a surge of air from Antarctica. She had a clear view to the barn from the front windows. *There's a light.* She spied a light glowing from the indoor arena, too panicked to notice anything else in the driveway.

"Oh my, Anna!"

When she reached the door, her hand grasped the knob, and simultaneously it began to swivel like a washing machine.

Bandit snarled, aware someone was on the other side trying to enter.

Becky froze, her heart pounding. The door clicked and pressed into the toe of her sneaker.

"Step back..." a man ordered.

Becky shoved the door, slamming it, but she was no match for his power. Bandit transformed into a wild sniffing frenzy at the frame. Becky searched for anything for protection, then eyed the fireplace poker. She raced to the grate, seized the poker, and positioned herself behind the door.

"Just you and me, Bandit."

As the door inched, Becky raised the poker like a hammer, ogling the massive figure as he angled a shoulder in the opening, then tipped his brimmed hat to reveal mesmerizing cocoa eyes.

That was the last thing Becky remembered.

CHAPTER 14

The drive home to Seven Springs and Tunnel Hill Farm was mostly in silence, at least on Jess's part. She eyed the digital clock on the dash of Sam's Mustang—2:57 A.M.

Jess had refused to ride in his car, but was forced to yield when she struggled just to stay upright after seeing Buddy's body in the tack room. Sam had secured her, steadying her walk. Jess only wanted to shove him away, but she was too weak to contest.

Tonight, Sam had made a fool of her, not believing her, brow beating her about why she went to meet someone without notifying him. Then he'd blatantly denied he had contact with a Lola. The worst was when he put down Jess's so-called detective work.

In the last few months, Sam was regressing to the man who broke her heart decades ago and fled to join the FBI, ignoring all his responsibilities at home. Maybe this was Sam's true MO, and Jess had been too blind to see through her veil of dreams.

Wake up, Jessica McCoy. Wake up from this fairytale.

The last thing she remembered at the scene was Sam requesting Sergeant Burns to send someone to a movie set. *A movie set?* She must have a concussion, as the doctor at the hospital surmised. Jess thought she even overheard Sam say, *"Go to the movie set and tear up the railroad tracks for drug needles."* Jess must have been delirious.

At this point, everything was foggy. She was positive her imagination was playing tricks on her. A movie set in south-central Pennsylvania, especially with her employed by the *Chronicle*? She surely would have been aware of such an event.

By the time Officer Martin coaxed Jess into the front seat of Sam's Mustang, Ty Burns was right behind them. Standing at the passenger door, he confronted Sam, flaunting this was his territory and he would damn well do as he pleased.

Jess swore he touted, *"That movie's bringing us a lot of revenue. Plus, powerful people are involved."* He proceeded to threaten Sam, saying he would have his badge if he stepped foot investigating this case or even in his territory again.

Jess had to be drifting in and out of reality. She didn't have the energy to call Becky to ensure all was well. Martin claimed he had verified they were fine and insisted both Anna and Becky were most likely snuggled in bed. The next thing Jess could clearly recall was the luminous lights of the emergency room, beaming down on her as she lay flat on her back, headed for a CT scan.

She had refused assistance from Sam to the gurney or back to the car. Even though she was unstable from the dose of anxiety drugs the doctor prescribed, she declined Sam's help with her seatbelt. "I can do it," she insisted, jabbing him with a piercing glare. Her head felt as if a freight train was rumbling right through her skull.

Sam was enthralled on his phone, in and out of calls, while Jess rested back, trying to avoid sleep. The highway was basically free of traffic at this hour. Only a few glowing headlights, magnified, made her head throb even more. Sam's hand drifted across to her after he shifted gears.

"Don't," Jess ordered.

"I'm concerned for your safety. This isn't a game. Buddy is dead."

"Don't patronize me. *My safety* must mean making a fool out of me because you did a great job at that." Jess nudged his hand off hers. "And Buddy was my friend! Maybe like Lola was yours?"

Jess scowled. She had to squint because her vision was so distorted. But he didn't react. Instead, he focused on the road. Heavy gusts were swirling, spinning the leaves to the ground from the late summer trees.

Her feelings for him were hazy now too. Jess studied his chiseled profile, the flecks of grey in his dark hair, his square jaw, defined lips perfectly etched by his mustache, a dimple which she rarely witnessed any more. She was so in love with him, ready to be his wife. Yet, he could not soldier behind her, believe in her when she needed him most. Too handsome for any one woman, perhaps. Her stare didn't seem to impact him.

He immediately bluetoothed his phone when it rang, appearing relieved to fully engage in a conversation with Sandra at the Seven Springs station.

"What do you mean they lost them? How could that happen?" He listened, then responded. "They didn't have enough men to chase the car that was tailing me to the West arena?"

"Another thing, am I on speaker?" Sandra's voice weakened.

"Yes. Why?" Sam said.

Jess perked up because it sounded like Sam's assistant was implying he needed to be alone for her to speak.

"Oh, it's not important. Everything is okay. Uh. Everything is fine." Sandra was stuttering obviously to change topic.

"Sandra?" Sam cued for more.

"Everything is okay... at the farm... I mean. No worries... not at Tunnel Hill. Per Martin. But I'm sure you will handle the... things... It's all fine now. Bye."

Sam eyed the direction of the speaker. Waiting. His face puzzled.

"What did she mean by that, Sam?"

Sam only shook his head. "You know Sandra. She's a little flakey."

"I never thought of her as flakey," Jess refuted, but Sam remained distant.

He didn't even need to click the phone off. Sandra had hung up without allowing time for him to do so. "What the hell's going on around here?" he muttered to himself. "This entire case is a fiasco."

Jess struggled to focus. Sam was struggling to unwrap a piece of gum while trying to drive. He shoved the stick in his mouth, then stretched his mouth open wide several times. One hand gripped the steering wheel. The other returned to a plastered position on the gear shift and not her hand.

He was certainly alluring. However, she was observing another man in the driver's seat, not to mention presently she was feeling quite nauseous.

"Lola called me, again. She sounded desperate. Sam, there was a dead body in the stall, and a hammer with blood. Lots of blood. And…" She expected his support.

He abruptly palmed the gear shift so tight his veins thickened. "Like I asked, what were you… and Buddy doing?"

"I was trying to uncover the use of illegal drugging. I repeat, *illegal*, Sam, at the equestrian center. Plus, you must admit your relationship with this Lola is suspicious."

"Well, maybe you ought to try keeping an eye on Anna instead, and stop worrying whether I'm having a fling. Anna's been in trouble at school, her riding abilities seem to have deteriorated and the horse is growing ever more dangerous. She is going to end up hurt or lose interest in a hobby she excelled in. At shows, you hide in the trailer and write, per your friend Tina Prickler!"

Jess was stunned by his remarks. Her stomach churned. "First, Tina Prickler is not my friend, and you know it. Second, don't tell me how to engage in work or be a mother. Besides, Anna is *my* daughter, and I'll determine how I raise her, not you."

Jess purposely added the punch. She knew Sam loved Anna, no matter how he felt about Jess. "And third, I could care less who you might be flinging with because I was wrong about us. Start packing…"

"Not when your job is interfering with a case—a very dangerous case. There's no clear evidence of any illegal activity, and not your job to investigate. Buddy was murdered. Strangled, Jessica, if you hadn't noticed. And it's my job to take it from here."

"I'm going to do everything in my power to find out who killed Buddy," she snapped, then cracked the window open. She let the wind whip her cheeks and steal her breath, hopefully stirring her to alertness. The vile feeling in her stomach was building into her throat.

"Over my dead body! You are not, Jess," he ordered and leaned over into her space to continue. Instead he hesitated, "Are you… you look awfully pale…" His fingers lifted off the gear as if to brush her arm, then stopped. "Why don't you sit back and…" His tone grew quiet.

"You don't believe me."

Sam shifted in his seat and refocused on the double yellow line. The moon's glare was adding to Jess's already blurred vision and pounding head.

"I saw a body, a bloody body, and I will find out who murdered Buddy. He was my friend! Why would… anyone want… to kill him? He was there first, but… I never saw him. Just his truck." Her voice was fading. Her thoughts were not reaching her lips in formatted sentences. Instead, they were slipping away like the tears down her cheeks. The salty drops landed on the edge of her lips, then drifted into her mouth and mixed with her building queasiness, leaving a repulsive lingering taste.

She rambled on, "You are not watching over me… the wedding is off. You are… you are moving out."

He stared straight ahead, seemingly not hearing her. She questioned if she had even spoken any words. Was she imagining this conversation? "I'm asking you to move out. Go to the springhouse until you find a place."

"Like old times, huh?" Sam grunted, his voice dry.

His lack of further response blistered Jess's heart. Sam didn't even challenge her, try to change her mind or preserve their relationship. He was silently weaving Dead Man's Hill, as they neared the bridge and then the incline to Tunnel Hill Farm.

"And one more thing…" Jess added.

He waited, almost nonchalant. Jess knew her next statement would change all that, cut him like a knife, and Sam would immediately veer into action.

CHAPTER 15

Sam thought he had eyed flashing truck headlights hidden in the trees as he crested Dead Man's Hill, but there was no time to investigate. As soon as he heard Jess's urgent request, he diverted off the main road.

"Pull over! I'm going to be sick." Jess wrapped her abdomen and lurched forward.

Sam certainly didn't need Jess retching in his car, so he heeded her cry, parking on the berm and darting around to the passenger door.

Jess clutched the handle and opened the door mere inches, just in time. She edged her legs out, then pressed her head between them, facing the ground for a rough series of dry heaves.

Sam eased over her and brushed her hair to the center of her nape. He secured a hand-held ponytail as softly as possible, trying to prevent any disdainful reaction from her. His heart saddened. "Baby, I'm sorry. The doc said this might happen," he whispered.

Jess swallowed hard. "Skip the baby stuff, Sam." She cleared her throat.

Sam said nothing and continued to hold her hair in place behind her head. He couldn't avoid letting his fingers roll against her soft skin. He eyed the sky, stars brightly shining, the wind pushing the clouds across as daylight soon approached.

Sam wished he could explain, reveal to Jess that he had spoken to Buddy right before the incident... that he too suspected illegal activity at the equestrian facilities. But there was no way he wanted to have her involved or threatening to write an article with new knowledge.

"Let's face it. I knew you couldn't stand the thought of me barfing in your precious car," Jess snipped.

Sam squeezed his eyes closed as if imprisoning any insolent response he might have the urge to say. He knew she certainly was suffering from the events this past evening. He wished nothing more than to embrace her. In fact, he hungered for her, but that wouldn't help his intention to scare her enough to quit.

"Jess..." His tone grew more adamant.

"I don't have the energy to argue." The woman he loved sat back and pressed her head against the seat. "And yes, just like old times," Jess reiterated his prior statement. "You can move to the springhouse."

Sam quietly returned to the driver's seat and proceeded toward Tunnel Hill's gravel lane. He meditated, shocked that Jess had told him he had to move out. He would call Sandra back as soon as he had a private moment. The woman was not a night owl, so there was definitely a reason for her call.

The trees that lined the lane swayed in the wind, trembling like his heart, blowing and tumbling leaves across the road. Leaves that wanted to hold on to summer a little longer, but weren't strong enough. He eyed the lush pastures, glowing in the moon as it slid down to meet the earth. Normally, dark shadows of horses would litter the fields on late summer nights, but tonight it was far too gusty. The pastures were empty, as the horses were tucked safely in their stalls.

They slowly crept toward the log house, passing the springhouse to the right. Jess must have eyed a truck and trailer parked between them, directly in front of the barn. She leaned forward. It was evident to Sam that her head pounded as she gripped the dash. "God, I feel so woozy." She squinted. "Who the heck... are my eyes playing tricks?"

Sam sensed Jess gaze his way. Again, he ignored her, reflecting on her last remark about him moving out of the main house. The lights of his Mustang illuminated the trailer etched with the name JAXSON BAY, painted in a swirling oversized design as magnificent as the Australian himself.

"Jax? Is Jax here?" Jess questioned. As soon as the car stopped, Jess sprang to freedom, unfortunately too quick. She had to brace her body with the door and remain stationary.

Sam rushed to her even though he knew that touching her would trigger another rejection.

Jess had no choice but to allow him to stabilize her as she mounted the stairs onto the wraparound porch. They walked together to the front door. She tried to see in. The front wall was entirely floor-to-ceiling windows. The shades were drawn, and only the light of the room was visible. Jess's eagerness mounted as Sam opened the door.

Upon entering the great room, Sam waited, holding her inside the door as Jess scanned the large open space. Stairs rose on the left. Bookshelves from floor-to-balcony of the loft lined the wall straight ahead, then the massive hearth was to the right. Bandit was nestled on the rug in front of the fire almost at the feet of a man who was bent over its enormous stone masonry, stoking the rising flames. Though not the normal time of year to light the hearth, the fire warmed the chill from an early deep cold front that had swept into the valley.

Anna was curled up on the oversized armchair, sound asleep, covered in a hand-woven Indian patterned blanket, its bright colors vivid against the halo of the hearth. Becky was spread out on the sofa, also in a deep slumber, an empty wine glass on the timber end table next to her below the faint glow of an elk horn lamp.

Jess blinked, taken aback by the male stranger as he pivoted to face them. His brown hair was tousled, his shirt loosely buttoned and opened at the chest. Powerful arms curved from his broad shoulders when he set down the iron stoker. Sam knew she recognized the strong statured frame immediately.

"Jax?" Jess liberated her body with a twist from Sam's hold. He released her without hesitation, although he didn't want to. A sense of envy cloaked his heart.

"It is." The man nodded in affirmation, his accent warm and inviting.

Sam heard Jess sigh. Her relief upon realizing Jax was indeed present forced Sam to press his jaw tight. Jess wobbled and sucked in a breath uttering a soft, *"Oh my God,"* stirring Becky.

Sam tried to save her, but she slipped his reach with a shove. Becky quickly sat forward as Jess managed to reach the sofa and seize its back. Jax neared her.

"Hello, Jessica." He lunged forward to rescue her unstable body. "Are you okay?"

Jess didn't lose eye contact as she was suspended in his arms. "Jax."

Sam constricted his jaw even more and looked away, scanning the loft above.

Within Jax's expansive shoulders and muscular arms, Jess lost her balance. Luckily he cocooned her against his chest. Jess laid her head on his shoulder, giving into her weakness, igniting Sam's agitation. He questioned if the decision to invite Jax to Tunnel Hill Farm, especially in this current emotional climate, was sensible. He decided to hide in the kitchen until he could lasso his emotions. In addition, he could return Sandra's call, alone.

"Another secret," Jess darted at Sam as he brushed past.

"I wanted to surprise Anna... and you," he softly replied.

Jax was thinner than the last time Jess had seen him, but the man still offered sturdy support. His frame was bulging in firmness that she felt under his white shirt. His potent hands gently touched her shoulder and waist.

Sam dropped his eyes and continued past, appearing uncomfortable.

Jess could read the concern on Jax's face when she pushed back to see his smile slip.

Becky piped up. "We had trouble here tonight. Thank God Jax showed up."

"Trouble?" Jess inquired. Sam rotated back.

Anna stirred as Sam raised his finger and motioned toward the kitchen. He was perched in the doorway surrounded by the bookshelves.

The four convened in the kitchen, Sam leaning against the counter, his hands tucked in Levi's that sculpted his frame perfectly. His flannel shirt was disheveled, mainly due to the twenty-four-hour day.

Becky helped Jess to a chair, then headed to the coffee pot. Jax filled the doorway with his robust stature, his left arm stretching across as if propping up the frame.

"There was a man… in the barn. He grabbed Anna when she was about to ride Belle. She swore he was here to steal Belle," Becky blurted.

Sam and Jess chimed in unison, "What? Anna?"

"Is she okay? Why was Anna—" Jess attempted to stand.

Becky placed a hand on her shoulder. "Yes, she's fine. And Belle, too. But that's thanks to Jax."

Sam was already searching for his phone. "Is that why Sandra called? Why didn't someone just tell me? Did you see him? I need to…"

Jax stood taller to nab Sam's attention. "You might want to hold off a minute. At present, everyone is completely safe. Perhaps you could listen to the events of this evening and go forward. Anna may be less frightened that way. And Becky, once she came to her senses, called for help to your station…"

"I needed to see Belle," a small voice interjected. Hidden behind the Australian, she peeked under the shelter of his robust stature. Jax adjusted his stance and smiled. "Jax would have never wanted me to put her away on that bad note after the show today." Anna gazed up to his smile and he winked.

"You mean yesterday." Aunt Becky pointed at the range clock. "It's 4:12 A.M. My sweet mother!"

Sam took Jax's suggestion. He stepped back against the counter and folded his arms as he was about to listen. Both Jess and Sam still focused on Anna, clearly questioning why she had been in the barn so late and who would have tried to steal Belle. Not to mention, threaten Anna's safety.

"Anna! Are you hurt?" Jess couldn't help but want her daughter in her arms.

"Mom, I'm fine," she answered as if the thought was ridiculous. "Thank God the potion worked. And that I went to the barn to ride her. The man would have stolen Belle!"

Jax nodded to verify Anna's story.

"Potion?" Sam asked almost inaudibly. "All right, this is serious. Someone tried to kidnap you and Belle. Anna…"

"Sam!" Jess looked over her shoulder. "You are going to scare her more." Jax raised a hand. He didn't have to say a word as a repentant expression washed Sam's face.

"Sorry, but this had better be good. I don't want anyone here getting hurt. We need to be vigilant."

Jess intervened. "First off, we will discuss your whereabouts later, but why would a man come here to steal Belle and Anna?"

Jess almost rose again from the table until Becky rested another hand on hers. "I called Jeff and said I was staying for a while, at least until I know everything is settled down here." Then Becky stood to pour coffee.

Jax tried again to explain the events of the night but Anna broke in. "Aunt Becky passed out at the front door with a poker in her hand!" The girl rolled her saucer eyes. "She could have hurt Jax! But she fainted and he caught her fall!"

Becky blushed.

Anna continued, "Aunt Becky wanted to sleep in my room. I was like, uh no… we can just wait for Mom and Sam, right here, in the great room with Jax."

Becky nodded in agreement.

Briefly, Jess connected with Sam, searching for an answer.

"Anna, how about you and your mom go get some rest." Sam turned his attention to Jax. "Tell, you what. You stay here in the lower-level guest room for a night or two. Evidently, I was wrong about the springhouse—it's occupied right now, by yours truly." Jax eyed him cautiously. "I will add some extra surveillance around here after today."

Jess felt eased there would be a man in the house, and that it was not Sam. As much as they were friends, she knew Jax's hold on her always touched a nerve for Sam.

Sam didn't need much time to gather some belongings and head to the springhouse. Once settled, he would investigate the barn and talk to Jax about the attack. His mind was in heavy thought as he packed a small duffel bag and then loaded another with items from his home office.

Why would someone want to steal Belle? Obviously, Anna had foiled the plan and then become a target. Was someone trying to threaten Sam into halting the investigation? Or prevent Jess from writing an article? Then there was a crazy notion Sam had about the Qualifier Friday night. Would a participant go so far as to hurt Belle so Anna couldn't compete? That was a ridiculous thought, as Anna's chances of being a top contender in Sunday's championship had drastically diminished.

Sam also had every intention of checking out the location where he'd eyed headlights earlier. It was probably just a bunch of teenagers, but considering the events at the farm that night, he wanted to inspect the area.

Sam's concentration was distracted upon discovering Jess waiting alone in the kitchen. He had been on his way out of the office but decided to grab some coffee before leaving. Pausing for a moment, he said nothing and proceeded to pour a fresh mug. Jess rose as something jingled from her hand onto the counter next to him.

"You're forgetting something." Jess moved her feminine sculpted fingers to the edge. Sam recognized the gold ring he had given her when he asked for her hand.

Sam longed to wrap her against him. Instead he stared at the jewel, showed no emotion, and made no response as she left the room.

CHAPTER 16

Sam toted a duffel bag over his shoulder as he headed to the springhouse, a déjà vu from two years prior when he first returned to Seven Springs to investigate the murder of Jess's husband. Tonight, he never expected the love of his life to ask him to leave. Lying next to her was what he waited for each night. Yet, he knew this was best; he had knowingly and secretly pushed her away, distancing himself in the last months… and for good reason.

He stopped momentarily on the expansive porch of the log home, putting his bag down to set the rocking chairs in place that had blown the night before. Then he scanned the horizon as the sun burst to life. September was edging in and so was Jax. The Australian was at the trailer gathering his own small tote of belongings.

Sam tensed every muscle in his body. This had been his home for the last two years—his forever home with the woman he loved and their children. Bringing Jax here early was supposed to have been a joyous occasion. But the surprise couldn't have had worse timing. At least not from the perspective of his relationship.

Luckily, Jax had arrived exactly when Anna needed to be saved. *"Like magic,"* Anna had said. Sam wanted to be Anna's magic, too.

He studied Jax approaching. The dynamic man skipped two steps at a time as if overanxious. His knapsack bounced on his shoulders.

Sam's heart ached, thinking about sending Jax in the house, alone, with the woman he loved. Sam tried to cover his pain. "I hope you're okay with the sleeping terms. I need you in the house."

"Well, that wasn't what I expected, but I'm thankful to you for allowing my mates a rest in your lush pastures. And for opening your doors to us all."

Sam nodded.

"There's no wedding in sight, if you noticed," Sam mumbled.

"What I noticed is that there is considerable love in that house that should not be lost. So happens, right now, it's hurting. The goodness will find a way, Sam."

Sam hesitated, soaking in the words. He eyed the horizon again. "And thanks for saving Anna tonight. That girl is the love of our lives."

"She's a darling to me, too. Anything I can do, I'm here."

"Give me some time to settle in the springhouse. Then we can review last night. After that, I may need some help. I thought I saw truck lights flickering on the return home, tucked into the ravine by Deadman's Creek. And considering what happened here, I think it's best to check it out." Sam pointed to the lower valley.

"Funny, mate, there was a truck and horse trailer parked at the edge of the road where I came in last night. I noticed them because I was guiding the turns extra carefully."

Sam forced his hand to reach out, and Jax gripped it in a solid handshake. "You think you might be up to taking a little ride?"

"Absolutely, mate! You know where to find me when you're ready." Jax pointed toward the barn. "I'll be feeding and tending to the horses in a bit. Take a few minutes to rest." Jax swatted him on the shoulder.

Sam nodded, knowing rest wasn't in his blood right now. Caffeine was, and adrenaline. He was too keyed up not to take action. He heard the screen door close with his heart and stepped off the porch.

Sam fingered Jess's ring in his pocket. He reminded himself that it was a miracle he had sent Jax back to the house early last night. Sam never could've forgiven himself if something happened to Anna.

He continued across the gravel drive, past the barn, then onto the porch of the springhouse which had burned to the ground two years prior. The building, now remodeled, was an almost exact replica of what Jess had so dearly loved. He glanced back to the main log house to eye the smoke clouding from the mouth of the chimney against the blue morning sky.

Okay, Sam. Get your mind on the investigation, he coached himself. *Maybe Jax is right... the goodness will return.*

He had a lot to accomplish and would be lucky if he slept at all. As Dallas the coroner spouted, *"When Sam's involved in a case, there's little sleep and no time for anything else."*

Sam entered the springhouse and laid the gold ring on the small table for two nestled in the tiny kitchen. Tonight, he'd sliced their relationship with condemnation and harsh words. He secretly believed something indeed occurred in Stall 23. Not to mention, Buddy had been murdered. He pulled something out of his bag and positioned a framed picture of Jess next to the ring. Then he checked the time before sitting to listen to the multiple voice messages plaguing his phone.

Sam's first phone message cemented the fact that he would not be taking any catnaps today.

"Hey, Sam, it's Attorney Cousins. I need you to expedite that expert testimony. Could you have it done this week? The judge said he's tired of waiting. I really need verification how the horse was killed, who the responsible parties were, and who exactly receives payment. Weirdest case. I fully understand that you are busy. But the insurance company wants to blame someone. I'll catch you in the morning."

That was all Sam needed when he already had an overflowing plate. Early in the month, he'd received a request to look into an accident report for some insurance investigation. A horse escaped from a pasture and caused a horrible incident on Horse Haven Lane about fifteen minutes on the other side of Dead Man's Hill. He'd known Clancy Heidel since as far back as he could remember, but it was only in more recent years that the eighty-year-old and his wife opened a rescue. The horse was suspected to have escaped from Clancy's farm. Yet, Clancy was in complete denial. The case was an annoying investigation, and Sam wished he had not procrastinated, dealing with the issue that was sealed in a manila envelope.

An empty cup sat in front of him. He couldn't drink enough coffee as he began looking at several items he'd laid out on the table. First, the envelope for the insurance investigation, and second—and more dire—the ripped envelope and papers from the thorn bush.

The paper just held gibberish, like a crossword puzzle. Someone had scrawled words and names on one side, some even scratched out, then angled lines to what Sam assumed was another list on the other side, like a matching game in grade school. One half of the paper was ripped away, leaving no answers.

Sam was fully aware of Jess uncovering allegations of illegal drugs. He didn't want to dissuade her; he knew how much she loved her work. What Jess didn't know was that he had been maintaining an eye on her the entire time. Ironically, Jess was following right behind his own investigation.

However, he never suspected the crime of drugging would have a deeper web, leading to another vile crime—one involving powerful people inside and outside the little community of Seven Springs. Perhaps that image of a quiet, unnoticed community was the attraction to hide a crime so very sinister.

Unexpectedly, his investigation nosedived into this dimension when Lola surfaced. The informant claimed to have a list of names involved in drug purchasing, but that was only scraping the surface. She swore she could attest to the disappearances of grooms and horses at both equestrian centers. Lola insisted her life had been threatened.

When Sam wouldn't listen, she pressured him with hang-up calls to Jess. At first, he was sure it was just a tool to threaten him if he didn't believe her. He told her to call Ty Burns, but Lola claimed she couldn't trust him or anyone else in her county. Ty Burns was one of the names scribbled on the shredded paper from Ginger Jake's. Sam jotted the name on his own notepad followed by one word: Suspect.

Another name on the torn paper was Ernest, but with no last name. Several drug names were listed, as well as three other names, one being Lola Diaz. And one being Sam. The paper unfortunately made no sense. Nothing more than a senseless puzzle, he rubbed his moustache, then his jaw which was becoming extremely stiff from grinding his teeth. Sam worked his mouth open and closed several times. What he needed was chewing gum.

Why had Lola delivered the envelope for holding with Jake at the bar, then steal it back? Or maybe the thief wasn't Lola. Maybe someone else was assuring the list stayed out of Sam's hands.

Sam rose with his mug and went to the sink. The kitchen was tiny, with a black iron wood stove, brick floor, and a small, hatched door that led to an underground passage. The passage went all the way to the barn. A cozy hideaway, this springhouse, but not where Sam wanted to be. He shook his feelings off and rinsed the cup.

His first concern had to be the manila envelope and the simple insurance investigation. The case probably could be cleared up in about a day, so he could concentrate on Buddy's murder and the puzzle.

Sam turned and was suddenly staring at himself in a handcrafted horse harness mirror. He focused on his crystal green eyes and crow's feet that etched the corners. His dark hair was dabbed with grey. He pressed his thumb and index along the silver moustache that edged his lips. He examined the cut from the boot rowel the night before that could have used a stitch. Certainly it would leave another scar on his forty-year-old body. His face was drained, unlike Jax and Anna brimming with new magic.

Sam sighed. He had work to do. And he wasn't what one would call an expert on horses. What he actually needed for the insurance case was someone who was extremely qualified: Jax.

CHAPTER 17

Sam heard Jax whistling when he entered the barn. Although the Australian guest had arrived only a few hours prior, he already transformed back to the man Sam recollected. The black stallion Dundee was standing in the cross ties. The magnificent animal greeted Sam by puffing his chest forward which rippled the muscles in his raised neck. Then he released a whinny followed by a blow of the nostrils.

"Well, welcome home," Sam hailed. "You look a little different from yesterday too."

"He already feels relaxed." Jax peeked out from the stallion's stall where he had the wheelbarrow parked blocking the doorway.

"Sorry the accommodations are antiquated, and there's no mechanical manure bucket."

"Hard work never hurt anyone, mate. In fact, I would rather." Jax smiled and tossed a clump from the fork onto the wheelbarrow.

"Hey, that offer to help still stand?" Sam asked.

"Absolutely!"

"I want to ride over to a local rescue farm for this insurance case, about fifteen minutes up the ridge," Sam explained. "When you're done, of course. I need an expert. In addition, we can discuss the events that happened here in the barn last night."

"Ride? I'm always up for a ride." Jax stood tall as he leaned on the fork.

"Well, I was thinking of the car. It's been a while for me and..." Sam hesitated.

"Can I go?" a tiny voice questioned. Anna peered her head around the edge of the cross ties, standing under Dundee's neck. He nuzzled at her black ponytail which mirrored his coat. Bandit was dancing around the wheelbarrow as if ready, too.

"You hardly slept, little lady. What are you doing?" Sam quirked a smile.

"I couldn't wait to help Jax in the barn, and then, maybe, to let him see me ride Belle? The final Qualifier is this weekend. The top two will be determined for the championship. I may still have a chance."

Sam shook his head. "Yesterday, I thought you were throwing in the towel. You changed your tune, eh?"

"Well, the *magic* is here." She winked and kissed Dundee's muzzle.

"Tell you what, Anna. Let me take Belle out with Sam, out on the trail and assess her. Does Sam have a horse to ride? You and I can work all week on the jumping."

Jax must have read Sam's mind about not letting Anna be a sidekick, but still he wasn't keen on the horseback riding idea.

Anna curled her lip in a frown.

"And you, darlin', can ride Dundee with me when I come back. He could use a soft little bum on him for a change." Their eyes met and her smile inflated as if pulled by puppet strings.

"Agreed."

"You, my dear, are the magic," Jax added pointing to her.

Anna snatched up the wheelbarrow and proceeded past Sam. "I'll get your horse." She apparently understood Sam's apprehension. "I'll make sure it's a walk and trot babysitter."

Sam approved. He watched Jax stall Dundee, then tie and saddle Belle.

Anna headed toward them down the aisleway, almost dragging a brute of a horse. The beast clomped and lugged his sizeable metal shoes in substantial steps. She tethered Cowboy, an oversized and overweight chestnut gelding, next to Jax. The hefty horse stood idle as the girl brushed.

Anna tossed the saddle pad in an arch onto Cowboy, but there was no way she could wrangle the saddle. Cowboy was too tall. Sam moved forward to help, intercepted by Jax who was already holding the tack, prepared, knowing the outcome.

"Need help, Anna?" Like a sheet of paper, Jax hoisted a Western saddle over Cowboy's mesa of a back.

Sam studied the two as they worked in harmony. Neither uttered a word, both intent on gently caring for their horses.

Magic. Hmm. He stifled a breath. Sam wanted to be the family magic.

Before they finished the horses, Sam slipped away to gather supplies in a saddle bag, then investigated the aisle and barn for any clues from the night before.

He phoned Officer Martin. "You're headed out to Tunnel Hill this morning like I asked, correct? Becky said she'd prepare a heck of a breakfast for you. Should only take a couple hours and I'll be back."

"On my way, Sam!" Martin replied, with an ever-loyal tone.

"And Martin, not one of those ladies leaves the farm. Jess isn't supposed to be driving, anyway, and Anna should not go to the barn alone. All eyes on them."

"Got it, sir!"

When Sam returned to the barn, Anna had skipped away, headed to the house. Jax waited for Sam to straddle Cowboy. He was leaning over the horn, stroking Belle's neck. It had been quite some time since Sam ventured on a horse. He had been too busy.

Jax seemed to read his concern as he pointed to Cowboy. "You'll be fine, mate. That gentleman looks like a real babysitter. Soft eye and a kind heart, like someone else I know. Now, lead the way." He tipped his hat.

Sam visually swept the expansive field that connected to the wood line just before the ridge. Then he nudged Cowboy with a squeeze. The gelding lumbered past Belle. The mare attempted to dash behind Cowboy instantly, but Jax edged up his rein. "Follow Cowboy's pace, my dear." His gentle words appeared enough for the little mare as she did hesitate.

Sam knew the winding back trails from Jess's forty acres through the game land that eventually connected to Clancy Heidel's hundred acres. The game land encompassed the area called Dead Man's zone. Its winding curves etched down the ravine, across the creek, through a narrow culvert, then scaled up another crest to the back of Heidel's house. Sam was apprehensive about the trails, thinking three months of summer was sufficient time for them to become overgrown jungles. For that reason, he had tucked a large set of clippers in his side panel.

The Heidel spread was not entirely visible from one location even though Clancy Heidel's home was situated on the rising crest overlooking his farm. The land sloped down off the front into another valley. Once a cattle ranch with fields of soybeans, rows of corn or whatever else to harvest a living, Sam understood the Heidels had struggled with money woes most of their eighty years. In addition, they had lost an only son in a hunting accident and recently his wife of sixty years was extremely ill.

Sam's nerves chilled when he realized nothing unnerved Cowboy who selected his steps like a champ. A frisky Belle occasionally trotted behind, the Australian reining her back with his voice. Yet, Belle was nothing out of the ordinary, not displaying any adversity as she had done at the show grounds. Her happy, forward demeanor tackled anything she faced.

"Jax, that's where I saw lights flick last night," Sam verified.

Jax nodded. "That's about where I eyed a truck and trailer." The two angled over the trail, toward the water. The creek roared louder as they neared, rushing current over rocks and debris.

Once they reached the open spot by the creek bed, Sam dismounted with a grunt. He already ached. "Dang. You are a hefty fellow, Cowboy."

Sam kicked the red clay glued to his boot, stickier and lighter in color than the earth had been as they descended. This soil, dampened from the overflowing creek, with each step sucked his foot in with a squishing sound.

"Someone didn't know how wet this area can be from Dead Man's Creek," Sam remarked. He could smell the wet mud and dampened moss lining the bank.

"I found that out two years ago, when I met the same fate." Both men chuckled. Jax added, "Luckily, this mate managed to drive out."

"Who would park a rig here, unless it was absolutely necessary?" Sam studied the tracks. They inspected the water's edge. "Looks like a good spot to cross," Sam suggested. Jax nodded.

Sam moaned on the remount. He suspected he was going to ache in the morning. He pressed Cowboy who proceeded into the water on first request.

Belle hesitated, though. Sam thought perhaps from the scarred memory of her near fall two years prior. However, Jax's quiet persistence initiated her forward until they waded to the other side.

"Atta girl."

The horses' hooves sucked into the thick clay on the other side, but with powerful leaps they rocketed to the bank.

"There!" Sam pointed up to the back of Heidel's home. "It is quite a climb." The roof line of the house emerged, perched on the crest above.

"Piece of cake," Jax encouraged.

They weaved up the rocky terrain that twisted through thick wooded thicket toward Clancy's. Sam halted Cowboy along the journey to trim overgrown briars as he briefed Jax on the Heidels.

"Horse Haven is the name of this respite. Clancy is in his eighties, retired from cattle and farming. I heard he broke his back both literally and physically." Sam continued as Cowboy executed the ascent with a sure foot. Sam nabbed some of his chestnut mane and lifted out of the saddle. "He offered his pasture for lease to any horse outfit whose equines need a break—summer camps or eventers, high end jumpers, any discipline where the horse needs rest. They could live as Clancy says, 'Horsin' it up'." Sam heard Jax rein back Belle as she tried to gain on Cowboy.

"Sounds like a great idea," Jax added.

"Well, I've heard rumors that Clancy is struggling to manage. His wife is sick, and too many people have abandoned old or problem horses right on the lane without any warning. I believe Clancy has his hands full."

Anna heard the sizzle, simultaneously smelling the aroma of bacon frying as she entered the back door. Aunt Becky was breaking eggs in a bowl for her signature scrambled quiche. Unlike her mother, Aunt Becky was a top notch cook.

Bandit whipped past Anna. The dog sniffed and licked the air as if tasting the aroma.

"Has Officer Martin arrived?" Anna asked.

"No Uncle Martin as of yet."

"He is not my uncle," Anna mouthed toward Bandit.

Aunt Becky was clanging the bowl with the whisk. "I bet you can't wait for the special eggs I'm going to whip up especially for you! Now, go feed Bandit and then check on your mom."

Anna nodded as if following directions. She had a slightly different plan.

She glanced up to scan the loft. Her mom was talking on her cell. "Yes, Ben. I know, but Buddy was my dear friend. I'm staying on the article. I can handle it. We both worked for your paper. I have a duty to follow through. I owe it to Buddy."

Her mom evidently was pleading to her boss, the owner of the *Chronicle*. That conversation was going to keep her mom distracted for some time. *Good.*

Anna exited out the front as Bandit tagged along. She shut the door and slipped into her riding boots that were sitting by the porch steps. Bandit attempted a small groan in anticipation.

"Shhh, we don't want to get caught." Riding alone was going to get her in trouble, lately her middle name. But technically, she wasn't alone if Bandit chummed along, right?

"What could possibly happen in broad daylight?" Anna shrugged as if Bandit would answer.

Anna and Bandit sprinted toward the barn, weaving behind a row of pines. As she slid the barn door closed, Anna eyed Martin's car driving down the gravel lane. She quickly pinched the door shut.

CHAPTER 18

Sam was positive that inviting Jax as an expert would cement the investigation and aid in quickly wrapping up the case. The two rested on their mounts by an abandoned shed waiting for Clancy. Sam examined the property, noticing several outbuildings that appeared in distress.

He was about to remark about the sweet, three-horse, gooseneck trailer connected to a "cowboy Cadillac" Ram truck. The rig appeared fairly new and was parked next to two matching white four-wheelers. Then the sound of another vehicle caught his attention. A souped-up John Deere gator headed toward them, weaving down from the house on the winding driveway.

The neon green gator, with four sparkling chrome mag tires, sputtered and grinded to a stop. The brakes screeched loudly, causing Belle to go on alert. The driver, an older fellow, grinned. Cowboy never flinched. He was busy teething on the bit in a series of repetitive chomps.

"Well, if it isn't Sam Quaid. When Cousins said you were the investigating expert, I thought it can't be." He pointed to Sam while eyeballing Jax. "I knew this kid when he was only knee high. How old are you now?"

"Not a day over thirty-nine," Sam teased.

Old Clancy appeared weathered. He wore a matching neon green ball cap, not enough protection for his skin after decades of laboring in the sun. His physique was thin, drowning in his Carhart overalls. His face was scruffy and his hair, in need of a cut, edged out of the ball cap.

Sam dismounted with a slight wince. He wanted to squat up and down a few times to stretch his legs, but he reached out immediately to shake Clancy's hand. Sam felt the strength that tamed plows, steered tractors, and bailed hay from morning until night.

"I like your ride." Sam admired the vehicle and then joked, "Had to cost a pretty penny?"

"This? I can't afford the jacked-up version with extras, but it's become a necessity. I can't walk the property anymore, and my old gator gave out. My partner thought I needed a better ride since I check the livestock pretty much every day," he continued. "Saw you looking at the rig over at the barn too. Same deal. Not mine, either."

"Partner? You mean your wife, Margaret?"

Clancy paused as if to backtrack his words. "Oh... uh..." He rested back in the gator seat. "Yes, Margaret. She's the boss. It's all hers." The older man shifted in his seat as if uncomfortable, then seemed trapped for words.

Perhaps it was his age, Sam considered. "This is Jaxson Bay. He's the horse expert. Maybe you heard of him?"

"Nope, can't say I have," Clancy answered with an abrupt air. "I haven't left this place in years between farm work and Margaret's sickness. Or didn't you quite understand? She is wheelchair bound and needs full-time care." He whipped his hat off, revealing only a few strands of hair across the top. Then he veered his head in a sharp gesture to the porch where a wheelchair was parked. "Thank God we have private nurses and aids round the clock, so we can stay here, in our home. Lord willing, she'll die here." Simultaneously, the porch door opened, and a small-statured woman with a dark ponytail reached for the apparatus.

"So, let's get on with this investigation. I'm a busy man." Clancy's sudden agitation with the discussion forced Sam to keep his next thought to himself. Either farmers had great health insurance, or Heidel had a nest egg. Or maybe there really was a secret partner.

Clancy waved his ball cap in the air. "I assume you boys are riding, so follow me." He floored the pedal. The gator shot off like a streak of lightning and Belle jarred her head in shock. Cowboy was still chomping away undisturbed.

With speed and confidence, Clancy followed the high tensile fence that lined his property. Both Jax and Sam had to instruct their mounts to engage in an extended trot, sometimes even rolling into a lope. Sam was forced to grip his legs with enduring strength to avoid falling to the ground from the jarring ride.

The group jogged past pastures filled with horses and run-in sheds between sections of wooded areas until Clancy stopped with no forewarning. Jax had succeeded in tagging closely behind on Belle. He was experienced enough to effortlessly sit deep, bringing Belle to a smooth almost reining slide. Sam, on the other hand, bumped and jostled in the saddle, hopping to a stop as if on a pogo stick.

"You all right, mate?" Jax smiled.

Sam smirked. "Sure, but could be a problem tomorrow morning."

Clancy had parked in an area where the high tensile fence was recently repaired. He swung around and stared at them.

"First off, the fence is electrified. So, touch that and it'll throw you back there on your ass." He pointed down a few feet. "Fair warning."

His curt tone made Sam decide to restart the conversation. He evidently had hit a nerve. "Clancy, I'm sorry to hear about Margaret. And I am sorry I have to investigate. I know you labored hard and take pride in this place. But it's protocol."

Clancy nodded as if accepting the apology. "Honestly, I was a little taken back when Sandra told me you were investigating an escaped horse that caused an accident. Absolutely, it wasn't any fault of mine. I want that proven. No horse of mine escaped. I already explained the story."

"A woman was killed after hitting a horse. Your fence was down, and you did report a horse missing shortly thereafter. I believe the report said two days later."

"Not my horse, Sam. Isn't that in the report? I want it in the report." Clancy was stringent with his demand.

Sam reached into his backpack and flipped through the document pages. Quite frankly, he had not even read the report. Too much had transpired in the past days that took precedence, like the loss of the most important person in his life. He had only made a quick scan of the report. Right now, he felt like a fool.

"Clancy, we're just trying…" Sam shuffled the papers, "to get to the bottom of…"

"That accident happened a few miles from here. If a horse had escaped, you think one of them made it through that terrain—hills, curves, Deadman's Creek. What about your horses?"

"Clancy, my horse didn't escape." Sam was still nosing through the packet.

"Someone is trying to blame me. It's probably all about insurance money, if you ask me. Well, I don't have any insurance money, so relay that to Attorney Cousins. Besides, I found my horse."

Jax patted Belle loud enough to gain attention. "First instinct for a horse would be to stick with the herd. Seems likely he'd follow natural instinct."

Sam knew Jax was trying to diffuse a tense conversation and could plainly see Sam had not done his homework. "Well, who the hell lost a horse? We're standing in the middle of Horse Haven, so it would seem obvious." Sam gritted his teeth trying to restrain his temper at the case and himself.

"People drop horses off here all the time," Clancy said. "So, let's clear this up. We had a storm. It was late. I checked the fence like I do, but maybe that was the next morning or maybe two days later. Whatever. And yes, lightning did split a tree, and it partially landed on the high tensile wire." Clancy folded his arms. "I panicked, scanned the field and thought I was missing a horse in this section. Horses normally hang out at the feeding area. Maybe this one was hiding in the shed when I did the head count."

Clancy pointed to the area near a round bale of hay, where a herd of six horses huddled.

"I say partially on the fence because only the top wire was down. The rest was still electrified. They smell the electric." Clancy waited for a response.

Jax spoke first, as if talking to himself. "One of these horses left the huddle, out into a scary storm, near a smoking hot fallen limb that left a partially broken electrified fence. Then the horse jumped to run away from the safety of the herd? That's a hard one to swallow, mate."

"So, right here it reads that Clancy Heidel reported a missing horse from his property two days after the accident." Sam exhaled with ease at the jubilation of discovering the line. "It says right here, you called about a chestnut horse."

"Sam, you see one chestnut horse, you seen 'em all. Mine had a star," he snapped.

Jax again interjected in a soft tone. "Clancy, do you maintain each herd together that comes from the same owner or situation?"

"Some. The first pasture near the house, well, those horses are used for college competitions. The second group is on break from a summer camp up north. They arrived yesterday."

"Clancy," Sam interrupted, breezing further through the report. "I see you retracted your claim. And found the horse."

Clancy turned back to Sam. "I even went down to the station and examined the horse to help identify it. No mark, by the way."

"Do you have papers to validate ownership on these animals? Records?" Jax inquired.

"Papers? I don't keep records like that. I know what's important. Whose is whose. That day I thought I was missing a chestnut mare with a white star on her forehead. I don't forget. I can tell you what color the cows were in this field in 1969. I have a memory for stock."

"This group, are they on break?" Jax asked. "I see this herd has a number painted in white on a hip."

Sam was enthralled in reading, not listening to the two. "So, the horse lay in a morgue somewhere for you to see it?" Sam was confused with the entire story.

Clancy volleyed back to Sam. "No, the horse was destroyed, immediately. There is no morgue for horses, to my knowledge. The police had a picture. Don't you have the picture in the packet?"

Clancy pivoted back to Jax. "That is the mark I was referring to. On the dead horse. He had none. If he came from this field, he would have a number. These horses go to the abattoir."

Sam flicked his eyes up upon hearing the odd word. Stopping his search for a picture, he was in time to watch Jax's face wash with a disturbed expression. Sam had been about to ask for a definition, but his cell rang. He scrambled to reorganize the papers in order to locate his phone.

"Martin?" Sam answered immediately. He quietly listened, then shoved the phone in his pocket.

"We'll have to continue this conversation later, gentlemen. Seems there's a runaway back at Tunnel Hill."

The two men cantered toward the Heidel house. Sam observed the herds of horses grazing on the hundred-acre spread. *No way Clancy's doing all this work alone.*

He caught a glimpse of the house and the nurse again on the porch, this time with an older woman slumped in the wheelchair. Obviously, Margaret. They slowed to a trot, weaving between outbuildings and the trailer. Sam noticed the two four-wheelers were gone. The truck and trailer were sparkling except for thick mud glued to the tire tread and hubcaps and splashed across the bottom undercarriage.

"Something doesn't add up, mate." Jax angled his head back as if reading Sam's mind.

They reached the ridge to enter the woods as the gator could be heard behind them veering toward the porch. They halted momentarily before starting the trek home. "Two things," Sam said. "First, what's an *abattoir*? You looked like you saw a ghost when Clancy mentioned the word earlier."

"Fancy name for a slaughterhouse," Jax answered. "I'd jump the fence, too. But if I was that horse, I'd take my mates with me."

"I wasn't aware that was in existence anymore."

"What's your second thing?"

"Escorts. We have two." Sam twitched his head toward the crest off to his left. Two four-wheelers were parked in the distance, visible through the thicket.

"Why would that be, mate?"

"Maybe to make sure we leave and don't find our way back to Clancy's. We'll make it easy for them today."

CHAPTER 19

Anna scurried down the barn aisleway with the plan to jump on Snowball bareback. The pony would carry her everywhere, even with just one eye. She would follow Jax and Sam. She wanted to see Jax ride Belle with her own eyes.

Anna grabbed the bridle with a gold plate labeled Snowball from the tack room. She dashed to his stall so she could head out before Martin figured she was MIA. As quirky as Aunt Becky sometimes, he was still an officer of the law and didn't shy from duty. Martin would be on the search as soon as he realized Anna was missing. And he would know where to look—Anna's favorite spot, the barn.

The stall inhabited by the barn cats was between Dundee's on the left and Snowball's on the right. As Anna lifted the latch to approach Snowball, she noticed the pony was pawing the connecting wall and peering through the bars with his good eye. "Snowball, there are no cats in the stall right now. What are you so upset about?' Anna tried to calm the pony. Then she was alerted by Dundee who was even more agitated, dancing on the other side. He was rotating in a circular pattern, then flipped his head up and down with blowing snorts.

Anna stopped. This was very odd behavior for the two horses. Snowball had only one fear—men with cattle prods. Something in the stall between them had sparked terror in both animals. Anna scoured over the edge of the wood between the bars into the stall.

"It's okay. You two sillies, there aren't even any cats in here." Anna did notice a large mound of straw in the corner. That was odd. She had fed the cats earlier. It hadn't been there then. Anna studied it now, inching into the stall. The straw was breathing, inhaling then exhaling.

Anna had little fear, even after last night. Bandit would never let anyone hurt her. She focused on Snowball and placed her finger over her lips, "Shhh, boy." She crept in further, forgetting about everything else. Bandit zipped past her, knocking Anna over. She released a boisterous *whoa*.

The dog nose-dived into the straw, thrusting and snorting. Anna caught a glimpse of red wiry curls. Then two spindly legs were thrashing in oversized boots. Anna braced herself, ready to dash.

Bandit shifted the bedding until a person popped up like a Jack-in-the-box. Feathered in straw, it was a boy also prepared to bolt. He was petrified, as scared to see Anna as she was to see him.

The boy hesitated, giving Bandit enough time to jump onto his chest. The boy lost his footing. The border collie wrestled him flat to the ground. The redhead was pinned between the dog's four paws, too weak to ward off the obsessive licking tongue that was washing his face.

"Bandit, stop. He won't hurt you." Anna crawled across the stall floor and clamped onto the dog's collar. The boy wobbled to stand. "Don't run, please. It's okay." Anna's voice seemed to settle the freckle-faced boy. He exhaled and relaxed into the straw. "Who are you?"

Bandit's tail batted the bedding. The boy didn't answer until he touched the soft black and white head of the dog. "Wyatt Evans." His gangly chest puffed up like Dundee trying to intimidate something. It wasn't working. Anna smiled.

"I hitched a ride in the back of the Australian's trailer. And I ain't going back! So I'll be on my way now." He huffed, then surrendered. "If I could just have a little water, please. I can even drink from a horse bucket."

"You need more than water!" Anna observed. "You look like you need a hot meal and a bath." Anna fluttered her fingers in front of her nose. "Woo wee."

"Please, I can't go back. Don't tell anyone I'm here!" he begged.

"You have my vow of silence." Anna rose. She saluted with a cheering bark from Bandit. "I know where I can get you a hearty breakfast. But let me get you some protection first. Here." Anna unhooked a horse blanket from the front of the stall door. "Softer than the straw and better to hide under if someone shows up. Bandit can stay. He'll protect you. I'll be right back."

Aunt Becky was rummaging around the kitchen so Anna hid in the mudroom until the other woman went in search of her for breakfast. The twelve-year-old quickly snagged a container and her school lunch bag. She filled both to capacity with any item she could stuff and slide in—napkins, chips, eggs, bacon, two cans of soda, a bottle of water, six pieces of toast and two cinnamon muffins, including one for her.

Heading out, she nabbed a sweatshirt and sneakers from the mudroom. Wyatt seemed about her size. Her arms were practically exploding as she slipped out the backdoor.

She stuffed a muffin in her mouth, leaving a trail of crumbs which followed her as she took cover in the row of pines. Her cheeks puffed like a chipmunk. Tiptoeing between each tree, she prayed not to be noticed. Once in the barn, she jammed the last bite in her already overflowing mouth and fled toward the cat stall.

In horror, Anna froze. She must have imagined a shadow standing in the aisleway. The girl blinked again.

Officer Martin.

Anna stopped chewing. His arms were plastered on his hips. He was stopped precisely at the end of Dundee's spot and the start of the cat stall.

"You've been called to breakfast. But by the look of your arms, you knew that. Something I should know about out here?"

Anna's eyes widened. She swallowed the dry muffin with a gulp. The pieces jammed in her throat, causing her to choke. She coughed to clear her voice. "No, Uncle Martin. Why?"

Martin scrutinized her as she dropped a shoe. "Running away?" Clearly the additive of *Uncle* hadn't won her any pity.

"No." Anna could only watch as Wyatt suddenly attempted a breakout. The boy darted around Officer Martin from the stall. In a quick pivot, and one long stretch, Martin had a grip on his bony shoulder. Bandit nipped at Wyatt's heels in an effort to corral him to Martin.

"Whoa there, cowboy."

Jess was not supposed to sleep because of her concussion, but she was exhausted. She'd closed her eyes once, only to be awakened by a nightmare. A body was face down in the straw, everything else around her dark as she knelt. She turned the body over, and it was Buddy, a leather rein around his neck. The dream was as real as when she witnessed him in the tack room… dead.

Jess's thoughts bled together. She couldn't be clear who she had rolled over in the stall. Since the dream, she was wide awake, repetitively reflecting over the past events. Her thin body was stretched across her bed when she decided to call Ben Donahue, her boss at the *Chronicle*.

Ben had already learned about the murder. "News hit the headlines this morning. I was about to call you. Your work on the drugging article is over," he insisted.

"Absolutely not. With or without your support!" She turned her cell off, but not before dialing Lola Diaz on a whim. As Jess suspected, there was no answer.

Jess could smell the aroma of Becky's cooking from the loft. After hanging up, she realized she hadn't changed clothes or showered since the incident, so when Becky called for her to come to the table, Jess responded, "Start without me."

By the time she managed to make it to the kitchen, she was in a trance devising a game plan, but she had a splitting headache. Holding her temples, she stopped in the doorway. A strange child was shoveling in scrambled eggs. It was followed by a bite of toast as fast as Becky could slide more on his plate.

"Slow down, honey. My dear boy, you don't want to get sick," Becky suggested.

Anna was sitting directly across, appearing hypnotized by the boy's voracious appetite. Her fork dangled from her hand. Bandit had his head on the thigh of the skinny red-haired boy about Anna's age.

Everyone appeared still, as if in a wax museum—Becky suspending a pan over the boy's dish, Martin pressing a cup of coffee to his lips, Anna's mouth hanging open. The only sound was the boy chewing. Then he slurped down an entire glass of orange juice.

Martin was the first to realize Jess's presence. He cleared his throat.

"I see you all have a secret to share with me," Jess stated. She stared at the boy.

"Mom, listen, do we ever."

"Maybe you want to sit, dear, and have a cup of coffee?" Becky pulled out a chair with her free hand. "Give your mom a minute."

"I really think what I need is two aspirin." Jess headed toward the side cabinet, her eyes never leaving Anna.

"Mom, this is Wyatt Evans. And his parents don't want him. He had to work as a movie star, can you believe that! Then he stowed away in Jax's trailer. He's on the run with no food and no water. We can't send him back. They're criminals, drugging the horses! That's what your article is about, right?" Anna could barely breathe.

Jess stood stationary with the aspirin in her palm.

"Now, Anna..." Martin soothed.

Jess's hazel eyes squinted. "That's a mouthful, little lady. I'm sure this boy—Wyatt, right?—is not quite a movie star. His parents must be searching for him."

"Nope," Wyatt jumped in, his voice flat.

Jess ignored him. "And drugging horses is a huge implication and not something to take lightly. We should call the authorities. So, let's settle your imagination."

"Mom, Martin is an *authority*, and need I remind you the police chief is Sam?"

"Anna," Becky scolded.

The boy placed his glass down. "Miss, may I speak?"

Jess nodded.

"It's the truth. My dad is gone and my mom… well, she shipped me off to the movie set. She needs the money."

Jess tossed the aspirin in her mouth, followed by a swig of coffee.

He continued, "I think Mr. Prickler is part of a drug ring where people go missing. That's the talk anyway with the actors. Something is going on over there!"

Jess raised her hand to stop the boy. She already knew Prickler was Tina's powerful ex father-in-law, responsible for the elite horses Maria rode. He might be a ruthless man, willing to do anything to win. But drugs, missing children? Jess read the panic in Wyatt's eyes.

His voice quivered. "The last boy on the set—the one before me—I never saw him again."

"That doesn't mean he was kidnapped."

A knock on the front door interrupted conversation. The group had been so intent on Wyatt's story that they jumped in unison. Jess did a kaleidoscope around the room until she met Martin's stare.

"Are we expecting someone?" he asked.

"No," Jess assured.

"You three, stay put here in this kitchen," Martin ordered. He dodged into the mudroom momentarily. "I locked the back door. Don't open it for any reason."

Becky almost dropped the skillet, forcing the eggs to slide and splatter onto the counter. Then she rammed the kitchen curtains shut, pinching them tight with her fingertips.

Jess eyed Martin. He touched his black holster as she passed, proceeding with caution toward the front door, knowing the deputy would follow.

CHAPTER 20

Sam and Jax descended the ravine through a dense section toward Deadman's Creek. The two four-wheelers stalked them from a distance, ensuring their path was toward Tunnel Hill.

Clancy Heidel's investigation was not proceeding as Sam had hoped. Instead, it was manifesting into a baffling case with a lot of unanswered questions.

Sam caught a glimpse of an ATV driver where the forest was not as thick, but the man was shrouded in a black shielded helmet. Sam had an eerie sense that the best choice was to avoid confrontation and head home. That day would come.

"I can tell you one thing for sure, mate."

"What's that?" Sam asked.

"That nice truck and trailer were somewhere recently that consisted of the same clay as we saw in the ravine."

They rode in silence, Sam flooded in thoughts about the case and last night's events. He thought about Jess, how she felt betrayed by him, and his heart sank. He wanted nothing more than to marry the woman he loved. To follow through on a forever promise that was an impossible dream right now.

Sam could see Jax engrossed on Belle as he quietly asked her to maneuver the woods. She was alert to him. Her ears pricked, rotating back and forth, sometimes simultaneously as she responded, performing side passes or jumps over logs. Not until they reached the forest edge did either say a word.

Jax stopped. "We have company."

Sam gazed across the wide-open field of long grasses. In the distance he could see movement at the back of their log house. Darting through the grass was a figure. A young boy was running in the opposite direction, not noticing Jax or Sam. Anna pursued him, madly racing, Bandit was by her side and then Becky. Becky was fumbling to gain her feet after skipping off the back porch steps. She was clearly trying to catch the children.

"What in the world?" Sam questioned, rising to stand in his stirrups. He aimed to call out, but Jax held up his hand. Belle jiggled under him from the mysterious commotion.

"I got this, mate. Girl still needs a good run." With that the two were off, both with an exuberant excitement.

Sam cantered behind as Jax galloped up to parallel the sprinting boy. The skinny kid had no defense against Jax. In seconds, the man's powerful arm scooped him up into the saddle behind him.

Jess peeked out a blind slat. "God, it's Ty Burns." She eyed Martin, then opened the door, quickly skirting onto the porch.

"Ty?"

"Jess." He was taller, about Sam's height, but beefier, from a little too much weekend Coors at Ginger Jake's. He studied Martin behind the screen. "I see Sam is providing you with a bodyguard after last night."

"Sam doesn't protect me. In fact, he doesn't even live in this house anymore. Martin's a family friend, Ty. And Buddy was my friend, too." Jess stared directly at Ty as confidently as possible. "I assume you're here about Buddy?"

"I am sorry about your friend. I know how close you two were." Ty backed up a step with a slight bow. She'd noticed his face lifted when she remarked about Sam's new residence.

Jess knew cooperating with Ty was crucial for any information she needed to gain. "Thank you, that's more than Sam could offer."

"I saw that last night, you and Sam..." Ty raked a hand through his greying blond hair. The man momentarily seemed knocked off guard, then cleared his throat. "I'm actually here about two concerns. Yes, I would like to go over the events of last night, which—"

"Ty, I'm exhausted. I haven't slept a wink, and my head is pounding." Jess raised a hand to her forehead yet kept an eye on him. Time to act like a frail woman. "Maybe we could arrange a time when my thoughts are clear, maybe just you and me?" She rolled her eyes up slightly as if pointing to Martin out of his line of sight.

Ty reached his hand up to touch her arm. "Uh, sure we can do that. Seems like you need rest."

"Sam will not be keen on that," Martin muttered behind the screen.

"Sam doesn't get to know my business." Jess kept her hold on Ty but meant her remark for both men.

"Here, take my card and use my direct line," Ty said. "Call me later today after you've had some rest and cleared your head. Maybe jot your thoughts down so we have an outline to base our discussion on. This Lola you mentioned... I've been trying to find her for weeks, for one of the owners. She stole a lot of money, not to mention she took steroids from his stock. We suspect she's reselling them underground. Ben at the paper told me you were working on an article. He suggested you turn that information in—to me—for your safety. And of course, you should stop working on the article."

Jess tried to show no emotion at the mention of Lola, but especially her article. *Bet my ass.* "I appreciate that, Ty." Suddenly, she could hear obsessive barking in the distance. It sounded like Bandit. *That couldn't be.* He was locked in the kitchen.

Ty's hand was still wrapped around her arm. Jess wanted to rip it off and catapult him off her porch. Instead she cocked her head with an angled smirk. "And the other issue?"

Ty seemed unable to concentrate between his touch on her and the barking. He refocused. "Yes... about a missing boy."

Jess was blindsided. She had forgotten about Wyatt Evans stowed away in her kitchen. She blinked herself to attention. "A missing boy?" *Bandit, please stop barking.*

"Yes." Ty hesitated a moment as if he was going to ask about the dog. Luckily, he continued, "I'm sure you heard about the movie set? I'm here about a runaway. He was last seen climbing into the Australian's trailer." Ty pointed to the rig in front of her barn. "His mother... and Mr. Prickler, whom I suspect you also heard of... are desperately searching for him." Ty flashed her a picture. "Why the hell is that dog yapping?"

"Wyatt?" The name slipped from Jess's lips unintentionally.

Martin intervened, Jess's word shocking them both. "The dog must be chasing a rabbit. No worries."

"I didn't say the boy's name. So you know him?" Ty was no longer concerned about the barking.

Jess ignored the question. "And you think he's here?"

Ty gripped her arm a little snugger. "There is the trailer. You said the boy's name. So how do you know him?"

"Well, I can tell you, there's no boy on this property." Jess turned to go inside, but Ty didn't release her.

"How did you know his name?" Ty shifted her back.

Martin clicked the door handle to open it.

"Go ahead, Martin, but I'm going to take a look in the house."

"Ty, you're hurting me." Jess tried to pry his fingers from the soft part of her elbow.

"I smell breakfast and I'm quite hungry," Ty insisted.

Martin moved outside. "Over my dead body."

"That won't be necessary, Martin," another man's voice echoed. "Because Ty here will be off the porch, into his truck and out the lane in a matter of seconds."

Jess instantly recognized Sam's tone. The three turned in his direction. Sam was stationed on the corner of the porch.

Bandit had stopped barking. The abrupt interruption gave Jess the chance to free her arm from Ty.

"Well, Sam Quaid. I think Jess will be the one telling me what to do, considering she says you don't reside here anymore."

Jess flicked an eye toward Sam. She expected a reaction, but his disdain for Ty didn't waver. She immediately scanned the line of pine trees leading to the barn—no horses, no Jax. How had Sam dismounted and appeared like a ghost on the porch? Surely, she would have seen the two men return. Or at the very least, seen Sam head in from the barn.

"Seems like you all have something to hide around here."

"I heard you," Sam said. "You think we know about a woman named Lola and some missing boy. Well, we know nothing." Sam patrolled forward. "Get a warrant. You're the one out of your territory now."

"Funny, Jess here even knows this boy's name." Ty returned his stare to her, his blue eyes bombarding her for an answer.

"Ty, look. We discussed the plan. I have your card." She pivoted back, tripping into Martin.

"That's unacceptable. How did you…" Ty tailed her.

Sam was almost upon Ty, and Jess realized she needed to prevent a confrontation, especially with the guest she was sheltering since Sam had no clue.

Jess examined the picture in Ty's hand. It was a typical grade school picture with scribbling on the back. She prayed and acted. Her sculpted fingers reached like a whip and snagged the photo.

"Lord, Ty. It's written right here, on the back." Her heart pounded as she flicked it over. She would have two options. First, if the writing wasn't Wyatt's name, her intention would be to snatch it, run inside and yell, *"Thanks! We'll keep an eye out for him."* Thankfully the second option came through. Miraculously the word *Wyatt* was penned on the back.

She held the photo to Ty's face.

Crossed-eyed, Ty looked perplexed. Jess instantly looped her arm into his. "Come on. I'll escort you to your truck."

She veered around in front of Sam, shielding Ty. Sam remained stone faced, except for the steam of anger that she felt resonating from his body.

Jess promenaded with Ty to his pickup. He was fumbling with the school picture, surely questioning at what point Jess had seen the back.

He regained his composure. Jess rotated and glanced at Sam. He was at attention on the edge of the steps.

"Jess, really. Let's talk right now. Get rid of him."

"Lord, Ty, you know his temper. That's why I had to kick him out. Appease me here. We can go for a nice dinner, maybe tomorrow night."

Ty assented. "At Ginger Jake's? Or maybe you would be my date at the Ball on Saturday night? Sam would just cringe."

Jess tucked some loose hair and tilted her head as if blushing. "You mean the Equestrian Ball, the night before the championship?"

He gave a hard nod.

"I would be honored," Jess said, practically lifting him into the truck and shutting the door. "We can talk tomorrow night."

As he drove away, Jess inhaled her confidence and faced the two men on the porch. Proceeding with a sway, she intended to pass right by Sam. She had no idea how she would tell him about the boy in the kitchen.

"You have some secret you want to tell me?"

She stopped. "What are you talking about?"

He waited, unyielding.

"Me and Ty?" Jess snarked, hoping to cut him with her words.

Rather, Sam smirked, almost in delight. "I really don't care about you and Ty." The remark serrated her heart. "I'm asking about you and Wyatt."

"Really, Sam, you think I know a Wyatt. You don't believe anything I say," she scoffed, about to walk off.

Suddenly, Becky appeared behind Sam on the porch. She was breathing, rather panting. She bent over, then popped up again. At that moment Jax, mounted on Belle, plodded into her vision on the front lawn. Wyatt was clinging to him from the back of the saddle. He and Belle were breathing almost as hard as Becky.

Belle flexed her sweating neck to tug on the reins. Finally, Anna, tethering Cowboy who was attempting to graze, paced in behind them.

Anna looked at her mom and shrugged her shoulders. "He knows."

CHAPTER 21

After Ty had driven out the lane, Sam watched Jax take the horses to the barn with Anna and Wyatt tagging behind.

He and Jess remained on the porch. He advanced to a mere step away from her. She was trying to explain her account of Wyatt's appearance on Tunnel Hill, but he couldn't focus.

Jess began to fidget, then bumped into the door when she tried to lean away. "Wyatt managed to escape the kitchen to flee out the back door. He's petrified. You can see it in his eyes when he talks." She stopped. "Sam, are you listening?"

"Hmm?" was all he could succeed in saying.

"Apparently you believe Wyatt about as much as you believe me."

He stumbled to answer. Sam could smell her aroma, and this shook his concentration. He took a step back. "I believe Wyatt," he said, "but we can't hide him here. I'll call Carol at the children's home and discuss the matter." Sam's heart was pounding. He was positive Jess could see the vibration of his checkered shirt.

He studied her high cheek bones, captivating green eyes, and tantalizing lips. Although she was glaring at him, Jess was still beautiful. Sam was driven to apologize. He almost did so, but squeezed his jaw shut at the last moment. At this point, she certainly was not about to forgive him.

A chill breezed across the porch between them. Fall was fast approaching, and the warmth of summer was shifting away. Neither said a word as the two locked eyes for what seemed like minutes. Then Sam freed himself and headed toward the springhouse. He had a lot of work to do.

When he reached the door, he glanced back. Jess had already disappeared. He scanned the horizon. The thought of leaving this beautiful farm broke his heart, but saying goodbye to Jess would crush him. He was determined to solve this case and mend their relationship before everything became irreparable.

Once inside, he studied the material scattered across the small breakfast table. Sam was not the most organized detective. His specialty was in the field. He pulled out a chair and glanced at the clock. This day was half over.

The Friday night Qualifier was only days away, then the Saturday night Equestrian Ball. Sunday would be the finale. Two of the five equestrians competing Friday would enter the championship. This weekend would certainly set the stage to catch illicit drug users, sellers and maybe even kingpins.

Time to get organized. Sam laid his phone on the table to key in some notes. He gathered the pile together to reassemble.

First, he examined the newspaper from his office. An equestrian publication, the picture on the front showed a woman in the winner's circle leading a horse. Her face was shrouded behind the steed. The name in the caption was Lola Diaz. Finding Lola was his highest priority for the next day, meaning a possible dinner stop at Ginger Jake's. He stockpiled the clipping on the left.

Next Sam observed the torn paper from the bush under the restroom window at Jake's. He surveyed the words, appearing to be a list connected by horizontal and angled lines. Senseless. He shifted the paper to the right. He would not need it the next day.

Sam slid the documents from the manila envelope regarding the missing horse investigation. What an ass. He'd performed shoddy work by only skimming the information. He fanned through the pages and found no pictures of any kind as Clancy suggested, including the dead horse. He pressed his hand against the envelope and unsuspectingly felt a hard object in the bottom.

Quickly, he flipped the opening upside down. Metal clanged against the table, and Sam recognized the silver items—a chain and dog tags. He examined the inscription which clearly was the property of a Marine because of the MC notation before the identification number.

He inspected the name. Sam blinked. He tightened his jaw in disbelief. "B.B. Sterling." These dog tags had belonged to Buddy. Sam never recalled Buddy without those tags. He closed his eyes and reminisced the night as Dallas examined the cause of Buddy's death. Sam had a talent for visualizing every detail at a scene. Buddy had no dog tags.

He glanced at the date on the front of the report. June of that year. About the same time Sam began investigating the drugging reports.

Why would Buddy's dog tags be in the envelope unless he had been at the scene of the accident? Could this incident at Horse Haven Rescue be related to his investigation? Ironically, Jess had never mentioned it, though she and Buddy were inseparable at the paper. Come to think of it, Sam could not recall this incident being published in the *Chronicle* at all. That was extremely odd; everything that happened in Seven Springs hit the *Chronicle*, even if it was Sandra, his receptionist, eating a donut at Mimmo's Café.

Could all this be entwined? He touched the framed picture in the middle of the table next to the gold ring. The one he had managed to swipe from his office, the one of Jess, Anna and his daughter Sela. They meant the world to him. He would do everything to protect them.

Searching for clues, Jess was in the office rummaging through Sam's desk. Why had someone targeted Buddy? Clearly, the murderer had an opportunity to kill her too, but chose not to. And was the woman Jess believed to have been lying dead in the stall really Lola? She was trying to find the article she had noticed on Sam's desk before. Jess leaned down, her nose almost touching the top of the desk while she searched under the edge.

"Jess?" a voice inquired from the doorway.

Startled, Jess bumped her head. "Ouch." She stiffened to attention as if caught in a shameful act. A large bare chest curved in bulges stood before her. It was Jax, guarding the doorway and rubbing his wet hair with the white towel she had laid over the guest bed. He must have showered after returning from the barn. His aroma stirred her to her senses.

"Sorry. I was just checking on you. Are you missing something?"

Jess pressed her hand to her already thumping forehead. "Jax." She sighed as if he was there to save the day. "I need to find out who and why someone killed my friend Buddy."

"Jess, you need rest. I guarantee Sam will find them. Maybe we could concentrate on Belle and Anna."

This was not the response she aimed to hear. "It was my article that got him killed. You remember my passion for writing. I was working diligently to uncover the drugging of horses at the facility. I was hoping this would be my big career break." Jess thought that the accusation of drugging horses would spur Jax to her side.

"That's why Sam should manage from here. The investigation could be dangerous. Anna needs you."

"Anna needs *you*," Jess insisted, surprised he hadn't appeared to understand. Had he forgotten that he was the one to reignite her writing? She dismissed his advice. Obviously, Sam teetered Jax to his side, so she changed the subject. "I don't know what's happening with Anna or the horse. When Belle enters the ring, it's like a switch flips. Perhaps, Anna has let the pressure of others affect her nerves?"

She met Jax's stare, then shifted as if guilty. His brown hair danced in waves on his head, some drops of water dewing on his massive shoulders.

Jess cleared her throat. "No one could believe a fifteen-hand quarter horse could compete and win against the likes and abilities of thoroughbreds and Hanoverians. Anna worries too much about others laughing."

Jax was silent, but his eyes said he was baffled. "Maybe Anna worries too much about winning?" His soft remark speared her heart. He had stopped drying his hair and held the towel by his side. His abdomen muscles rippled in waves. There was a firmness to his words even though he spoke barely above a whisper. "Do you believe she can do it?"

Goosebumps dotted Jess's arms, causing her to rub the exposed portion of her neck. She imagined her cheeks were flushed in a soft rush of red.

Jess slapped her side with her hands. "We probably should have kept Belle and Anna in a Western program, uh... like reining or barrel racing? She despises everything English anyway." Her voice trailed off.

"I asked if you believed in her. My advice is to follow your heart, your horse's heart. It should not be about winning or others' comments."

Jess was bothered by what he was suggesting. "You know that's great, Jax, but how does that include me staying here? You're the expert."

"She is your everything. As I said, why don't you spend today with us? I think Anna could use some adjusting as much as Belle. And she could use your support."

Jess slumped her shoulders, refusing his advice. "Why did you show up here? Now you're not only a famous horse whisperer, but an actor, too? There are so many people you should help."

"Sam reached out. I'm on a movie set donating proceeds to the children's hospital. I thought there might be a wedding, and my mate, Dundee, needed a break."

Becky interrupted and popped her head in next to Jax. She handed him a steaming cup of coffee. The sight of his bare chest almost buckled her to her knees. "Din... din..." she stuttered, "dinner time."

Jax nodded but remained locked on Jess. His aroma fused with the fresh black coffee as she reflected on his words.

He sipped his smoking coffee. "It's awful when you know something is true but no one believes you."

Jess's eyes widened. *Yes, it is.* She didn't have to say it; he *knew.*

"Think about what I said," he added.

Jess's phone vibrated in her pocket, easing the tension. She tried to skirt past him as she peeked at the name. She shuddered.

LOLA.

CHAPTER 22

Sam couldn't sleep. He had been awake most of the night scouring through past events. He nabbed his keys and the items stashed in the manila envelope. There was a lot to accomplish before a possible final stop for dinner at Ginger Jake's that evening—coincidentally, the same time and location where Jess was to meet Ty Burns.

The clear night sky was lit up by a symphony of stars even though it was giving way to morning. As he approached his Mustang, Sam examined the main house. Unexpectantly, the lower level was aglow. Sam touched the car, his imagination running wild.

Jax had said he would be up early to ride Dundee, but 4 A.M.? The idea of the Australian with Jess today helping Anna haunted him. He wondered why he had even attempted to surprise her with this visit amidst the current issues burdening their relationship.

He imagined Jess smiling perhaps at something Jax said—a smile Sam had not seen in the last month. Then Jax touching her shoulder. His thoughts gnawed at him, spurring Sam to flee into the car. He could not bear envisioning the two tete-a-tete.

Martin had promised to watch diligently this time. Sam had asked for two reasons. First was to protect the family. Clearly someone had tried to harm both Anna and Belle. Secondly, it would keep Sam informed about how Jax and Jess spent their day.

He shook off the rampant thoughts. *Jax would never undermine our friendship... at least I hope not.*

Sam jingled the contents of his pocket before heading to his office in Seven Springs. He needed to be positive that he still had Jess's car keys. An extra precaution.

The police station was totally dark at the end of town when the Mustang parked. The small facility housed three offices, a front desk, two interrogating rooms split by a glass window, and several holding cells in the back. He knew Sandra Drover would not arrive until 8 A.M.

Sandra doubled as a receptionist and secretary, and sometimes tripled as an investigator. After the two had graduated high school, Sandra retained the job, never married, and still lived with her mother, the owner of Mimmo's Café and Pizzeria.

Sam was positioned at his desk by the time Sandra burst around the corner. "Good morning, boss. I heard the news... about Buddy. I am so sorry."

Sam spun around. Sandra was already wrestling the coffee pot. He strolled out to her holding a yellow sheet of legal paper. She didn't stop fiddling with the coffee machine. Her grey hair was a mess of short curls. "Here, I brought you a muffin." She slid a bag toward him, Mimmo's insignia on the outside.

He smiled. "Your mom's homemade muffins are certainly irresistible. Thank you."

"They are. And as you can see," Sandra rolled her hand across her middle, "I don't need another. I see you also have a full list of things to tackle." She pointed to the paper.

"I do."

"Well, I have one question first." She stopped, holding a coffee cup filled with fresh brew. "Is he here?"

Sam knew she meant Jax. "Yes." Then Sam's tone lowered. "Everyone's hero is at Tunnel Hill."

"Hmm, not a good subject?"

"Don't ask."

Sandra snatched the paper from his hand, simultaneously passing him the coffee. She shuffled through her purse for reading glasses. "Okay, let's see. Research Sir Prickler. The director?" She glanced over the glasses. "He directs some award-winning movies, by the way." She continued to scrutinize the list, not giving Sam a chance to respond. "Clancy and Margaret Heidel? Lord, Sam, they're in their eighties and Margaret's been sick... don't have a penny to their name. But whatever you say, boss."

"That's what I thought."

But Sandra acted hard of hearing and kept going. "Call Ben Donahue's paper and inquire what he knows about the accident at Horse Haven Rescue. And why it didn't make the paper. And was Buddy there?" She looked up with scolding eyes. "And ask him if there are any clear pictures of a Lola Diaz."

She raised her eyes over her reading glasses. "Seems like Jess could help you with these questions, but that's none of my business." She rambled on. "And finally, what's a... *a-bat-toir*?" She sounded the word out slowly. "What in the world?"

"A slaughterhouse. Where is one located in the area, and who manages it?"

She glanced up over her pince-nez again. "This will require a raise." Her voice was sour.

"I knew you would say that. How about dinner with Jaxson Bay, the horse whisperer?"

Sandra lit up like a Christmas tree, her round cheeks expanding like balloons. "Really?"

"In fact, he is guest of honor at the Equestrian Ball on Saturday. I invite you to sit at our table." Sam sipped his coffee, waiting for an answer even though he knew it would be a yes. "Now, one more request. Could you call Carol at the children's home? I'd like to drop by."

"No need to call Carol, boss. I just left her eating a muffin." Sandra began to pour another coffee for herself.

"What would I do without you?" He crashed the mug on the counter and winked at Sandra. "You're the best."

"Are you headed to the crime scene? Because I think you should be warned... Ty Burns is watching for you to cross into his territory."

Sam smirked. "Guess I better watch my step, huh?" He winked again.

"Lord, we know how you like danger."

With that, Sam disappeared out the door.

Sam arrived in the nick of time. Carol was about to leave a booth when he slid in. "Have a minute? It's business."

"For you, Sam, of course," Carol responded with a handshake.

Mimmo Drover dashed over with a muffin. Sam raised his hand to politely decline. Mimmo had no part of it. "You look a little thin. Maybe you need to get married."

Then she thrust the decadent treat across the table.

Sam wanted to address the issue of Wyatt Evans. Carol had been receptive to anything concerning children, and the conversation regarding Wyatt went well. Carol was quite concerned upon hearing of possible abuse and adamantly agreed to meet the mother and be in touch with a possible court order to protect the boy.

Sam had not realized how much time had passed. He and Carol had discussed a smorgasbord of subjects ranging from conditions at the home to her family. He even asked if she had heard anything about the director, Sir Prickler. She agreed she would check him out.

"Thank you for all you do," Sam commented as he stood. "I have to run. To think, we talked for almost two hours."

"And back at you. Good friend and good eats. If I eat one more of Mimmo's treats, I will burst!"

Sam's next task was to investigate Buddy's death. But no doubt Sandra was right; Ty Burns would have the West Equestrian Center crawling with security, patrolling for him. Since investigating the crime scene was not a good idea, he'd just visit an infiltrator for pertinent information—Dallas the coroner.

Jess glanced at her phone. She was nestled in the oversized chair in her bedroom where she must have passed out from lack of sleep after twenty-four hours.

Her mind foggy, she retraced the happenings from the evening prior. When her phone had vibrated, she'd slipped past Jax and announced to Becky she was too tired to eat. Then she'd raced upstairs to respond privately to a text from a dead woman.

Lola.

Jess now focused on the floor at her phone. She had attempted to dial the number repeatedly, but no answer. That's when she'd fallen into a deep slumber, only now to see the single text still flashed across her screen.

I will meet you on Friday night. My terms. I will be at the Qualifier.

Don't try to find me. This will only cause me to run.

I will find you.

The Qualifier was edging closer. Jess was not a patient woman. She eyed the time—7:50 A.M. Had she really slept that long? She catapulted out of the chair, doused her face with water, and headed to the kitchen.

From the sink window, she could see Anna, Jax and Wyatt. Jax had designed a course in the field, an arrangement of jumps— parallel, oxer, upright pole, even a plank. Anna and Belle were confidently clearing each one at his direction. Jess disregarded a tinge of guilt.

Perfect timing to slip unnoticed to the springhouse. Jess needed to search through Sam's things, perhaps finding a clue, anything regarding Buddy's death.

She pivoted around to pass stealthily out the back door only to be startled by a man in the doorway. Jess grabbed her chest.

"Martin!" She had forgotten about him. "Really, the men around here need to stop sneaking up on me."

"Sorry, Jess. Only doing my job keeping an eye on you." He was dressed in his official uniform, a light khaki jacket and matching pants. "Are you going to watch Anna?"

"Uh, well, maybe later. I was going to..." Jess scanned the kitchen for an escape. "I was going to take one of my extra coffee pots to the springhouse. There isn't a working one over there.

Thought I would sort of… apologize… with a nice gesture." Jess curled a flirting smile. "You know how Sam likes his coffee."

Martin delayed any response. "Well, let me help you. You can't leave this house alone."

"Martin, really. I will be right over there." She pointed toward the outside. "I am a big girl."

"Should be okay?" His voice crawled to agreement.

Jess fumbled to gather the extra pot from the pantry. "Now, I am only going to the springhouse. It is wiser for you to keep an eye on the children, don't you think? I can scream if I need help." She zipped past, praying he didn't follow.

Inside the springhouse, she explored the kitchen. If she was right, Sam hadn't slept a wink, shuffling through evidence. In luck, she eyed the items on his kitchen table.

A plastic bag containing a set of dog tags caught her attention. She had seen them before. B.B. Sterling. *Buddy.*

CHAPTER 23

Sam ascended two steps at a time to the entrance of Dallas's office, checking back at his Mustang when he reached the door. How lucky that a tan Ranger he observed a block away pulled out from a corner space by the alley. Parking could be an issue in front of the coroner's office, and he didn't want to double park.

He found Dallas standing in his office facing the wall decorated with numerous wooden framed pictures. He was listening to some diabolical concerto, his robust short stature admiring a particular drawing. His chin rested on his fist, only his index finger moving to the tempo.

"Good morning, Sam," he said without turning. "You're late."

"Dallas. Thanks for seeing me." Sam moved beside him to study the picture. "Nice work."

"Work? Sam, this is art." He reached to the shelf and silenced the music. "I am a collector of bones."

Sam raised an eyebrow. *First, he thinks I'm late, now he reveals he collects bones.*

"Not people bones, but charcoal etchings by the famous artist Mason Bones. They invigorate life in me. Just spellbinding."

"They are... *unique.*" Sam hoped to proceed directly to business, but no rushing Dallas.

"I just purchased this one. Ironic, a scene of a horse jumping. That is the topic of the day, isn't it? Horses. This drawing is of the infamous *Ernest Earner.*" Dallas straightened the picture. "But I don't have time to admire, do I, Sam?"

Sam cocked his head and stepped closer. The intricate charcoal etching was indeed of a horse soaring over a hedged fence, but it was the inscription on the bottom that caught his attention.

"*Ernest*? Where have I heard that name before?" He tried to recall. "Are you a fan of horses?"

Dallas thumbed his red suspenders. "I don't know much about horses, but I do love Bones. His charcoal drawings are exorbitant in price, so I make a point to read the attached information." He handed a piece of parchment to Sam.

The paper noted the artist and then described the print. "Seems *Ernest Earner* was a leading money winner in the sport of jumping. Hence the name. To this day, his offspring are some of the most expensive in the discipline. If they carry his name and bloodline, you better have an open wallet. The element that tempted my purchase was the artist and the stud's ties to the tri-county area." Dallas glanced at Sam, to see if he was listening.

Sam stood, arms folded, pressing his lips together while his head bobbed up and down. He was still trying to remember where he heard the name Ernest.

"I see. No time to admire, not when you're involved. No rest for the weary or your better half?"

Sam wondered what the heck Dallas was referring to. However, he didn't have time for light conversation. Dallas's eyes were magnified by the thick lenses of his Harry Potter styled trifocals. They bulged as if he let something slip, and he nervously coughed. "I know why you're here. I have the file out, right there on my desk."

Sam watched Dallas reach to the antique oak desk which was etched on the corners with ornate carvings. The desktop was spotless, containing only one ball point pen, a file marked B. B. Sterling, and an old-fashioned ringed notepad he traveled with to every scene.

"Where's Buddy's body?"

"Ty had the body expedited to the lab. All the information is here in this file. My work is impeccable, as you know." Dallas handed Sam the neatly organized bundle. "By the way, Ty mentioned foul play."

"Foul play?" Sam smirked. "Buddy was murdered, so that's an understatement."

"Let me finish, Samuel Quaid," Dallas scolded as he tucked his stubby thumbs under the suspenders. "Ty requested fingerprints suggesting that they might match you or your precious wife."

"What?" Sam ignored the *wife* comment.

"Your jealousy over Jess and Buddy's working relationship, it seems, suggested to Ty that it might be jealousy that drove you to murder Buddy." Dallas's eyes magnified again. "Ty's theory was you lured them both to the location, pretending to be an informant named Lola. Then *voila!*" Dallas moved his hands from under the suspenders and encapsulated both sides of his neck as if in a choke hold. "You strangled Buddy in a jealous rage."

"You have got to be kidding." Sam raked a hand through his hair. "The two were friends, with an age difference of thirty years, I might add."

"I do not joke about murder. In any case, Buddy's body has been sent up north to the forensic lab for autopsy. If it's any consolation, I don't believe the account for a minute."

"Well, that's a relief. Someone is on my side."

Dallas grinned. "You can handle Ty. I know you've dealt with some of the vilest criminals in the world when you were employed by the FBI."

Dallas swatted Sam's shoulder. Sam whipped an envelope out from the inside of his jacket with his free hand. "Listen, I was delayed in opening this report about the Horse Haven Rescue investigation. I was a little shocked when Buddy's dog tags fell out."

Sam now searched the manila envelope, but the tags were missing. He even held the envelope upside down and let the contents scatter on Dallas's desk. But Sam must have left the dog tags on the table at the springhouse.

Damn it. Focus, Sam, he badgered himself.

"I see you can't stand to let me enjoy a clean desktop." Dallas began to help Sam organize the material. "You aren't the first to inquire about that topic today." Dallas's voice was almost inaudible. "Buddy was at the scene of the accident, I assume for the *Chronicle*, snapping pictures, or whatever he did. He happened to be leaving the scene when I arrived."

Sam closed the envelope. "I find it strange that Jess was not involved in reporting the incident at Horse Haven. Her and Buddy were inseparable as working partners. She reported, he snapped footage. Not to mention, nothing made the papers. As if the accident never happened, yet someone was killed. That's news." Sam stroked his thumb and index finger down his moustache.

"Can't provide an answer on any of the above. I placed the dog tags into the file when I discovered them hanging from the mirror of my car. I assume someone must have found them on the ground and thought I would find the owner. I had every intention to return them to Buddy. I even called him." Dallas paused and slid into his desk chair. "Something else was strange that day, now that I think about it."

Sam pressed his fists on the desk and leaned in. "What?"

Dallas fiddled with his pen. "Well, when I told Buddy about the tags, it was as if he was expecting me to call and inform him I had them. He said, 'What took you so long?' He was adamant I give them to Jess. *Only Jess.* I asked why he wouldn't just come and retrieve them himself. But then he said something even more bizarre."

Sam waited. Dallas appeared in a daze, mesmerized in his own thoughts, until Sam banged on the desk with one of his hands. Dallas jumped. He whipped his glasses off in a fit of disgust, staring at Sam. The coroner rubbed his eyes which returned to a normal size without his specs.

"Buddy said he'd send Jess over to get them... and not to give them to anyone else. Then he got cryptic. I remember the words almost exactly. He said, 'Hey, Dallas. You love to read and can appreciate a good book. I'll send along a copy with Jess of *The Child Spy.* Have you read it? It's a classic.'"

Sam was bewildered by the conversation, trying to understand Dallas's point.

"Well, I am a voracious reader. But I've never heard of *The Child Spy.* Anyhow, when Attorney Cousins ordered the paperwork to be sent to his office ASAP, I neglected to remember about the dog tags."

Sam paced to the wall of pictures. "Why would he want you to give his tags strictly to Jess?" Sam rubbed his chin. "At first sight, this case didn't appear to be difficult. A horse jumps the fence in a storm and causes a terrible accident. Now, it's a tangled maze."

"All mazes have a way out." Dallas came up alongside Sam and pointed to the picture. "Even if you have to jump the fence to find it."

"Dallas." Sam's green eyes lit up. "I need to see the horse— characteristics like its markings, male or female. Where is the body, or maybe a picture? Clancy Heidel claims he examined a picture of the deceased horse. Yet Attorney Cousins swears they were not in the packet he received."

"Body? Where the hell would you store a horse? I can tell you the body isn't here. And I'm not aware of a horse morgue. I would say check the glue factory. And all pictures went to Cousins in the file."

"Come on..." Sam's voice intensified, and he reached for a fresh piece of gum only to find a toothpick.

"Sam, this is a small community. You will never find the horse's body. 1-800-dead-cow was called to the scene to remove the dead animal. That's protocol, unless you have money and time for a pathologist to perform a necropsy. A horse's body starts to disintegrate quickly, so where would one be housed in Seven Springs? I'm a coroner. My job is to announce death and time. Who or why? That's your job. In my professional opinion, the horse jumped the fence, *boom*, car accident and a passenger is dead."

"Who owns the Dead Cow company?" Sam glanced over at Dallas who was once more intent on the charcoal print.

"Not sure. But Clancy Heidel seems to be involved. Somehow. He's been a contact for the retrieval of dead animals, holding live ones for slaughter at the Tri-County Auction House, plus a respite for the over-worked animals who need a change of scenery. Or a place to hide."

Sam read the horse's name again. *"Ernest Earner."* Then it hit him. "Ernest. That was the name Tina Prickler called her daughter's horse."

Dallas had returned to his desk. "Look at the time. I have a meeting. I don't know why the two of you couldn't have come together."

"What do you mean?" Sam eyed Dallas.

Once again, the stout man appeared he had let a secret slip. "Look, the file is from the crime scene at the Equestrian Center. Ty had his crew scour Stall 23 with a fine-tooth comb. There wasn't a dot of blood, no hammer and, as I told your wife, no other body. Honestly, as much as I loathe Ty, he was precise. He would go to every effort to exceed you."

"Did you say my wife?"

Dallas started to apologize. "Oh, that's right. You aren't married..."

Sam raised his free hand. "That's not the point. Jess called you?"

Dallas snapped his suspenders as if scolding himself. "I wasn't supposed to say. But I like you, Sam. I like you a lot. She tried to convince me you wouldn't mind."

"Mind?"

"Jess was here. This morning."

"Here?" Sam pulled out his phone.

"She knows about Buddy's tags. In fact, she had them in her possession," Dallas defended. "I examined them in front of her. The clasp wasn't broken, as if Buddy purposely removed them. Odd. And I googled *The Child Spy*, and found no such literary classic."

"How on earth? Was she with Martin?" Sam was searching for the officer's number on his phone. Then he remembered the tan Ford Ranger pulling out of the front space. He was too far back to realize that it had been Martin. He was supposed to have been at Tunnel Hill anyway. At least, Sam thought he was. Jess must have somehow bribed him to drive her to town. Sam's mind flooded with concern for the kids. Why would Jess endanger them?

Dallas scratched his head. "No. She was by herself."

Sam froze as if x-raying right through Dallas. "She wouldn't put them in harm's way. They are her world," Sam spoke his deduction out loud simultaneously realizing Jess had been alone.

"Sam?"

"Did you happen to catch where she was headed, Dallas?"

"Buddy's office at the *Chronicle*. She was determined to find out why he'd been at the scene of the Horse Haven investigation without her. You better take care of that girl. Buddy was strangled. Someone is not playing games. It's in my report." He pointed to the file in Sam's hand.

Sam didn't answer, instead spun toward the door.

Dallas tailed him offering a word of advice. "You might have to jump the fence to work out of this maze."

CHAPTER 24

Jess swerved the Ford Ranger on to Main Street after leaving the coroner's office. She was upset that Dallas had been reluctant to answer her questions. He was stalling, waiting for Sam. She fiddled with the metal chain and tags she'd stuffed into her pocket. She had not examined Buddy closely enough the night he was strangled to notice they were missing. Buddy always wore his tags from the moment she met him years prior.

"What the heck?" she whispered. "Buddy, why didn't you tell me about the incident at Horse Haven?"

Jess wished she could have stayed and talked to Dallas, but it was too risky. Colliding with a fuming Sam right now would probably land her in handcuffs.

Dallas had insisted, "Sam should be here any minute. I'm sure he'll be fine with me releasing information, but I'd rather wait. Understand, it's protocol."

Jess eyed the dog tags she'd presented to Dallas. The silver shimmered under the fluorescent office lights beaming directly overhead. She had stormed in to inquire about the incident at the West Equestrian Center. Instead, she opened a can of worms.

Jess was still seething that no one would believe her. She'd tossed all night, convinced there was a body in Stall 23. She barely gave Dallas time to move, except for his mouth which fell open in shock.

He'd fingered the dog tags momentarily. Jess could tell he had seen them before. "Good," he said. "You have these in your possession. I am so sorry about forgetting to give them to you." Dallas appeared to lapse into thought as his hand brushed his forehead. "I guess Sam passed them on to you. Funny, I don't recall telling him that Buddy insisted you have them."

Jess let out a small gasp. "You spoke to Buddy before he died?" She studied Dallas and remained dumbfounded.

"He was adamant about you having them. Weird, maybe he had an intuition of some sort." He snapped his suspenders and leaned back in the chair. "Persistent, he was. But it slipped my mind. I apologize."

Jess's eyes welled in tears. Dallas had not really answered her, and she was more puzzled. "Was Buddy alive when you arrived at the scene?"

"Alive? Well, of course. He was there shooting footage for the paper. I did wonder where you were, as the two of you were joined at the hip." Then Dallas must have read the horizontal lines scrunched across her forehead. "Oh God no, Jess." He let out a rare hearty bellow. "Sorry, I wasn't clear. You must've assumed I meant at the equestrian center. He didn't utter a word there. Certainly not." Dallas's voice became as flat as a plateau. "I am not talking about the murder scene."

Jess's cheeks flushed. "Then what are you talking about?"

"The Horse Haven investigation. The one Sam is working on as expert."

"Expert?" Jess had no clue what Dallas was saying, but she didn't want to appear stumped. She stood tall and stepped back from the desk. "Horse Haven," Jess echoed, determined to play along if she could just join in with the game.

"Yes, Horse Haven Rescue." Dallas appeared to stumble, not sure he should continue. "You know, Buddy must have been called to take the photos. Quite frankly, I was surprised you were not with him. You were aware of the incident, right?"

Jess could not hesitate. "Yes, of course!" Her voice sounded an octave higher as she shouted in defense. "Geez, let me see, I believe that was the night Anna had a... something... some function."

Dallas relaxed down into the office chair. "I guess Sam knew how much they would mean to you. He must have forgot he gave them to you." Dallas leaned over the tags. "God works in mysterious ways. Maybe Buddy sent him a sign from the other side. I see stuff like this in my line of work all the time."

"Stuff like what?"

"Like when I called Buddy and told him I found his dog tags hanging on my car mirror when I went to leave the scene of the dead horse accident. He wasn't surprised—said some angel must have placed them there."

"They called you for a dead horse?"

Dallas stopped, completely flummoxed. "I thought you said you knew about the incident? The dead woman was the main reason why I was called there."

"I knew that part," Jess lied.

"In any case, these tags weren't part of the investigation. Buddy had been adamant I give them only to you." He pointed to Jess and removed his glasses. "They were stuffed in the envelope. Guess Sam had a mysterious intuition you should have them. Because I never discussed the matter with him."

She ignored his question, enthralled in her own thoughts. Jess assumed Sam had the tags in his possession from the murder scene. She had to pretend to be aware of the entire happening.

"Since you work for the *Chronicle*, why was that accident kept so secret? It never made print. A few days later when Attorney Cousins called, he threatened to file a court order if I didn't immediately hand everything to him. He claimed the case was being transferred into someone else's hands higher up. Honestly, I didn't have time to worry about it and passed the file to his office immediately. I never heard another peep about the incident."

Jess had to change the subject before Dallas grasped that she didn't have an inkling. "We don't have time for that," Jess explained. "Sam told me to get a head start here regarding Buddy's murder." She tried to control her fidgeting hands by tucking them in her jeans pockets.

Just about everyone knew this coroner favored Sam, including Ty Burns. No doubt, Ty had a conniption when he realized Dallas was filling in for their county's coroner. Jess watched as Dallas's face transformed as if locked up. He pressed his thick hand flat on the single file lying on his orderly desktop.

"I have the file out, but I am waiting for Sam."

"I have a right to have my questions answered. Don't I? Buddy was my best friend." Jess tucked hair behind her ear and blinked her almond eyes.

He opened the file, methodically ironing down the center crease with the side of his hand. Yet the coroner said nothing. He was moving in slow motion as he glanced at his watch, hesitating on purpose. Then he licked the tip of his index finger, touching each page corner before turning it.

"Dallas, please. I saw another dead body. A woman. I saw her. Who was she? Where did she go? I can't clear the image out of my mind! I touched her. I held a bloody weapon. I'm absolutely positive." Jess's words fired at Dallas, hardly stopping for air, tears cascading down her cheeks. "Whoever did this to her is probably the one who killed Buddy." Jess paced toward a wall littered with artwork, then pivoted to face him.

Dallas maintained composure, not giving in. He abruptly closed the file. "There was not one hair, not one drop of blood, nor one clue in regard to another body. I'm sorry that's not the answer you desire."

Jess crept closer to Dallas behind the desk. He turned at an angle to confront her. The file was now pressed against his chest as if he feared she would snatch it from him. The thought had crossed her mind.

"Dallas, someone hit me over the head. Do I need to show you the bruise?"

"I am only providing the facts." He skirted the office chair further from her. "Sam will be here in five minutes. Have a seat."

"I really have no time. I'm heading to Buddy's office. I have to figure out who killed him... and who the woman was."

Jess swiped the tags off the desk. Frustrated, she swiftly delivered them back into her pocket.

"You really need to sit and calm down. This is not a game. And you are in no condition to go driving to the other side of town. Come on, sit."

Jess did not adhere. She headed to the door.

Dallas rose to attention. "Let me ask you something... about Buddy."

Jess halted, prepared to spring for the door.

Dallas moved toward her. This forced her to sidestep away. "Have you ever read *The Child Spy?*"

What kind of question is that? Jess thought.

"It's a children's novel, a literary work," he continued.

"No, but I think I've heard of it." Jess scanned her brain. The name sounded familiar.

Dallas attempted to surpass her to reach the door. The stout man was gaining on her.

"I'd love to get my hands on a copy. Buddy was the one who suggested I read it. He said he was intending on sharing his copy with me. So, if you come across the book in his office, could you deliver it to me?"

Dallas's free hand now crossed in front of her, grasping for the doorknob. He was trying to force her to stay. Jess darted, barely edging past. She avoided eye contact and hollered back, "Thanks. And mum's the word on telling Sam I was here, please. I'll keep an eye out for the book though."

His scolding voice came from behind her. "Jessica Quaid! I thought you said Sam was fine with you being here."

She turned to walk backwards, calling out, "It's still McCoy. And will probably stay that way."

As she rushed to the car, Jess struggled with the fact that Buddy had been at the scene of an accident without her. She didn't have a clue about Horse Haven Rescue. The thought crushed her—Buddy kept something from her involving work. Nothing surprised her anymore about the men in her life.

Jess understood it would not be wise to ask Ben Donahue's permission for what she was about to do. Her boss already demanded she back away from the article regarding the inside world of show jumping, insisting she take time off. Ben would never agree that she visit the one place that might hold an answer—Buddy's office. Her next stop.

Jess steered through the center of Seven Springs. As she headed east, she passed familiar entities she had known most of her life… Jake's Hardware, Millie's hair salon, Mimmo's Café and Pizzeria and the little stone church St. Mary's. The Ford Ranger bumped across the railroad tracks that ran dead center through town–the railway that connected sleepy Seven Springs to all the major hubs in the tri-county area.

She tried to digest the conversation with Dallas, including the fact that there was no evidence of another body. How could she fathom such a scene? Did someone manage an elaborate set-up just to murder Buddy?

Jess was sitting at a green light when the car behind her beeped. She inched forward and realized the police station was just ahead to her left. She pressed the pedal to whip past. Her heart two-stepped thinking of Sam. First, she was so angry at the man she once trusted enough to marry. Second, he was probably on her tail in hot pursuit.

Chapter 25

Jess hoped Officer Martin would forgive her for stealing his truck. He was such a kind soul. Well, technically it wasn't stealing. Her car had not been returned since the night of Buddy's murder. And when she couldn't find the keys to her truck, or any of her vehicles for that matter, there were Martin's. Jess had a good inkling whose possession her keys were in. Sam had left her no choice but to get creative and borrow Martin's truck. She could play Sam's game.

Her exit from the farm went like clockwork. Martin and her sister Becky were hanging over the fence behind the house, observing Jax who worked diligently with Anna on Belle. Wyatt was pressed by the Australian's side while Jess drove out the lane completely unnoticed.

She was positive it was only a matter of time until Sam was hot on her tail, probably barely a step behind. As soon as he would find out she stole Martin's truck, most likely he'd alert every officer in the county. It was her own stupidity to let her next stop slip to Dallas. He would surely inform Sam. That's why she decided to park in a space around the back about a block down the alley from the 1950's building that housed the *Chronicle*.

The *Seven Springs Chronicle* had been in the hands of the Donahue family from its onset in the 1800s. Ben Donahue, the present owner and Jess's boss, was the great grandson of the original owner. He also was the grandfather of Penny Donahue, a member of the Tri-County Pony Club. The same club where Anna was a member. The same club that surprisingly had three members headed for the state championship.

Maria Prickler and Penny Donahue were completely expected to vie for the title, but Anna McCoy's rise was nothing short of a major upset. The outcome to announce the reserve and grand champion winners out of the top five would be determined tomorrow night at the Friday night Qualifier preceding the championship on Sunday.

Ben Donahue's newest purchase for his granddaughter Penny had cost a mere $100,000. For Donahue this was nothing more than a trip to the bank. He'd developed something of an obsession after Maria Prickler's grandfather announced his latest gift to the girl. Grandpa Ben made a mad dash before the season to find a competitive steed for dear Penny.

Although Donahue's hobby was horses, and he had several prolific studs on his elite farm, he had nothing competitive for Penny in his possession at present. Unfortunately, Penny would age out of the youth circuit at the end of the year. He didn't want his granddaughter disappointed, missing out on a $100,000 purse, not to mention the notoriety. Had it been sheer luck that Donahue succeeded in finding an equine of matching bloodlines and talent? *A three-year-old powerhouse* was the description in the club paper announcing the competitors and their mounts.

As Jess turned to veer down the alley, she passed the building that housed Buddy's office, the same location where she had worked for the last two years. An iron six-foot clock was a landmark in the front. It read 11:54 A.M. She didn't need that information to know it was almost lunchtime. Jess had not eaten much in the last two days.

She caught a vision of herself in the rearview mirror before jumping out of the truck. Not only was she hungry, but the woman staring back at her looked exhausted. The trials that had occurred in the last two days were tearing at her soul. She was in the middle of something sinister. Someone murdered Buddy, attempted to capture Belle, and then attacked the joy of her life, Anna! Why? And why would no one believe her story? Jess was left no choice but to pursue matters on her own.

She lifted the pink hood of her sweatshirt before strolling toward the building with her head tucked and sunglasses pressed over her eyes. She noticed the flag in front was flying at half-mast. Before entering, Jess read the posted note on the door: *Due to the grave sadness of B.B. Sterling's death, the offices of the Seven Springs Chronicle will be closed for five days. Staff will answer calls remotely, working from their home offices.*

Ironically, Buddy's death provided Ben an honorable reason to close. The truth was that he was having the building remodeled. Although Donahue appeared to be an upstanding citizen who donated a vast amount of money back into the community, he was also cold. He bared his teeth at anything or anyone who tried to outdo him. Those who worked there knew never to cross the owner.

Jess sighed in relief when the double glass doors were unlocked, and no guard was stationed between the first and second entrance. The strong odor of sawdust flooded her senses as she entered. The building appeared completely vacant, but Jess knew better by the distant sound of construction. The humming of saws and tapping hammers vibrated at the end of the hallway. Contractors at work. The *Chronicle* had grown, and Donahue was expanding.

She skimmed the foyer. Its large rotunda had a glistening white marble floor and was trimmed in ornate gold. Massive columns supported the second level balcony while the rest of the expansive room was an open two stories with a domed center. The reception desk marked the middle. The large staircase climbed behind the desk and led to the balcony where there were two offices: one for Ben Donahue and the other for his personal secretary.

Jess gazed upward. The Donahue office door was closed, but the muted glass was illuminated. Jess could hear a muffled voice, definitely Ben. His words were inaudible, but not the loud bang that suddenly resonated through the entire rotunda. Ben had appeared to pound something on the desk, and her body jumped in response.

Ben must have been captivated by a phone conversation. *Good.* Jess decided it was time to move quickly toward Buddy's office. She would hopefully go unnoticed. The pang in her abdomen said it was best not to disturb her boss. The fewer people that knew she was searching through Buddy's files, the better. She didn't want Donahue to even know she was in the building.

Jutting out from the circular waiting area were lengthy hallways. The newspaper building was split in two divisions: reporting to the left and publishing to the right. Two conference rooms were nestled at the end where the construction was taking place. In the last years, Jess had spent many a day working long hours on location. She was dedicated to write that one promising article that would skyrocket her career and provide the notoriety she dreamed of.

Jess practically tiptoed past the main reception desk and examined the left corridor where her office and Buddy's were located. She whipped her hood back and zipped past the first room housing the cubicle she shared with several part-time reporters. Jess didn't store any items of importance at her desk space so there was no need to check it. She focused on one goal—Buddy. The photographer's office was at the end of the hall right before the conference area.

Well past the rotunda, the hallway darkened. The one fault of the building design was its lack of windows. Jess didn't want to bring any attention to her arrival by flicking on lights. As she closed in on Buddy's office, Donahue's voice diminished, the hall darkened, and the construction humming grew louder. Jess shivered with hesitation.

She checked back down the corridor. *Shake it off, lady.* It was like a reenactment, a déjà vu from two nights prior.

When she reached her destination, she touched a laminated sheet of paper pasted across the same muted glass that was inlaid in every door. *Do not enter, contents under investigation.*

Jess edged her hand down to the knob and turned. As she suspected, the door was locked. She could no longer hear Donohue's muffled shouts. Every sound was deafened by the racket of construction. Although Jess had been prepared for the door to be locked, she was not prepared for the eerie feeling that the message on the office door was meant directly for her.

Ben was aware that Jess and Buddy were tight. She knew he would assume Buddy entrusted her a key to his office. The photographer was notorious for locking himself out, and other than the janitor who could rarely be located, he needed a good friend to save him with a spare key. Ben probably assumed Jess was that friend. But he was wrong. Jess held no extra key. However, she knew where to find one.

Buddy kept a spare hidden nearby. Jess checked right, then left to verify the coast was clear. She knelt to the floor and sought the hairline tear loosened from the molding strip. She was never sure if Buddy had discovered it in the carpet or made the slice himself. That was the secret spot under which he slipped an extra key. Jess loosened the edge back and fingered for the key with victory.

Quietly dipping into his office, instead of turning on the lights, she raised her cell phone flashlight and viewed the room. Buddy had few possessions. He was an avid mystery reader, an exceptional photographer, and easy to work with.

After returning home as a Marine from Vietnam, Buddy lived alone, never married and worked freelance. When he retired, he took a job with the *Chronicle*. The soldier loved his country and claimed his dog tags were one of his most valuable possessions. He lived as a minimalist, and other than his books and pictures, which filled his office and home, he journeyed through life completely satisfied.

Jess expected to view what she always did upon entering her friend's office—books stacked on the shelves and clusters of pictures nailed haphazardly on the walls. That wasn't the case. As Jess scanned the room, she shuddered. Someone had already cleaned house.

The pictures and photos, the ones Buddy tagged as his greatest masterpieces, were barely hanging, some angled in different directions, some broken on the floor, pictures from his tour in Vietnam to the latest events in Seven Springs. The entire premises was in disarray. File cabinets popped open, drawers emptied with only remnants of loose pieces of paper, paperclips speckled the area, pens strewn on the floor, and one stapler next to his computer on the desk.

What was the chance the computer still functioned? Jess knew the password, but so did the IT department. Jess inspected the door. She raised the office chair back on its wheels, sat and turned his computer on. To no surprise, nothing displayed except a black screen. All his files and his pictures had been deleted as if he were never here.

She exhaled what was left of her energy... nothing.

Jess continued rummaging through the two-drawer desk with a final hope. Her head was deep in the lower drawer below the desktop. She never heard the door click or open. Not until the bright fluorescent light flashed on.

Jess jumped to her feet, too quickly. Her lack of nourishment and lingering headache set her body in a spin like a merry-go-round. Bumping the desk chair sent it plummeting to the floor with a crash. She dropped her phone to grip the desk for support. Jess attempted to focus on the blurred image blocking the door.

She squinted and muttered, "Ben? Is that you?" It had to be. He was the only other person in the building that cared if she was in Buddy's office.

"Jess," her boss's voice held no sympathy for her unstable body. "This office is off limits. Did you read the note on the door?"

Jess nodded. Ben was a man in his early seventies. Thin and tall, he avidly worked out. His head was clean shaven which made him quite attractive. He was perceived as a beacon in the community.

He generated a condescending stare, which he was very proficient at doing. Removing his reading glasses, he stepped closer and kicked the door with his heel. To her dismay, the door shut behind him, leaving Jess trapped.

"Your colleague was murdered. This office is part of a police investigation. I'm shocked Sam didn't warn you about coming on the premises."

Jess could barely respond. She was gathering herself and restoring her vision.

"Was there a reason you were shuffling around in Bud's office so secretively?"

The hair on Jess's arms spiked. Something was wrong with the way Ben was talking to her. He was the one who had personally given her a job, the same man who insisted Anna join the pony club. *"It would be great to have a Western discipline rider in the English* club," he'd touted. *"The girls need a little diversity."* At present, Jess sensed a negative rush of emotions that tormented her.

"That is a funny thing…" she started to defend herself.

"Humor me, Jessica."

"Quite honestly when I tapped the light, it didn't work. I figured the construction workers had the electric off."

Ben proceeded to flip the light switch on and off as if machine gun fire. Every time it shone, she caught his torturous smirk. On the final time, his sneer disappeared, and he cut her the demeaning glare.

"I know it seems funny that it apparently works quite fine now but…" Her voice drifted off as if admitting she had been snagged in a lie.

"And suddenly, let there be light?" Ben added in a tone matching his expression.

Jess pretended to cover her eyes, searching the floor for her phone.

"I'll have the workman check this out." Then he extended his hand. "Your key, please."

"Excuse me?" Jess met his penetrating grey eyes.

"Your key," his voice raised.

"I was just searching for pictures Buddy snapped of Anna at the show. I have so few." Jess stretched her arms out. "Who emptied his entire office? It looks like a disaster zone, more like someone was tearing it apart to find something. I knew they would be confiscating the contents of this office, but like this?"

Jess stared at his stationary open hand.

"My search was innocent, Ben, and it's not my key. It's the extra one Buddy had stashed away."

Her boss wiggled his fingers, dismissing her remarks.

She held the key out to him. Ben snatched it up. There was no reason for her not to go. Nothing was left here.

"And yours?"

"Mine?" Jess balked. "I told you, I don't have one of Buddy's keys."

"To *your* office."

"Ben… are you… letting me go?"

"I advised you to keep a low profile. Yet here you are trespassing through Buddy's *off limits* office. Are you aware how serious a crime that would be if I chose to press charges?"

"Press charges?"

"Funny, Sam really should have informed you of the consequences."

"Are you kidding me?" Jess scaled the floor in a quick glance to locate her missing phone. She was feeling uneasy.

"I don't kid. I also don't need allegations of drugging when one of the largest horse show events is about to take place. The income and benefits for the tri-county area are crucial to our economy. Not to mention the valuable experience and notoriety for each rider, owner, and trainer involved in the competition. Or maybe that isn't so important to you now that your daughter is struggling to keep her status? Jess, I am beginning to question why I ever allowed the little Western girl to join our club."

"Little Western girl join *your* club?" The remark spliced Jess like a knife. She would never forget Ben's true character she was witnessing at this moment. "Don't you bring Anna into this. I'm warning you."

He continued his harassment. "I heard the Australian is once again visiting Tunnel Hill Farm. Or should I say, the magic Australian?" Ben released a snarky laugh.

Jess's body surged with heat. Time for her to take flight as soon as she pinpointed her cell. But she had one more question. "Why was Buddy at the scene of the Horse Haven Rescue accident without me? He didn't even mention it. The entire incident was hush-hush." She returned a vice gripping stare and thought best not to mention the dog tags.

"No idea. I believe I was in the islands, vacationing." The lock between them lasted for what felt like days until Ben broke the hold. "Perhaps, Buddy was tired of working with you. Maybe he wanted his space?"

His blow was final. That's when Jess eyed her phone and lunged. Donahue beat her to it. Ben scarfed the device and dangled it in the air. Fear sickened her.

"The Qualifier is this weekend. I am so sorry Anna's horse is experiencing issues. She was a surprising candidate. Lucky, she was in the top five. Certainly, a one-time honor on such an inexpensive little quarter horse." He swirled the phone in his hand. "If you don't mind me saying, you didn't really think they could possibly win, did you?" Opening his hand, the man extended his arm, teasing her to seize her phone. Jess inched her hand, gently touching the device.

"You need to stop stirring up bad publicity. And tell your Sam, his secretary needs to stop her questioning, too. I can demote her just as simply as you."

Jess never anticipated his hand closing and caging hers. Jess yanked hoping to steal her hand and the phone, but Ben refused to let go and tightened his grip.

"That is a fair warning." He dropped her hand with a shove. Jess sighed in relief, at last gripping her device.

Jess palmed her own office key and dropped it on the desk, avoiding his space.

Ben shifted aside and hailed an arm as if escorting her out. Jess skirted past.

"If it is any consolation, I liked the man. Unfortunately, you both were snooping in the wrong places. Better leave well enough alone. I warned you... Buddy's murder is on your conscience."

CHAPTER 26

Sam revved the Mustang at the same time he established Martin on the cell phone. "How the hell did Jess manage to drive away in your truck? Tell me she didn't talk you into letting her borrow it!"

"No sir, I guess... she might have stolen it." Martin paused.

"Might have?"

"I don't want to press charges or anything, sir. I like her, lots. But she is one tough cookie to keep tabs on."

"Tell me about it," Sam mumbled. "Listen, just stay glued to the others. If you have to corral them all in a stall, you have my permission. Whatever it takes. Don't lose track of any of them. I got Jess."

"Yes, sir. And, sir, don't be *too* upset with her. She has good intentions, and she's been through a lot in the last few days." Martin cleared his throat. "If I may say so, you have not been the most sympathetic."

Sam grunted a goodbye as Martin's words lingered on in his heart. He had barely left Dallas's office and was headed out Main Street in search of the woman he loved. Martin was a genuine person, always considerate, always loyal. Sam could hardly be angry at him, although he wanted to let loose on someone.

At the first red light, he took the opportunity to text Jess. He didn't expect a response. But he hoped to talk some sense into her if she would possibly answer.

He re-read his message before pressing send: *What the hell are you doing! You need to head back home to Anna. Call me!* Martin's advice echoed in his ear so Sam decided to soften his tone.

Jess, where are you? Could you call me, please? I
simply want you and Anna safe.

As he proceeded through town, Sam eyed every crevice along
his course in search of the tan Ranger. Despite his knowledge of her
next stop—thanks to Dallas—Sam still sensed it necessary to check
his surroundings. Jess may have detoured for another destination.

Sam observed Millie placing her fall scarecrow on display and
adding mums to the window boxes of her salon. The manager was
sitting in front of his hardware store slouched in the rickety folding
chair having his lunchtime smoke break, and Father Bob was
sweeping the steps of St. Mary's. A few teens were riding bikes and
mothers pushing strollers. All were oblivious to any indiscretions
below the surface of sleepy Seven Springs. Each recognized Sam by
his charged black Mustang rumbling through town. Each tossed
him a wave or tip of their hat except for Father Bob who motioned
Sam to attend church. Sam curled a corner of his lip.

All people for him to protect.

As Sam passed the station, he wondered how Sandra was
making out, if she had any luck researching his battery of
questions.

He arrived at the *Chronicle* office and cruised both front and
back areas. No luck locating the tan Ranger. The parking lots were
vacant, except for a few construction vehicles. He noticed Ben
Donahue dressed in a tailored black suit and carrying a gym bag.
The sophisticated man was locking the double front doors, then
parading down the steps toward his shining black BMW.

Sam intended to pull in directly behind him to block his exit.
Perfect time for a discussion. But his plan was interrupted by the
vibration of his phone. Instantly, he thought of Jess. He whipped it
out to read the name. His jaw stiffened. It couldn't be!

It's Lola. Tomorrow night, at the Qualifier, I will
reach out. Don't look for me, I will run.

Impossible. He pressed redial and listened while gazing ahead.
No message and no answer. Sam sat in disbelief realizing Donahue

had noticed his vehicle. The older gentleman immediately dialed something on his cell. By his expression, there was a good chance Ben was calling security.

Sam refused to be intimidated. He clicked his door to step out. But the sight of a tan Ford Ranger brought him to a dead stop. The truck darted across the back alley and onto the main street.

Jess!

He ditched his phone on the passenger seat, simultaneously slamming his door and leaving Donahue with a bewildered stare. Sam wasn't about to lose sight of her.

He thought to flick on the flashing alert lights but stopped himself. The day was overcast, with a low haze, even a fog in some lower areas which was strange. This weather would make the perfect conditions to trail her inconspicuously. Good way to discover just what she had on her radar next.

As he followed her out of town, Sam had a good intuition where Jess might be headed. And if his hunch was correct, he had enough time to call Sandra for an update.

"Good afternoon, my favorite secretary."

"Ha, you mean your one and only," Sandra joked, obviously munching something. "Don't try to sweet talk me. This list is over the top."

Sam knew she loved her job. "How are you making out? Sounds like you're breaking for lunch?"

"I was about to. Whew, am I exhausted." Sandra pretended to be agitated. "Where do you want me to start?"

That was when the typical Sandra rambling began, talking without a breath.

"I haven't heard anything from Carol at the Children's Home. I am aware you spoke to her. Things may take some time. I put my feelers out to start researching Sir Prickler, the movie mongrel. Did I tell you, he directed some great movies? I do know he has a lot of money invested in the equine world. Haven't heard from Ben Donahue himself, but his secretary was quite snippy. Makes you appreciate me, huh? I've found not one published word about your Horse Haven case or why it was so hush-hush. But here's an interesting fact."

Sam imagined Sandra was running her index finger down a list.

"We don't have a slaughterhouse or an incinerator in the county. Thank God. But unfortunately animals from the Tri-County Auction House are transferred. Clancy Heidel appears to oversee the dirty work of pick-up and delivery. He takes them directly to the train station. Block 5 to be exact. Where is Block 5, you ask? Right at the auction house located at... drum roll please..."

Sam could hear Sandra make a tapping noise across her desk.

"It's one stop after the Expo Center, just a few miles outside of the city. So, if his show horse doesn't perform to spec, Sir Prickler can drop and dash. That's a joke, by the way. The train rolls out of the Tri-County Auction House once a month on a Saturday night. This coming one, to be exact. While we are wining and dining at the Expo Affair, a few miles up the road these beautiful creatures are marching to their demise."

Sam watched as Jess made a turn ahead, just as he'd predicted.

Sandra sighed. "Really it's ironic and sad. I hate the thought of animals having a horrible life. I want to save every one of them. Funny, I thought that was what Heidel's horse rescue was all about. That's why I have five dogs, fifteen cats and a goat. But, as with many equestrians, I guess the only concern is winning."

"Take a breath, Sandra. You might need a raise with all those critters." Sam had actually slipped a sentence in. He wondered if she heard his smile.

"Nice to hear you say something funny. You haven't been yourself these last months. Why don't you just say you're sorry?"

"I am sorry, Sandra. These past few months, there has been a lot happening."

"I don't mean to me. Apologize to someone else." Sandra could be heard taking another bite. Sam knew what she meant. She had a heart of gold, like Martin.

"One more question, then I have to roll. My subject is gaining ground on me."

"Shoot." Sandra's answer was garbled as she continued to eat.

"Who owns the Auction House?"

"That is another ironic twist. Yours truly, Doug Kinard, the Humane Officer. Can't say I ever cared much for him. You remember him from school, Sam? He used to tease the heck out of the underclassmen and our mascot. That helpless little bearded goat. How is it Doug Kinard could climb to the top and be appointed to such a noble profession?"

"All good questions... and answers," Sam commented.

"You better... clean... dinner... with the magical Australian," she declared with a giggle. "You owe me!"

His cell service was fading in and out. "Look, Sandra, you did great! I must be losing service out in River Hills."

"Okay... *Marco*."

"Marco? What does that mean?" Sam asked quickly.

"You respond with *Polo*."

"Polo?" Sam was completely bewildered.

"A game, like say, tag. You're it. You know... I call you, *Marco*... and you answer with *Polo*. It's like a code. Marco Polo. That's it, a secret code."

Sam grunted, "Tag?" He didn't quite understand.

"Oh, forget it. And River Hills? What... are... doing?" Sandra was cutting in and out. But her last words were clear. "Be safe."

Jess assumed that Buddy had resided in River Hills for most of his life after returning from Vietnam. At least that's how he spoke of the little cottage he seemed to adore. Bungalows littered the cliffs overlooking the Susquehanna River but were far enough apart that neighbors were not visible. Buddy was a loner and liked it that way.

She drifted along the brim of the gravel road reading numbers slapped on mailboxes, some half missing or peeling away. The area was overcast and foggy, and she couldn't see well until right on top of each one. She made a sudden stop at 443 River Hill Road, the address of B.B. Sterling.

She eyed the cottage's slate roof. Several slabs were missing. Others needed repair. Only the roof of the bungalow was visible because the rest of the house was snuggled into the side of the cliff that dropped to the river.

Already the temperature decreased since leaving the center of town. *About five degrees*, Jess thought as she opened the car door. The combination of a heavy foliage canopy and cool air rising from the moisture below, Jess zipped up her hooded sweatshirt and proceeded toward the edge.

She surveyed the area. Not a soul around. An eerie fog blanketed the gully like smoke. Odd for that time of day. She could only hear the water rumbling as it cascaded over the rocks in serenade with a jungle of chirping birds.

Jess reached the crest of the ridge. She stood next to a neon orange *No Trespassing* sign and studied the entrance to Buddy's cottage he called home. Her foot stepped on a splintered piece of wood, the first step on the only way down to the bungalow. A rickety wooden staircase that was a far cry from the staircase at the Donahue building led the way to Buddy's front door. The boards cut the cliff in zigzags like a quilt pattern, some darker, older and weathered, beside lighter, newly replaced sections. All were in need of attention.

Jess surveyed the board and batten cottage with a screen porch jutting out over the ridge secured by what appeared to be only four wooden posts that disappeared into the haze. The screens, like the boards, were in need of repair, ripped and curled with age.

Jess had been to Buddy's cottage only once to pick up photos for a story while computer systems were down. Buddy met her at this exact spot, the top of the steps leading down. She never noticed how the place was a fire trap.

She tightened her ponytail and inhaled moisture and the smell of fresh green moss hugging the trees. Her skin was wet, dotted in dew. Or at least she hoped it wasn't sweat from anxiety. She couldn't imagine crossing these wooden steps several times a day or night and feeling safe. She gripped the wobbly banister and shook it. *Ouch.*

Jess scrutinized her hand, already one splinter too many. The banister was split or cracked in multiple sections. She carefully managed each step with control. They were especially steep, but most intimidating was the open space between the stairs, giving full view of the ground below. The haze canopied and hid the full depth at places, making the thought of a fall even worse.

Jess sighed a sense of relief went she reached the porch door. She made it.

CHAPTER 27

Jess entered the screened porch which was in a state of disrepair. A mutation of a musty odor mixed with stale kitty litter and cigarettes hit her. She noticed a cat box under a hickory twig stand next to a wooden rocker. Jess cautiously moved into the house. The screen door squeaked and slammed behind her.

She remained stationary and looked over the small, open floor plan. She should have felt no surprise that Buddy's house was in similar condition to his office. Still Jess was shocked. His computer had been smashed into smithereens on the kitchen floor, dishes broken and tossed from the few cabinets mounted on the wall, bookshelves demolished, and chair cushions upturned.

The bungalow was a mere 800 square feet, enough living space for Buddy. Jess stood in the kitchen, with its café style table and chairs. She peered into a small living area, where books were strewn across the floor. A small TV was shattered like the other devices, along with the CD collection Buddy boasted about. Every case was open and the discs split in half. There was only enough room in the tiny den to hold two recliners which had been shredded. Billowing white foam puffed out.

Jess could see a bedroom and bath in the back corner. The same musty smell infiltrated her nostrils as she softly stepped between the broken objects and books like a childhood game of Twister. The walls were whitewashed with tan trim, in need of a good coating of paint. The ceilings were extremely low, almost closing in on her. Wood floors throughout were probably original from the 1950s.

She could see the bed covered in a green military blanket. An old-fashioned claw foot tub stood in the bathroom. Black mildew speckled the chipping ceiling from too many steam baths.

She raced back to the kitchen feeling claustrophobic. The sink was filled with dirty dishes, probably from Buddy's last meal. The wood stove was hanging open. She couldn't imagine a fire in this small timber house. It was mere kindling itself.

The scene accentuated the truth that Buddy was dead, and it tugged at her heart. Her eye zoomed in on a picture of the two of them, its glass cracked on the floor, causing her to step further back, bumping into the settee.

Ben had been right. Buddy was dead because of her. She raised her eyes up, fighting back tears when she eyeballed the top of the Kelvinator.

The refrigerator towered a mere three inches from the ceiling. Just enough room to rest his cookbooks. Jess was far enough back that she eyed three books resting there with their spines facing her—two cookbooks, and the other *The Child Spy.*

Jess blinked and whispered the title aloud. That was the book Dallas had been asking about that morning. Then she remembered Buddy, the night she'd asked him to meet her. He had mentioned the same book. Unfortunately, she blew him off and told him he could explain later. The book was tucked between the other two, oddly untouched, on top of the old Kelvinator.

As Jess pressed against the table, a sudden dark flash soared into her peripheral vision. A mound of fur plummeted through the torn screen. Jess had barely a moment to block her face and chest before the animal landed on the table, then went airborne in her direction. The varmint lunged for her, clawing on her forearm to gain stability instead of falling.

Jess belted out a loud screech, coinciding with a similar one from the yellow furball. On final release, the critter catapulted to the floor, taking off in a race toward the other room. Jess lost her balance and reeled backward to plop hard on the wood floor.

Sam was finished with the cat and mouse game. He had parked below Jess on the gravel road, far enough back that she hadn't noticed him. He watched her through his binoculars, positive she had disappeared where he presumed the entrance was to Buddy's cottage. He could not tolerate sitting here, waiting. Sam had to know she was okay.

What Sam really needed was a strong cup of coffee. His head was growing cloudy from lack of sleep. He hopped out of the Mustang. It was good the environment invigorated his senses—the chilling dampness, the sound of rushing water, and the smell of moisture. They both needed rest. He would go into the bungalow and demand Jess return safely home.

Sam paced himself until reaching the edge of a dilapidated wooden staircase—an aged timber passageway to the cottage. He stopped, his cheek muscles twitching from the pressure in his jaws. Sam surveyed the situation. Then his hand touched the bright orange *No Trespassing* sign that Jess completely ignored. Sam gave the rail a good shake only to hear a crack. *Hell, all you need is one match to take this thing out.* He was surprised to think of Buddy traveling across it several times a day.

Suddenly, there was no more time to think because a piercing scream resonated from inside the cottage. It was Jess. Coinciding with another high-pitched screech which was not Jess. His heart stopped.

Sam didn't waste another moment worrying about footing. He dove to action. Scaling the decking stairs two and three at a time, he reached the porch screen door. His twenty-plus years of FBI existence immediately sent him into protocol. He pulled his pistol and slammed the door with the side of his arm, flinging it open. Sam spun the weapon around the circumference of the porch scanning the area. Then he called her name.

"Jess?"

No answer. He busted through the second door with the identical procedure, almost tripping over the woman lying flat in front of him. Jess was there on the floor, a small yellow cat purring at the base of her legs.

His gun was locked and loaded. He held a stance over her while checking the room at every angle. Sam leaped across and shifted into the living area, then surveyed the bedroom and the bath just like every drug bust or crime scene he'd ever engaged in.

"Sam, no one is here. It was this kitten. The little rascal lunged at me... jumped in through the screen."

Sam did not respond. He was still in attack mode, absorbed in his surroundings. He kicked the numerous items littering the floor as he headed back to her almost tripping. Someone had been desperate to find something.

When he rounded the corner, Jess was gazing at the yellow kitten purring and whining at her feet. She remained stuck to the floor, dots of blood seeping through tears in the forearm of her pink sweatshirt. He remained silent in a rigid stand.

"You can put your gun away. I told you, it was this kitty. He must be hungry, but he scared the heck out of me." Jess leaned forward on her knees with a slight grunt. She cradled the kitten in her arms, then tried to rise.

Sam quickly disarmed his weapon and tried to assist, but she pulled away. He slapped his side and stepped back.

"Why are you following me?" Jess didn't make eye contact after her snappy remark. Instead, she went to the screened porch and nabbed the cat carrier sitting under the table.

"What are you doing here? This house is part of an investigation," Sam slashed at her. His heart had not stopped thumping since he heard her scream.

"I guess I'm investigating. You wouldn't believe me anyway." Jess acted like a damaged child. "And Buddy's kitten needs a home."

"Look, you're in enough trouble already. Now let's go."

"I will go when I want. You stole my keys." Jess was preparing to place the kitten into the carrier when his hand latched on to hers.

"You stole Martin's truck. That's a crime. What are you not getting about this?" Sam's crystal eyes held hers in contempt. "You could be arrested for the crimes you committed. You're also trespassing. Plus, you went through the investigation packet on my desk and stole evid—"

"You mean the dog tags?" Jess interrupted. She finished placing the kitten in the carrier. "You should have told me about Buddy's tags." Jess held them out to him.

He raised an eyebrow saying nothing. He wasn't even looking at her.

"Sam? Take them." She jingled them in the air. "Take them!"

But he was not paying attention to Jess. His head was raised and tilted slightly to the side. He sniffed the air.

"What's that odor?" He raised his hand.

"What are you talking about?" Jess snapped.

"Shh. Listen, Jess?"

Jess looked annoyed. She tucked hair behind her ear as if the gesture would help her hear better. "You mean that distant sound of a... a four-wheeler? We're in the middle of nowhere." Jess rolled her eyes. "What's the big deal about a four-wheeler?"

He shook his head. He'd heard the four-wheeler, too. Lots of people had ATVs there in nowhere land. "No, it's a hissing. Like air being released from a balloon," he softly suggested.

Jess listened. She touched the handle of the cat carrier.

The four-wheeler was growing closer. Sam did not like what he was thinking and tucked his gun back in his holster. He curled his hand inside her arm, then slid his other hand under hers to lift the cat carrier and maneuver her toward the door.

"What are you doing?" she balked.

"We're leaving," Sam ordered.

"Sam, I—" Jess stamped her foot, pushed his hand away and clutched the cat carrier in objection.

"Jess, this is serious." He didn't release her before he leaned into the porch screen to the side of the cottage. He examined the ground below and area above. The four-wheeler was near, at the top edge of the house, idling, waiting.

He heard Jess inhale deep, then cough. "What is that rotten smell?"

Sam couldn't answer. He saw the propane tank against the house, where someone had no doubt opened the valve. He could now hear the gas soaring freely into the air. He caught a glimpse of the white four-wheeler up at the cliff, inching back and forth as if challenging Sam to run. The rider had a blow torch strapped to the back.

"Gas."

"What?"

His powerful frame spun her around. "We have to get out of here."

"What, Sam? What?"

He yanked her to the second door, but Jess was pulling back like a raging bull.

"No, the book."

"What freakin' book!"

"*The Child Spy.* Buddy insisted I have it!"

"Too late! This place is gonna blow!"

Jess ripped her arm free. She was breathing heavy. "Take the cat!" She rammed the carrier toward him in the center of his chest.

He read the seriousness in her eyes. She had every intention to go back and locate a stupid book. "I'm not leaving you." But it was too late. She was already on a mission back into the cottage.

Sam heard the four-wheeler dig dirt to dive toward the house. "Jess!" He dropped the cage to nab her hand, but she rushed the door. He had no choice but to follow.

Sam raced back inside to find Jess standing on her tiptoes knocking books further back on top the refrigerator, until they slipped between the fridge and a cabinet. He seized her arm and jarred her back. "Jess, they're going to kill us."

But she was not relinquishing. Now she'd made matters more difficult. The books were jammed.

Sam released a potent grunt as heat rushed his face and neck. He heaved her back. "Get out! Take the damn cat and get out!"

His arm was struggling, wedged between the refrigerator and the cabinet. Sam could feel the vibration of the ATV against the house. He grunted again. His fingertips snagged the book, and he tapped it closer to his reach.

Now the attacker was under the porch. Sam felt the reverberation as the ATV circled around to do the job Sam feared.

He was shocked when he pivoted, book in hand. Jess was still standing there. She hadn't left. Instead she was waving her hands waiting on him. "Come on, come on!"

He busted out the door onto the porch. The ATV, revving underneath, had gotten stuck against wet rocks and viscous mud. It bought them time, perhaps the minute they needed. He scrambled to get Jess out the second door. Sam flung the book against her. "Take it." With one swoop of his arm, he grabbed the carrier. The furball was bouncing off the sides in terror. "Good kitty!"

Jess momentarily froze before bouncing onto the rickety stairs as she stared in horror at the four-wheeling hunter. Sam tailed right behind, scooted her forward and sent her body like a slingshot over the first steps. She immediately lost her balance to a weak section. Her leg straddled and dangled in the space between two boards. Sam looped her arm and pulled her body to stand. "Go!"

He glanced under the cottage and took a quick mental flash. The man was still fighting to free the vehicle. The enemy was gripping the torch, ready to fire as soon as the ATV was free. Sam spied a tattooed skull the width of the man's hand, just as Jess screamed.

The rail had split, and she was on her knees struggling for balance again. His attention flipped to her just as the four-wheeler squealed to freedom. "Damn!"

Jess tried to keep climbing. Sam worried there was not going to be enough time to reach the top and run far enough to be out of jeopardy. Rapidly he scaled the steps toward her as the kitty carrier banged against his thigh.

"No time, no time!" he chanted with every step.

Sam was left with one choice. He eyed the embankment of mud centered under Jess's position on the stairs. Then he surveyed the drop—twenty feet to the blinding haze, and beyond that, prayers.

He jostled Jess one-handed, pushing her toward the broken rail.

"What are you doing!" Jess yelled. "Are you crazy?"

"Jump! We have to jump now." His arm encircled her waist. The couple soared into the air as a firestorm erupted behind them.

CHAPTER 28

Sam struggled to cocoon Jess as much as he could while holding the cumbersome cat carrier. His hope was to protect her if possible. The heat and vibrations from the explosion behind thundered above them. The sky lit up in orange and yellow bursts. Pieces of bungalow surged to the sky like miniature rockets.

Their entwined bodies vibrated in waves as they split through the haze. The best outcome would be a padded landing of earth, leaves and mud. Sam tried to shift his weight sideways, positioning his body on the bottom.

Luck was on his side. The landslide of mud he'd analyzed above continued below the haze. Once hitting the slick earth, both grunted on impact. Sam was forced to let go of the carrier and unfortunately Jess on impact. They rolled and tumbled on an incline toward the river.

Finally skidding to a stop in a thick gushy riverbed, Sam braced himself to avoid plowing directly into her. Mud splattered. Then he crawled in the slush to Jess as quickly as possible to block her from flying debris.

He shielded her, pressing into the mud with his forearms. He could feel her heart pounding and her quick breath against his own. There was nothing more they could do. A series of explosions, pops and crackles blew and waned in succession. The debris could be heard falling, splashing in the river, hitting the earth, and searing through the foliage with whistling force.

At last, Sam raised his head. Jess was breathing heavy into his neck. His only desire was to stay there and hold her.

She coughed from the fumes and gas mixing, choking them both. Tangled together, he pressed his lips against her forehead without thinking. Aware their bodies were tight and sculpted, his rib cage throbbed with an ache. Something hard was wedged between them.

"Jess, are you okay?"

"I think..." she nodded. "I'll know for sure when I can feel my body."

He arched his own body higher to hover over her. Sam looked down and spotted the words, *The Child Spy*. The book. The damn book that almost got them killed was ironed between them. The kitten was crying in the cage a few feet beyond in repeating mews. Sam pressed his lips together tasting blood and brushed the mud from Jess's forehead to see if she was cut.

"Your lip..." Jess raised her shapely fingers and pointed, barely touching the split. "It's bleeding."

"Not the lip again." Sam slumped and then grunted as he rolled off, letting the mud suck him in. Sirens rose in the distance. He lay there, in the wetness for a moment, thankful they were both alive. He wanted nothing more than to kiss her voraciously, consume her. But he knew the timing was wrong. He wasn't even sure she would accept his hand to assist when he stood up.

Jess melted into his Mustang, wrapped in a blanket the medical tech had supplied after checking her out. Her body was beginning to ache in areas she didn't even know existed. The kitten was in the crate resting on the back seat. The yellow tabby had finally settled and stopped the obsessive meowing.

Jess bent down the visor mirror as tears welled. Her face was smudged in mud, her hair crusted, and scratches streaked across her cheeks and chin. Her side seared in pain. Fortunately, she was alive. More than she could say for Buddy.

Jess watched the firemen for what felt like hours as they doused the flames. All that remained was rubbish and char. The bungalow had disappeared in a matter of minutes. Not even a scorched wooden beam endured. Nothing was left, including Martin's truck, now just a metal frame glowing and smoking. The odor was asphyxiating. The book on her lap was the only relic that Buddy ever existed.

Jess brushed her palm across its cover. The book felt different, odd. The pages between the cover were hard. Jess raised the outside jacket to discover the book was really a box, a fake, like one that holds Whitman's chocolates at Christmas time.

Jess saw Sam chatting with the police. Then the familiar face of Ty Burns appeared. Buddy's cottage sat split between two counties—half in hers, and half with Ty Burns. How strange. And because Buddy was part of an ongoing murder investigation with Ty in charge, of course the sergeant made a cameo. At that very moment, Ty Burns was headed straight toward her.

He ran his fingers through thick ashen blond hair as he leaned down to the passenger window.

Oh my gosh. The box! She snapped the lid shut and nonchalantly dropped the box under her legs, tugging the blanket tight. She prayed Sam's tinted windows had masked her maneuver.

Jess inhaled. She really couldn't stand the man and wasn't in the mood to talk. Then she remembered... *dinner tonight.* She'd mentioned something about having dinner with Ty at Ginger Jake's that evening. She slowly lowered the window.

"Jess, are you okay?"

"I am. Shaken up, though."

"Well, you should be. What the hell were you doing out here with him? You know this was posted land. Man, he's crazy not to worry about your safety."

"It's a long story. Maybe we can talk over dinner? But not tonight. I'm exhausted."

"Want me to take you home? I don't think you should be alone with Sam. And I agree... you don't look like you're in any condition for dinner." Ty glared at Sam who had just noticed Ty's whereabouts.

"Not necessary. How about we just wait for the Equestrian Ball on Saturday night? Remember, I had mentioned that earlier." Jess realized she had to wrap up the invite before Sam reached them. "I'll meet you at the center. Okay, great. It's settled." Jess started to close the window.

Ty seemed befuddled. He nodded faintly. "Uhm, at the Ball? Saturday? I guess I'll see your table, right?"

Jess nodded and mouthed a response through the closed window when Sam opened his door. "I'll call with the information."

Sam moaned as he fell into the driver's seat, then checked his lip to secure the butterfly bandage in the mirror once settled behind the wheel. Jess could almost feel the anger his body generated due to Ty's presence.

He started the car with a hard push on the ignition button. "What did that idiot just say?"

"Nothing. Let's go, Sam. Go."

The drive back was quiet. He definitely wasn't making Ginger Jake's tonight, which wasn't necessary because Jess wouldn't be on a date with his arch enemy. There was so much Sam wanted to express to her but could not bring himself to do so. He was confident he'd heard her arrange a date with Ty to the Ball. *Great, our table.* The invite flooded him with jealousy. He thought about reaching for her hand, to apologize, until he saw Jess pick the book off the floor and place it on her lap. Jess reverently touched its cover.

"So that's the book that almost got us killed. I hope it's a classic."

"That's not funny."

"I don't think any of this is funny."

Jess hesitated. Her voice seemed paralyzed. "It's not a book."

"Well, what might it be then?" His tone edged on snarky.

Jess slowly inched the lid open to reveal a box. Inside were contents.

Sam raised an eyebrow and idled the car at the next stop sign. "Well, what do we have here?" Inside were two black capsules which, upon examination, appeared to contain computer USB chips. He reached over and pushed the lid as far back as he could. That's when Sam detected the label on the inside top cover written in black marker.

Jess shuddered and clasped her mouth.

The word read *Lola*.

The sound of his car's Bluetooth announcing a call caused them both to jump. Jess threw a hand across her forehead. "Lordy!"

Sam accepted the call. It was Sandra.

"Boss, are you okay? And Jessica, is she…"

"It's all good. We're a little bruised, but alive."

"Oh my God, we heard the explosion all the way here in the center of Seven Springs! I swear." Sandra was out of breath. "I wanted to give you some information. I thought you might like it as soon as possible."

He shot a glance at Jess. She was leaning on the passenger window. His heart dropped because the woman needed rest.

"Yupper, fill me in. But remember to breathe," he coached.

"Well, you know your neighbor Clancy Heidel. Apparently he's been paying cash for every single bill at the hospital. My mom knows Ginny over there in collections, and she got the details. We're not talking a thousand dollars in cash. More like hundreds of thousands of dollars. Now, you tell me how a lifetime farmer with little or no insurance, with IOUs out all over town, comes up with that kind of cash. His parents were farmers, too, you know. I don't know what happened to Clancy after his only son died. He was such a good husband and father, and he loved Margaret with every morsel in his body. He would do just about anything for her."

Sandra was rambling, her usual MO. Sam cast another glance at Jess as he made the turn onto Deadman's Hill. The corner of Jess's lip twitched, and he thought she might smile at Sandra's dramatic rendition of the report.

"Take a breather, Sandra."

"Well that's it, boss. That's the latest. I'm so thankful you're both alive."

"Hey, nothing in regard to Lola Diaz yet?" he asked, seeing Jess perk forward at the question.

"Nada, but I think we should make that our new code name— Lola." Sandra let out a forced laugh. "Ha!"

"Code name?"

"Yes, boss. You do remember our earlier conversation, right? The game Marco Polo?" Sandra huffed. "Can't teach the guy anything."

The dried mud on Jess's cheeks cracked from her scrunched expression. Sam winked at her.

"Okay now, over and out. L O L A. You get it?" Sandra emphatically announced the name.

Sam temporarily smiled, but instantly dropped the corners of his mouth after he shut the phone. He was descending Deadman's Hill and whispered the word the same way, "L o l a," as he stroked his mustache. "A code name. Interesting."

Neither said another word until reaching the house. Sam glanced at the time—7:32 P.M. The fog had lifted, but a fresh haze loomed over the entire valley from the explosions, miles away. Jess clicked her latch. Sam raced around the Mustang to help while his body screamed in pain. He was sure Jess shared a similar agony.

Sam hoisted the cat crate onto the porch where Jax stood. Sam gave him a nod. Upon seeing the Australian guest, Jess started to cry. Jax reached for her shoulder, sending Sam a pang of envy. Her tears were Sam's clue to quietly surrender to the springhouse.

He turned to Jax before backing away. "If you're up for it, I'd like to take another ride in the morning. Time to visit our friends over the hill."

"You bet, mate. I'm all game for that." Jax tipped his hat.

Later, after Jess showered, she returned to the porch for one last sip of coffee before a much-needed sleep. She rocked alone on the porch swing. There wasn't anything about her that was not shrieking in pain, including her heart.

She never expected to hear the loud jingle of spurs approaching from the barn. It was Jax. As usual, tending to the herd.

"How are you?" Concern washed over his face.

"I'll live. I'm glad you're here. For Anna."

He nodded. "I am too."

"Tomorrow night is the Qualifier. Do you think she can do it?"

He tilted his head. "Are you asking if I think she can win?"

She stumbled over her reply. "Yes… I guess."

"It's not about winning. And it's not one-sided. It's about working as a team and listening to her horse. Even the underdog can win, whether a pony or a horse, if the win comes from the heart. Now, ask me if I believe those two have the heart." His voice was even toned, and direct.

"Do you?"

"If they work as one, I believe so. But losing is not a failure. It's learning." Jax rotated and stared across the horizon, then focused on the kitchen light in the springhouse.

Jess traced his stare.

"And Sam?" she asked.

"Do I think you and Sam belong together?" Jax remained focused in the direction of the springhouse. "I do," he affirmed. "I believe it's in your hearts."

There was a lengthy silence between them. Jess studied his massive shoulders and long powerful legs. But the quality she found most attractive was his gentle heart and stalwart nature. The hush did not feel uncomfortable. Jess was never awkward anymore in his presence. She understood Jax. He belonged to his mates. He was one with the horses.

"But you both have to find the connection, feel the oneness, follow your hearts. Selfless. Egos aside."

His final words along with his jingling spurs were the only sound that lingered as he entered the house.

Magically, he knew.

Sam was sitting bare-chested at the mini kitchen table, his wet hair slicked back and damp from the shower. His face still unshaven, at least the rest of him felt refreshed. He should be exhausted, but there was no way he could sleep. He had written the name *Lola* fifty times on a piece paper. He had examined the torn list from the bush at Ginger Jake's and had the Heidel investigation spread in front of him. The box holding the USB clips was open and pushed off to the side.

Sam really couldn't concentrate on any of it. He was too busy dwelling on Jess and Jax on the porch. Jax's hand was touching her shoulder. Sam's heart withered with an ache that overshadowed every other part of his body.

Sam couldn't hate Jax. The Australian was innocent. A good man. Sam was the one making him guilty of something Jax had no intention of exploiting. Sam placed his gun on the table and attempted to relax. It was his problem, Sam's jealousy. He raked his fingers through his hair. *Here I am again.* He touched the picture of Jess resting on the center of the dinette.

The knock at the door aroused him from his drowning thoughts. He peeked underneath the curtain to discover who his guest might be. He was shocked to find Jess, her freshly washed hair softly cascading over her shoulders shining under the porch light.

He cleared his throat and opened the door. "Come in. It's chilly."

Jess was wearing a V-neck white t-shirt and jeans. "No, no..."

Sam opened the door wide and tucked behind it, realizing he wasn't looking his best. "I don't care if it's just a minute."

She conceded with a bow and entered, her arms folded tight across her mid-section. Her open chest area glistened with a fresh coating of moisturizer. Immediately she took in the material on the table. She approached and touched the box with *Lola* marked on the lid. Sam closed the door behind her, studying her thin shapely frame.

"I was just reviewing the..." He lifted his hand and pointed toward the table, then raked his hair. "I guess... maybe... I couldn't sleep." He was stumbling to find words in her presence. He wanted to tell her how much he was sorry. To express that she was the only woman he loved.

Jess rotated to face him. Her well-defined lips opened slightly as if about to speak but appeared caught off-guard. She was inspecting his bare chest, his well framed shoulders... then her eyes descended his abdomen to the edge of his Levi's. Sam watched as a rosy blush filled her cheeks, and he flushed with a warm surge as well.

"Sam... you're hurt."

When Jess arrived, he'd forgotten about the bruise that rimmed the edge of his waist, up his side to his rib cage. The black and blue colors were bursting to the surface where he had buffered her fall at the bungalow.

Jess reached out, almost touching him. Her hand stopped a mere inch away.

Sam tried to clear the awkward air between them. "It's okay. I'm tough. Now, see this little slit on my lip. I could cry like a baby."

She raised her eyes. Her long lashes fluttered higher as she examined his lip.

"Might need a magnifying glass to see it, huh?" He let out a phony laugh. Sam was overwhelmingly nervous.

He could feel Jess's breath breeze his bare skin as she surveyed his lip. Once more, her index finger almost grazed him. She dropped her hand.

Sam was lost in her spell. His eyes closed. Nothing else mattered. His head lowered and his lips skimmed her forehead. The sweet aroma of her hair and skin melted the pain in his heart.

"Sam?" She arched back. "I'm here to give you these."

He opened his eyes. Her tender demeanor had transformed, suddenly hardened. Jess did not seem to share the feeling they once had for each other.

She dangled Buddy's dog tags mid-air. "They're evidence, I understand."

Sam shoved both his hands in his jeans pockets. He shook his head. "No Jess, they're yours."

Jess dropped her hand. "Why? Why was Buddy adamant I have them?"

Sam pressed his lips together. "Don't know. There was something he was trying to tell us. Perhaps the key is in the USBs. I tried to pop them into my laptop, but they're encrypted. Tomorrow, I'll send them to the lab."

"You believe me, then?" Their eyes locked. Her arms folded, returning tight against her chest.

"Jess, I never meant..." Sam's voice maintained an even softness.

"That's not what I asked you." Her tone was sharp. "What about Lola, sweets? Remember her? You called her *baby*." Jess drilled Sam, spinning like a knife in his gut.

"Those words were not what you..."

"Not what I thought, *baby*." She accentuated the word. "You barely spent time with me, with us, all summer. Like we didn't even exist. Then, I uncovered a good story. No... make that an outstanding story. I had the potential to publish an article that could have exploded my career. My dream!" Jess's voice was quivering, fighting back tears. Her eyes were slits of anger. Obviously this had been stewing for a long time, scalding her inside, because now she was boiling over like a volcano.

"Jess!" Sam gripped both her shoulders, shocking her. Her ranting abruptly stopped, tears spilling over.

"I did what I had to do for your safety... and Anna's safety. You have to believe this." Sam squeezed her tighter as he pulled her close to his chest. "Now listen, tomorrow you are not to leave here. Jax and I will head out to investigate a little issue at Clancy's and then we will be back. The Qualifier is what matters. This family's safety, Wyatt's safety and the competition. Do you understand?"

Jess's eyes were like saucers, paralyzed with fear. Again, her lips quivered as if she wished to say something more. Instead, she bent her head, and he let her slip back.

"I'll walk you back to the house." Sam could have kicked himself for letting his emotions take precedence. He said no more, but grabbed a sweatshirt, pressed his pistol in the top of his jeans and walked her back to the house with the resolution of an FBI agent.

Perhaps intimidated by the firearm and the concern in his voice, Jess conceded. Neither spoke. The only sound was her soft sniffles.

Once inside, Jess watched Sam cross back to the springhouse. She inhaled a significant breath to reestablish control of both her mind and body. The combination of his alluring body, captivating eyes and woodsy aroma almost hypnotized her to drift into the sanctuary of his arms. She wanted to tell him about Lola, that Lola had reached out to her in a text. Lola claimed she would meet her tomorrow night at the Qualifier. But she didn't let it slip to him. Writing the article was far too important. Jess could find another venue to publish her work. This article could be her break, and she refused to let her dream go.

When Jess turned around, Jax was in the kitchen doorway, leaning against the wall. He sent her a torturous look of distress as if he'd read her mind. Feeling guilty, she remembered his words about unselfishness and working as one. Jess dropped her chin and headed to her room.

CHAPTER 29

Sam glanced at his watch as he stepped off the springhouse porch the next day. It was near 7:00 A.M. and Jax was ready, waiting in front of the barn. He had Cowboy tacked up in Western gear waiting on Sam. Jax was mounted on a different horse this time. Dundee began to prance as soon as Jax asked him to step forward, tugging on Cowboy's tether. The black stallion was a picture of beauty. His shining mane and tail danced in waves with every raised stamp of his hoof. He snorted several long puffs as if greeting Sam.

Jax lifted his hat slightly as Sam approached. He rubbed his forehead. Sam knew Jax was watching him check his handgun in his holster. Then Sam slid a rifle in the side pouch of his saddle, instead of the set of clippers he had carried on their last ride. He knew Jax was not a fan of weapons, but he also knew the Australian understood it was Sam's job.

"I have an extra if you would like some reinforcement," Sam teased.

Jax smiled and tapped the kangaroo whip curled at his waist. "Have my own, mate."

Jax could handle himself. Sam had witnessed Jax's ability with the whip when he had saved Sam's life in one snap against a venomous snake two years prior.

Sam nodded and stepped into the stirrup. Cowboy held a steady position, and Sam now looked forward to being back atop the horse. He just wished it was for a leisurely trail ride and not a confrontation.

The two men moved in tandem across the expansive field heading toward the woods. The morning was crisp but exquisite, sunshine shimmering over the treetops as they made their pace.

Sam explained to Jax that he'd asked Sandra to make an early morning phone call dropping an anonymous tip to Clancy Heidel that two trespassers had been sighted on his property. Hopefully, that would be enough to ignite a backlash involving his friends on ATVs.

"I expect them to take the bait," Sam said.

"Just tell me what you need, mate," Jax replied.

"Well, I hope to split them up. If you could possibly give a little distraction to deter the second man, I can deal with them one at a time."

"At your service." Dundee appeared to share Jax's sentiment. The stallion picked up his pace with exuberance. His ebony coat glistened in the morning sun as he burst out in front. Jax busied the horse with zigzagging side passes until they reached the forest edge.

Sam glanced back, praying everything in the investigation would be cleared up by the Qualifier that evening. That, he knew, would take a miracle and was nothing more than wishful thinking. But he wanted his life back.

Sam also prayed Jess would honor the vow that she made regarding not leaving the house. He was pretty sure she was on the same page with him, understanding the danger of the situation. He eyed Officer Martin one last time, posted on the back porch watching them about to disappear into the woods. Sam had ordered an additional officer to stand guard at the barn over Belle and a third at the top of the lane. Someone had attempted to hurt his family already, and Sam was not taking any more chances. As demented as it sounded, it appeared someone was willing to engage in kidnapping, as well as murder, to stop Anna and Belle from competing.

Sam dialed Sandra on the cell. "Could you also have a prisoner van relocated to Clancy Heidel's shortly?"

"Boss, isn't that a little premature? You didn't even catch anyone yet."

"Wishful thinking, I guess." He knew when he hung up that she would oblige.

Ten minutes later, before crossing Dead Man's Creek, the two stopped. "I think they took the bait. We have company idling on the ridge, mate." Jax pointed upward.

He was right. Sam peered through the foliage to the top line. He spied two four-wheelers as a muffled hum like a lawn mower echoed down the valley. Sam and Jax would be safe until they crossed the creek.

"Let's lure them in closer. Let the goons work down almost to us. I'll let you know when to veer off in the opposite direction," Sam explained. "Hopefully buy me some time."

"I can buy you as much time as you need."

The ATVs immediately jumped off the edge exactly as Sam had predicted. The two weaved forward through the trees straight in the enemies' path until Sam trotted along Jax.

"See that large oak up ahead. Shoot left there." Sam indicated with only his eyes.

Jax nodded and veered left at the exact location instructed. The Australian checked his hat affirming it was secure, then asked Dundee to turn. Immediately the two engaged in a gallop.

Sam observed a curled grin on the face of Jax.

Sam aimed toward the ATVs and saw the man he perceived as the leader point in Jax's direction and shout, "Devon, follow him!" The second four-wheeler swerved and dug in for a mudslinging take-off.

Once the two divided, Sam edged Cowboy right and cued him to a rolling canter. They mazed through the forest in search of the familiar rocky area lining the crest. He knew the ridge would provide excellent protection to dismount and take cover.

Sam was far enough away from his attacker to jump off behind the massive mounds of boulders and remove his rifle. He tapped Cowboy on the rump to send the horse off. But Cowboy remained stationary and curled his neck toward Sam as if in question. The ATV rumbled closer on the other side of the rocks.

"Come on, boy. You gotta go."

Cowboy left Sam no choice. He raised his hand and heaved the horse a healthy swat. Cowboy trotted off, but only a few feet. Sam grunted in defeat and turned again, but it was too late.

The four-wheeler was flying over the ridge, across the boulders just about shearing Sam's head. This time Cowboy charged off, leaving Sam ducking for cover, wedged inside the rocks and causing him to drop his weapon.

The vehicle hit the ground on a nosedive. Luckily for Sam, the driver lost his seat and flew several feet into the air, depositing him spread eagle on the ground. He vaulted up, pivoted toward Sam, and formed two fists ready to box.

Sam locked an eye on the tattoo he'd seen the day before on a man's hand. The same definitive skull. Sam was positive it was the man from Buddy's bungalow.

The four-wheeler had catapulted forward, and at present was rolling onto its side as the two were in a ground confrontation. The powerful momentum from the crash thrust the ATV down the hillside headed directly for them. Its roaring motor sputtered. The unseated driver became distracted, frozen in panic. Sam found the perfect opportunity to bulldoze him like a tight end.

The boy of eighteen steering the ATV thought the man on the black horse had underestimated his four-wheeling skills. Devon had every intention of showing off. Ripping his helmet off, it sailed through the trees while he screamed, "Yahoo! I'm coming to get you." He was relishing every minute of the chase. He could wear that horse out before he ever ran out of gas. He hollered another chant in the air, "You are mine!"

The horseman picked up the gallop. Devon had to admit the man was quite an expert maneuvering the beast between the trees. Suddenly, he realized the steed had reached an open field ahead. Devon was almost to the clearing when the beast in front curled head to tail in a 360-degree turn without warning.

Moving too fast to bear right or left, still between the trees, Devon wasn't sure what to do.

The black horse dug into the dirt and lunged forward in a full run. The mounted man raised his arm in the air, galloping straight at Devon like a charging knight.

What the hell…

Then he eyeballed the whip cracking in the air. Suddenly, the horseman was upon him, the lash soaring toward him from the hand of the rider.

Devon flashed a smirk and yelled, "You think you're Crocodile Dundee, man?"

The last thing Devon recalled was the sting of the searing whip as it sucked him off the ATV.

When Sam first saw Jax come into view at the top of the crest heading toward Clancy's, he didn't see the man walking behind Dundee. But as they neared, he heard the moans begging Jax to slow down. A young man was tethered to Jax's saddle with the leather whip.

Dundee stretched his neck as they approached.

"You lost your horse, mate?" Jax tipped his hat back.

"I guess I did." Sam grinned.

The paddy wagon was parked next to the barn, just as he had asked Sandra. Sam had every intention of taking the two back to the station for holding and interrogation. But he had some questions for them and for Clancy Heidel who was standing next to the van. Clancy had lots of explaining to do.

Sam spent time with Clancy after he asked Jax to search out his ride home. "I'm sure Cowboy didn't go far. He's as loyal as they come."

At least an hour had passed when Jax came whistling. He was trotting back on Dundee with Cowboy in tow. By that time, Sam had unearthed an entire scheme before having the two criminals hauled into the station. Turned out that the two eighteen-year-olds had been hired by the new managers of Clancy Heidel's property to ward off unwanted visitors.

"I'm selling the property in a lease-to-buy agreement," Clancy shared as he leaned against the van. The old man appeared weak. "I just follow directions. I had no choice."

"Clancy, those two goons, and now you too, are going to be up for attempted murder. Do you realize they almost killed Jess and me in that explosion yesterday?"

"We didn't know you were there," Devon chirped up from his position.

Sam ignored him. He knew the young man was lying. "You won't be much help for Margaret from a jail cell, Clancy. But if you tell the truth, I could possibly arrange the charges to be dropped."

"I'm an old man, Sam," Clancy sighed. "She needs me." He pointed to the elderly woman in a wheelchair on the porch with a short nurse. This time the aide was male with dark hair.

Sam affirmed with a check of his head. "I realize that. That's why I'm pleading with you to cooperate." He had known Clancy since he was young. He had been a good man then. "Clancy, do you hear me? Do it for Margaret."

The old man focused on the porch. "I was breaking. Years of giving my whole life to working this farm. Lost my son... I was completely broke and then, Margaret's sickness. I saw this ad about a large corporation in an equine paper. They were looking for open land to run a horse rescue. They'd take care of everything, all the help and equipment, and pay *me* rent in a lease agreement. Not to mention, preserve the land."

"Sounds like a dream come true. What did you have to give them?" Sam checked back as an officer loaded his prisoner on the van.

Clancy removed his ballcap and wiped his brow. "All I had to do was keep my mouth shut and wear a blindfold. In exchange, I'd get all the care I needed for Margaret, including 24/7 aides. What would you do for your wife?"

Sam didn't bother to mention that Jess was not his wife. He would die for her, married or not.

"Unfortunately, it looks like this *rescue* is a front for several illegal businesses. I'm beginning to believe that drugging, horse theft, and maybe murder are just a few. So where did the help come from. I need a name. Who do you contact?"

"I've only ever spoken to a manager by phone. All exchanges are done through the mail, Fed Ex or Doug."

"Doug?"

"The Humane Officer. These young boys are in charge of running the tattooed horses to Block 5 of the railway or picking up the dead ones." He pointed to the van.

"Good old animal lover Doug." Sam rubbed his jaw to relieve the ache. "Sandra was right. Is there a name for this corporation?"

"Ernest Equestrians, LLC. Horse Haven Rescue is owned by them."

"I suppose they have a division that supplies the aides for taking care of Margaret. What is that called?"

Clancy glared at Sam as if he was going to lock up. "I don't ask."

"Go ahead, Clancy. Give me something to go on. We can make a formal time to record all the information and your confession," Sam coaxed.

"There is one thing I find strange."

"Yes?"

"All the aides, every single one of them... whether male or female," Clancy broke and glanced back at the porch. "They are all called Lola Diaz."

Sam and Jax ascended through the woods toward home after crossing Deadman's Creek. Sam was still digesting the events and the collection of new information he had gathered. Clancy agreed to come to the station Saturday morning and provide an official statement. In the meantime, Sam ordered the two teenagers to be placed in holding for safe keeping, with an officer to guard Horse Haven Rescue. He deemed it absolutely necessary to protect Clancy and Margaret.

Sam was beginning to believe "Lola" was nothing more than a code name, like the game Marco Polo. Sandra was right on again, without even knowing. He loved that woman. Perhaps "Lola" was used to inquire or purchase illegal drugs at the equestrian centers. Even more sinister, maybe the code was used to hire illegal immigrants as grooms or aides for the wealthy.

The reoccurring connection to Doug Kinard was puzzling. He had to prove horse theft wasn't the only evil involved. Tri-County Auction was just a short distance from the Expo Center—money, power, greed, and horses.

The whole idea sounded crazy, but Sam, as a former FBI agent, had seen many outlandish methods utilized by criminals. Sometimes, criminals could hide illegal activity right in front of the eye because it was so bizarre. *Who would ever suspect?* The tri-county area was the perfect environment for trafficking, especially considering its proximity to major metropolises like New York, Washington, D.C., and Philadelphia.

Then there was the name Ernest. Another common thread. Ernest Equestrians, LLC and *Ernest Living* owned by Sir Prickler himself and ridden by Maria Prickler in the Tri-County Pony Club.

Sam was not positive about any of it, but one thing was sure. A Lola Diaz was trying to rip open the entire sinister underground. He prayed she... or he... would just follow through and reach out at the Qualifier that night.

Sam thought about the torn list on the kitchenette table at the springhouse. Someone had been trying to connect names and items in a simple word puzzle, matching them to each other just as Sam was doing now. Recurring names included Doug Kinard and Ernest.

Sam decided to dial Sandra and add another request to her list.

"Another?" her voice squawked. "I'm still working on the first list!"

"You can handle it," Sam insisted. "I want to find out who owns Ernest Equestrians, LLC. If my hunch is correct, I bet Sir Prickler's name pops up. I have a feeling *Ernest Living* is at the center of this investigation. That's the grandson of the horse on Dallas's wall. He has ties to the county. Since you love animals, I wonder did you know that?"

"Can't say I did, Sam. But that reminds me about Dallas." Sandra took a breath. "He called to talk to you. Sounded like it was urgent. He said he's been trying to reach you all morning, but you don't pick up."

"I hope you told him I was a little busy with this investigation."

"Nope. I said you were most likely at breakfast with the Australian movie star whom I will be having dinner with tomorrow night. Lola, over and out."

"Lola? Lola, right." Sam was behind Jax and Dundee wishing he had a piece of gum. His jaw was killing him. Cowboy trod along as Sam searched his contacts for Dallas's number.

"Jax, have you ever played a game called Marco Polo?" Sam asked as he searched.

"Can't say I have, mate."

"It's like tag. Someone is *it*. Marco is like a code name, and others call out Polo in response," Sam explained.

"Like mates. I have a lot of mates."

"I guess so." Sam thought about Lola and her true identity.

Sam pressed the dial button, while Jax side-passed Dundee off the trail to cut a path over three logs about three feet high. They soared onto the crest, quite a feat because of the angle. Jax patted the black horse who was dirty and sweaty after their adventure.

"Wow, that was tricky. I didn't think Dundee could manage such a feat... I mean... after what happened at the movie set when he sucked back across the tracks." Sam trotted next to Jax at the top.

"No feat, just trust. Trust and saying I'm sorry for not believing in him. Dundee just needed a break and a change of environment." Jax smiled as if he had championed the Olympics. "A week ago, we would not have been able to do it. All my fault." The Australian's eyes drilled into Sam's, as if wondering if he'd caught the deeper meaning.

Jax turned toward the log house, now in view across the field. Cowboy waited patiently as Sam dwelt on Jax's words. He sensed they were meant for him. *Apologize, Sam.*

Dallas's voice brought him back. "Sam, Sam is that you?" The coroner was hollering over the phone. Sam swore he heard Dallas snap his suspenders. "I've been trying to reach you all morning. Why the hell don't you answer your phone?"

"I've been busy."

"So I heard!" Dallas barked. "We don't all get to enjoy breakfast when working on a case."

Sam laughed. "What's up? You sound stressed."

"What's up? Better to ask what's dead."

"Dead?" Sam leaned forward in the saddle asking Cowboy to move forward.

"I have another body, Sam. How many are you going to deliver to me before you close this case? I haven't slept yet."

"What are you talking about?" Sam squeezed Cowboy for a little more speed.

"Well, if you don't know by now, you will shortly. Ty Burns should be arriving at Tunnel Hill any minute to make an arrest. Perhaps he's there already."

"Ty Burns? That man isn't allowed to set foot on this property." Sam jiggled the reins.

"Oh, he can if he gets a warrant from the judge." Dallas sounded like a defiant child. "You should have picked up your phone. I tried to warn you."

"Who the hell is dead?" Sam felt a surge of pain in his jaw, not to mention his aching side. The fullback tackle on the teen Devon earlier was starting to have an effect.

"It's in my report, Sam. But if you must know, Ty suspects it's Lola's body, days old. They discovered her in the back of the charred Ford Ranger above Buddy's cottage, in a melted body bag."

Sam rolled his eyes. "Who does Ty think he's arresting?"

"It's not Officer Martin," Dallas toyed.

"For somebody who says they like me, you sure have a funny way of showing it." Sam shoved the phone in his pocket.

He triggered Cowboy again, this time with a series of rapid-fire clicks. The field rumbled from the enormous gelding as he charged toward the house.

CHAPTER 30

Sam galloped through the field to catch the rolling canter of Jax and Dundee. "What's your hurry, mate?"

"My *good pal*, Ty Burns, thinks Jess is guilty of murder. I'm about done with that bastard," Sam shouted, his focus straight ahead.

They galloped in unison to the barn. Sam dismounted Cowboy in a flowing swing of his leg, never breaking until he touched ground.

Jax took Cowboy's reins while Anna and Wyatt rushed off the porch where they had been standing with Officer Martin. The deputy's thin frame was in a rigid stance, arms locked in a fold. His usual boyish face was etched with concern.

"They took Mom, Sam. They arrested her." Anna raced up to Sam, her teary puppy dog eyes pleading for help, a look that melted his heart. But there was no time for chit chat.

"Now listen, you two." Sam bent on his knees and pulled both of them close. Jax was not far off, tethering the two horses who were snorting and blowing. "I only want you to worry about one thing—tonight's Qualifier." He gripped each of their shoulders, huddling them closer to him.

Anna sniffed back tears. "Mom. I'm worried about Mom."

"Let me worry about your mom. I'm not about to let anything happen to her. You understand?" He squeezed Anna's shoulder, then wiped a tear from her cheek. "I'm going to bring your mom right to the Expo for the Qualifier. There's plenty of time. You two, go with Jax. And take care of Belle. Next time I see you, you are to be saddled up to show that horse tonight."

"No, Sam."

"Yes, your mom will be there."

Anna inhaled three deep breaths. "Do you promise?"

Wyatt appeared to be tearing up as well.

"You have my word and my heart."

Anna's arms surrounded his neck like magic, followed by Wyatt who encircled them both. "I wish I had a family just like this!"

Sam wrapped the two in his embrace, then released and directed them to Jax. The officer who was stationed at the barn nodded at Sam. They were in good hands.

Sam stood for a moment, watching everyone else head into the barn and out of sight. He was overcome with emotion, especially by Wyatt's words. This family had been nothing but broken since the boy had arrived, yet he claimed to have experienced more love than ever before? What had the boy's life been like?

Sam regained his professional demeanor and met Martin on the porch.

"I'm sorry, sir. Ty had a warrant. I attempted to stop him, but he had two officers with him. Jess, she said it was okay, and to tend to the kids until you got back."

"I know. You followed procedure. Ty Burns is nothing to worry about. I'll take it from here." Sam patted Martin's shoulder. "You did fine, Officer Martin."

The deputy continued, "He had one warrant for stealing the car. I adamantly told him it was my car, and that I wasn't pressing charges. But he had a second warrant for trespassing." Martin flicked his head. "Told me not to try to fight it, because he would be back with another warrant for murder."

Sam maintained his emotions and checked his shoulder a final time. "I'll let you know if I need you at the Expo Center tonight."

The fury to save Jess released a fiery sensation throughout Sam's body as he burned the Mustang out the lane.

He placed a call. "Fill me in on this body, Dallas. Ty's got Jess at his precinct. I'm headed there now."

"The body was several days old, before the night Buddy was killed. I assume somebody had to clean up a real mess in Stall 23. I can tell you this though... somebody was pissed. The poor girl was bludgeoned to death. My guess is, if we can obtain fingerprints from both Buddy's and this little lady's body, we will have a match to the killer."

"Any idea who she was?" Sam asked.

"She had a fake ID, homemade, which did say Lola Diaz. Again, my guess is, some poor immigrant working as a groom. Seems to be a lot of illegals at the stables lately."

Sam thought how simple it would be to create only one fake identification card with the name Lola Diaz. When presented on the black market, whether for a drug purchase or any crime, the felon would know the person was their contact. Not to mention, a way to tag them as property of whoever the mastermind was behind Ernest Equestrians, LLC.

"I emailed you the details before shipping the body north."

"Thanks, I knew you liked me." Sam heard Dallas laugh with a tug of his suspenders.

"As for Ty Burns," the coroner said, "you can weasel that jerk. Tell him you know who's behind this entire mess, and if he's a good boy, you'll let him take credit for solving the case. He'll believe anything."

"Good idea. He's definitely someone's puppet. I have another question since you did your homework on that new picture you acquired."

"You mean *Ernest Earner*? Art, Sam... it's art."

"Yes. Seems Sir Prickler owns an *Ernest Living*. I'm thinking an offspring. How many does that horse have?"

"Well, every time one of Ernest's prodigies wins, the selling price goes off the charts. However, there are many in the county. I know for a fact Judge Massey owns a filly."

"Good to know."

"Your little girl is competing tonight, so I'd watch out for crossing anyone riding an Ernest prodigy."

Sam was about to hang up. But Dallas cleared his throat. "One more thing. Do you have any idea when this will be over? I was hoping for a vacation."

"When all the manure is scraped clean in the barn." Sam slid the phone to off and slammed the gas pedal.

Jess was watching the news on television in Ty Burns's interrogation room. The grey walls, cement floor and metal door with only a slit of glass were making her feel even more exhausted. The guard brought in a cup of coffee, but it had gone cold.

"Ty, please," Jess begged. "I can't drink coffee with my hands in handcuffs."

"Oh, I have seen detainees do it all the time. Just place it between your two hands."

She rolled her eyes.

"Sorry, but you're a flight risk according to seniority. I'm just doing what I'm ordered."

"Who is your boss?" Jess asked.

Ty ignored her, standing at the door. He was in his mid-forties but had deep wrinkles in marionette lines and grooves across his forehead making him appear much older.

"My superior claims there's a good chance I'll have a third warrant shortly for you... for murder. Please tell me you didn't kill anyone."

"Really, Ty? Murder? And I only *borrowed* Martin's truck. You heard him."

"I'm waiting on the judge." Ty drifted toward the door.

That was an hour ago. The Styrofoam cup now had a film of residue on both sides. If Ty thought her offer for a date still stood, he was quite wrong. She checked the clock on the wall—late afternoon. It was soon time to leave the house for the Qualifier.

Suddenly, the silence was broken by a familiar voice on the other side of the interrogation room door. Sam. From the sound of things, he was causing quite a ruckus.

Geez, settle down or you aren't going to be able to bust me out of here. Jess plummeted her forehead on the table to block out the TV voices.

"Look, Ty. You better move your officer out of the way of the door. I'm done messing around with you. I'm going in."

"Sam, I have a warrant. Two, to be exact, and another on the way."

"I'm about to tell you what to do with that damn bogus warrant. And your murder was days old."

Jess heard a sudden expletive out of Sam. The guard at the door must have drawn his weapon. Jess shook her head.

"Ty, tell him to put the gun down. I'm not armed. Who the hell is putting you up to this, anyway? I want to see the warrant!"

Ty called the officer down, then opened the door to her interrogation room. "Wait here," he told Sam and turned. "I'll be back in a minute with the warrant."

Jess lifted her head from the circle of her arms, restrained by her cuffed hands on the table, to see Sam. Standing just inside the metal door, he caught sight of the restraints.

"Holy Moses!" He pivoted around and banged on the door. "Get these handcuffs off her, Ty." Sam hunched to peer out the slit of a window, both hands pressed on the metal. Nothing happened.

"Sam?" Jess called quietly.

"What?" He snapped but didn't turn to face her. Instead, he smacked at the glass.

"Sam." This time it came out as a command, and he glanced back.

His crystal eyes looked exhausted, and he was unshaven but quite handsome in his red flannel shirt and Levi's.

"Settle down or Ty will never allow me to see the light of day."

He nodded and faced her like a scolded child.

"You did come to rescue me, right?"

Sam said nothing but walked toward her, still imprisoning her stare. Her cheeks flushed. Nervously, Jess fidgeted with her neck with her cuffed hands, realizing her white shirt was unbuttoned lower than usual and disheveled from the top of her jeans.

"I hardly had time to dress when Ty came to the farm this morning." She watched him as he eyed her chest never expecting him to reach up.

Jess froze, unsure of his intentions as he fingered her shirt collar, then slid his fingers down. He stopped at the open button. Her body zinged with an ache from every touch. His familiar aroma drew her in the closer he came.

"Jess." He then touched her cheek. "I *am* here to rescue you."

With that, the door opened. In a second, the two quickly separated.

Ty cleared his throat. "I have the warrant."

Sam studied the document. As suspected, Judge Massey had signed it.

"Jess here is in a heap of trouble."

Sam proceeded exactly as Dallas had suggested. "This is bigger than all of us. I worked with the FBI for twenty years, so trust me when I say this could be the bust of the century. Whoever takes this organization down is headed for the record books."

Ty's blue eyes widened.

"And if it goes the way I suspect," Sam added, "you'll go down with them."

Ty jerked his head. "I don't think so."

"Really? Read between the lines." Sam faced him dead center, and Ty jumped back. "I know who's behind all this. This dead body isn't the real *Lola*. This woman has been dead for days. Dallas says whoever killed Buddy also killed this poor lady."

"Jess did it out of jealousy..." Ty blurted.

"Come on. Then she strangled Buddy? Listen to yourself. Who's filling your head with this notion?"

Ty moved back to the door.

"Tell you what," Sam said. "I'll deliver the whole case to you once I get the evidence to solve it. All you have to do is tell me who told you to arrest Jess."

Precisely then, Sam's phone rang.

He lifted his finger. "Do you mind if I place it on speaker?"

Ty assented and stepped closer.

"Sandra, what've you got?"

"Hey, boss. That Lola Diaz called again. I thought you should know, immediately. She wants to meet you at Ginger Jake's tonight promptly at 6:00 P.M."

Jess raised an eyebrow. *That's odd.*

Sam extended the phone to Ty who had stepped even closer to hear.

"See, Ty? No dead Lola. Come on. You're being played like a fiddle."

There was momentary silence in the room, and Jess felt a chill. In a flash Ty said, "Attorney Cousins. He got a call from Judge Massey, who produced a warrant. That's all I know. I do what I'm told... unlike some of us. Do we have a deal?"

"Hell yes, my man. You can meet Lola tonight at Ginger Jake's at 6:00 P.M. on the nose. Now, undo these handcuffs before I break that steel myself."

Jess rolled her eyes and mouthed the words *"Did you have to say that?"* while Ty bent to unlock the cuffs.

She rubbed her wrists as they walked out past Ty who was now holding the door. "I think we might have to cancel that date to the Ball tomorrow night if you don't honor your end of the bargain," she said. "Let Sam do his job."

For the first time in months, Jess eyed Sam's dimple as he winked and smiled at Ty.

Once outside, Jess and Sam rushed to the Mustang.

"Sam, was Sandra...?"

"Yup, a set-up. Perfect timing, too. Keeps Ty out of my hair tonight. And if he is any kind of detective, he might discover what I already suspect."

CHAPTER 31

Anna walked on foot to the in-gate, which was marked #4. She stood at the two white double doors dressed in her pristine English attire—a black fitted jacket, tan jodhpurs, crisp white shirt, and her velvet black hunt cap. Not a hair out of place. It was attire she despised. Anna would rather be in Western boots and jeans with a belt buckle three times bigger than normal. So what if the Tri-County Pony Club laughed at her.

Anna tried not to lean on the gate to avoid any speck of dirt landing on her, a calamity she had trouble avoiding. Gate 4 was the entry from underneath the arena. This area contained hundreds of horse stalls and two indoor schooling rings. The general public was not permitted to enter unless badged.

The gates had been chained shut, but Anna was tall enough to peer over the top. From her stance, she felt like she was rising from the gallows in Rome under the Coliseum. She remembered reading in Sunday school about Daniel when he fought the lion. This facility was massive. Rows and rows of bright blue and orange folding seats rose in tiers to the domed ceiling. Thousands could be seated, and they were already filing in row by row.

The barn area was usually crowded with hundreds of horses, but not for the Qualifier. Tonight, only a limited few made the stables quieter than other shows. The area had the aroma of hay, oats, and everything horse, but not at Gate 4. From this position, Anna whiffed popcorn, pretzels, and cotton candy.

She eyed the course. It was the same one she'd walked on foot with the other four competitors just thirty minutes prior. She remembered kicking the fluffy brown dirt with the tip of her black leather boot as she set paces between jumps in her head. Anna attempted to muffle the crowds as she concentrated on her turns, size of jumps and course direction.

What am I even doing here? Belle can't do this.

She checked the spurs on her boots. They were the largest size allowed in the rulebook for this discipline. Jax suggested she not even wear them. Belle, he implied, would be calmer and more yielding without them. But he allowed the decision to be Anna's. Jax didn't understand, Lately, in Anna's opinion, a poke with her spurs was the only way Belle seemed to respect her.

Why didn't Jax see that?

The arena was flooded now with crowds almost able to touch the dome of the ceiling. The sound of the announcer checked in with a powerful echo, and the piercing intermittent whistles of the microphone resonated through the stands. The crowd screamed to higher octaves, nothing short of a roar.

Anna noted four people gathered at the judging table. They were exquisitely dressed in formal attire, in a cluster with the ring steward and show secretary. This was Anna's cue to leave. Undoubtedly, the judges had already formed an opinion about her and Belle.

It was a no-brainer.

Anna had to walk away from the ten staged jumps staring at her. Her nerves were all consuming just thinking about showing in this environment. She quivered from nausea in her gut, like the time she got seasick on her uncle's boat in the middle of the ocean.

Belle and I are out of our league.

Wyatt and Jax were waiting for Anna at the stalls underground. Jax had brought not only Belle in the six-horse trailer, but also Cowboy and Dundee in the event Anna moved on to the championship round. Belle could use the support. Plus, Jax was already lining up a request to do a special presentation with Dundee on the final night.

Jax stood by the side of the rail while she was in the schooling ring. Plain to everyone, his presence was calming for them both. His voice remained confident and steady, as if he believed in her.

Anna couldn't say the same for the Tri-County Pony Club. The group of mean girls huddled outside the workout area accompanied by Maria Prickler's mom, doing what they did best—whispering. Maria didn't have to practice more than one go around before her trainer hollered, "Give it a break, Maria. You're ready to go."

Anna heard Ben Donahue's granddaughter, Penny, in an audible undertone, "Even the judges think they shouldn't be entered. I don't know what that Australian trainer sees in her and that *pony*." Ironically, Penny was the only member, when not around the group, who would secretly whisper to Anna words of encouragement. The girl didn't have the courage to speak up in front of the others.

Anna patted Belle. "Hear that, girl? They called you a *pony*. Now you have to show them..."

Is that even possible?

Anna tried not to be intimidated by their murmurs. Jax claimed the slurs were just echoing their own fears. He insisted the remarks had nothing to do with how Anna and Belle really performed.

"Belle will read your aura—the one you convey through your hands, body and soul," Jax touted. "Just believe in yourself." But Anna could not drown out the murmurs.

Belle was tacked. The little roan quarter horse stood in her English saddle, white leg wraps and freshly cleaned bridle. Her large black eyes and wispy lashes induced a gentleness about her, normally a soft puppy-dog stare unless she was rocketing through the air in defiance.

Belle was quite attractive with a solid black mane now in tiny braids cresting her powerful neck. Western horses could sport long manes, but not in the show jumping world. Anna remembered moaning to her mother when she had to cut Belle's locks, throwing a fit with every snip. The haircut almost killed Anna.

Should have stayed in the Western discipline.

As Anna approached, Jax smiled. "Are you ready?" His voice was softly excited.

Anna couldn't help but tear up. *No, and where's Mom?* She couldn't speak. Instead, her face cried of horror which must have scared both Jax and Wyatt. The Australian asked Wyatt to lead

Belle to the warm-up ring to give him and Anna a few minutes to talk.

"Darlin', do you want to see the draw?" he asked, indicating the order in which the riders would commence.

"Have you heard from Sam or Mom yet?"

He shook his head. "All will be okay. Sam promised."

Anna took the paper Jax handed over. *Figures.* Maria Prickler was slated to go first. *Great.* A guarantee the Qualifier would lead with a perfect score she'd have to follow. Maria could laugh at Anna and probably the rest of the competitors, too. She was no one's friend.

Next was *Splendor*, a seventeen-hand Hanoverian from Erie. Third was *Gutless Wonder*, another seventeen-plus hand thoroughbred giant, from Philadelphia, followed by Penny Donahue and then the laughingstock, Anna and *Hobby's Little Belle*.

Great... last. People will have a good laugh.

"Anna, you can do this," Jax encouraged. "Tell Belle she can do this, too."

Anna mounted and walked Belle around the schooling ring. Her nerves built into a lump of burning coal that rolled from her throat to her toes. The other competitors anticipated their go while Maria Prickler headed into the arena.

Anna didn't see a drop of sweat on her or *Ernest Living*. He shined like a diamond as he floated by them in an extended trot.

Although Anna could not see Maria or the ride, by the sound of the audience, things were going as Anna expected. Perfect. The crowd cheered and immediately fell under her spell to silence. A pin could be heard dropping from the peanut gallery as the two performed. On the final jump, the crowd roared. Anna suspected Maria finished the course with no faults and in an excellent time.

Anna shifted in the saddle as each subsequent entry performed. Belle tried to set off in a trot with each shift until she was sweating with nerves. The crowd continued their hushed behavior, only shuddering on occasion from tics and knocks that probably caused minimum faults.

Penny Donahue, fourth to go, had been tied with Maria until the last and most difficult jump—the oxer. Her horse had a severe hit, shattering the rail, a 4-fault penalty. The crowd roared in sympathy with an extended "*aww.*"

After a vet and staff spent what felt like hours examining the horse in the arena, Penny exited the ring, crying in hysteria with her horse limping. That score placed her in second. *Why bawl?* It wasn't like Anna was about to nudge her to third.

The announcer called, "222."

It was time.

Anna eyed Jax at the massive tunnel opening that led toward the in-gate. Belle was already a noticeable bundle of nerves prancing and circling at her own will. When Belle peered through the formidable, hollow tunnel leading her to the hell zone, she started to pirouette—the same graceful maneuver others paid outrageous money for Lipizzaners to perform. Only Belle was not a Lipizzaner or a ballerina. At the moment, she was an out-of-control rocket coming in for a crash landing.

Belle.

Anna checked the reins hard, locked her elbows tighter, and jabbed the little mare's rounded sides with her spurs in a repetitive kicking. The four competitors and their overpowering mounts gazed on with thick raised necks and bulging bug eyes. Belle and Anna were like two ants among dinosaurs vying for the same prize. Impossible.

The laughing has started.

Jax was by her side as they headed toward what felt like the guillotine. "Jax, I don't have to enter. Why bother? Mom isn't even here."

That's when Jax stabbed her with a hard look. It was the first time she remembered him ever delivering such a glare. He grasped the reins, stroked Belle's forehead with his free hand, and the roan instantly dropped her head.

"Anna, this is not about winning. I recommend you relax. Just pretend you are home on Tunnel Hill, riding the fields. And take off those spurs."

"Jax, I can't even remember how to ride. What is this about if it's not the win?"

"Jumpers can be any breed. Winners can be any horse. But what's important is to believe in her. She's fast, agile, and fearless... just like you. Take off the spurs and work together. Complete the course. It's that simple. No matter how you look at it, you will finish. Belle has everything she needs to conquer this course. And you have everything, too. It's not about winning."

"I hate them, Jax." Anna looked at her ogling competitors.

"But you love Belle. And that's all that matters right now. Those other girls are scared of your heart. Fear is driving them. Don't let it consume you. Take the spurs off. Believe, Anna. It's about your heart."

Jax was holding onto the dancing Belle. How could she? Anna was positive that as soon as he released the mare that she would become possessed as always and surge into a fury. Anna looked to Wyatt who was standing to her left leg. The red-haired boy nodded in agreement, encouraging her to listen to Jax.

The announcer again called, "222." The next time would mean elimination.

"Do it. I've watched you ride bareback over anything at the farm. Believe, like I do!"

Anna reached to her right boot, simultaneously stretching her left leg toward Wyatt. Each unbuckled a spur.

Jax led Anna and Belle as far as he could before the double gates opened. "Believe you are riding bareback on the farm."

As soon as the sold-out crowd eyed the barely fifteen-hand little roan, whispers clouded the dome. Anna glanced at the four judges to acknowledge them in politeness. They were crouched toward each other with crinkled noses and wrinkled foreheads. Anna surveyed the other side of the arena. To her relief, she saw her mom on the edge of the bleachers just above the Gate 4 entrance directly across from the judges. Her mother smiled proudly and waved.

Mom's here!

Anna released a heavy sigh. Sam had delivered on his promise.

She scanned the ten jumps inside the arena. Earlier, she had walked the course. She knew she would have to allow extra paces for Belle to keep the time competitive. The mare lacked the length and stretch of the sizable show jumpers. What Belle did possess though, like Jax enforced, was flexibility to twist the turns, switch the leads, and quickly gauge the pivots. The ground condition was soft and fluffy—Belle's favorite. Compliance meant speed and no faults regardless of the horse.

Anna asked for a canter. To her dismay and embarrassment, Belle popped half a buck. Instantly, some groaning giggles and snide remarks could be heard over slurred whispers.

She eyed Jax just behind the gate. "Give her a pat, darlin'," he shouted. "And picture yourself at the farm. No worries."

Anna listened to Jax, as she should have before. She felt Belle release air and relax with the warmth of her hand. Belle rolled into the familiar canter at the touch of a shoulder. Besides, they were not judged until they passed the timer.

Good.

The two were halfway to closing the courtesy circle before the timer when Anna felt a snap. The left side of her body buckled. She curled her head down to the left and blinked at the leather strap. Glistening iron was lying in the fluffy dirt. *No!* Her left stirrup had completely torn free. Anna's left foot had nothing to support her.

But the nightmare was just beginning. When Belle passed the timer, the right side of Anna's body jolted. The right stirrup slipped from its place as well, leaving only a dangling leather strap slapping Belle on her underbelly. The walloping strap forced Belle into a frenzy of terror as they leaped over the second metal stirrup left in the dirt.

Anna glanced up at the glowing score board which lit up the dome. The timer had started, leaving only one chance. Rules did not allow for tack failure. This was considered rider negligence.

So she closed her eyes. *No stirrups.* Her squeezing legs cued Belle into a flat-out gallop. The mare was doing what she was asked. Anna's body bounced from side to side, forcing Belle into a zigzagging pattern toward the first jump. She was on a destructive, disorderly runaway pace.

Anna had nothing to depend on for support. Her mind went blank, in shock, as the crowd noise rose into hysteria.

CHAPTER 32

Sam was positioned directly across the arena from Jess above Gate 4. He was watching over the opening from the underground entrance, waiting to see Anna and Belle enter the course.

Sam pivoted back and checked his surroundings from the first row of bleachers behind him, up the stacked rows to the peanut gallery. The arena was packed. Sam massaged his jawline, wondering if "Lola" was hidden or even standing a few feet away.

Off to his right was the judging area protected by a low iron fence. A cluster of horse experts sat behind a white tablecloth and in front was none other than Sir Prickler. His entourage was surrounded by a barrage of security because of his notoriety. Next to him sat his ex daughter-in-law, Tina, adorned in white just like Sir Prickler.

The fourth to compete, Ben Donahue's granddaughter Penny was currently in the center of the arena in tears. Her horse appeared to be lame after breaking the top pole on the oxer. The ring crew was in the process of readjusting the course. A vet was checking the magnificent eighteen-hand horse surrounded by the ring steward, their trainer and Ben Donahue himself.

This mistake was unfortunate for the rider, but a blessing for Jess and Sam. The time had allowed them to arrive and settle in the stands to see Anna and Belle. They had decided to split up. Sam thought it safer to be away from Jess in the event this "Lola" did reach out to him.

Neither had said much in the car after Sam ranted how dangerous this entire investigation was and that he wanted her and

Anna out of harm's way. Jess was anxious enough to get to the event and this concern only managed to shut her down.

She refused to discuss Buddy's death. Sam never even had a chance to apologize because Sandra called with information regarding the encrypted USBs and Doug Kinard. Why couldn't Jess realize he was just doing his job?

Sam glanced diagonally across the arena to Jess, her slim body arching against the rail in anticipation. In the bright stadium lights, she was beautiful as always, her brown highlighted hair sparkling, her full lips glistening, olive skin flushed with rose in her cheeks, and her white shirt veed open where he had brushed her skin.

Jess unexpectedly looked across to catch his stare. They locked eyes until she saw the familiar kangaroo hat. Jax was walking out of the tunnel to the edge of Gate 4. He was studying the situation in the arena. When he saw Jess he stood below and reached up to clasp hands. Sam cringed.

Jess was mouthing something, then she pointed across to him. Jax eyed Sam with a tip of his hat. Sam acknowledged, but not without a jealous pang zapping his heart.

There was no immediate connection to the other side of the arena. Management had erected barricades for crowd control around the judging and entrance area. There was no simple way for Sam to join them without walking the entire oval coliseum or up numerous flights of cement stairs to the peanut gallery, then cutting across the top and back down. The underground stable area was another possible route, but security kept the public at bay there, too.

Maybe there was one other way—Sam's badge.

The announcer's voice resonated over the chatter, calling the crowd to attention. "As soon as the ring clears, our fifth and final rider, Anna McCoy, will have her chance at this difficult course. I hope everyone is ready for the championship on Sunday. Who will be the winner and qualify tonight?"

The crowd cheered. Sam decided this was the perfect opportunity to pay his friend Sir Prickler a visit. Sam walked over and wedged open two iron fence barricades at a connection point. Immediately, a beefy security man denied entrance in an authoritative stance. Sam smirked, his lone dimple enjoying the flash of his badge. He assumed the man was one of Sir Prickler's bodyguards.

"Sir Prickler can't wait to see me. I'm a good friend," Sam touted. The man grunted, took the badge, then eyed Sam.

"He's a celebrity. It hasn't been easy keeping his fans back. I'm watching you." The man flicked the badge back to Sam, then pressed his fists on his waist to flex his bulky biceps.

Sam curled one side of his lip higher. "I am his biggest fan." He edged by the beast and thought he'd humor the guy by adding, "Nice guns." *Go ahead and try something. I'm in the mood.* Sam's distaste for this entire case and what it had poured down upon his life was getting to his last nerve.

Already, another gentleman appearing to be an assistant was bent over whispering in Prickler's ear. Both the director and his ex daughter-in-law shot puzzled glances in Sam's direction. Tina's face scrunched in disdain even though any visible wrinkles had been botoxed to a frozen expression.

Prickler said something to the man, then rose and proceeded toward Sam. His gold cane shooed away anyone in his path.

"Mr. Prickler." Sam nodded and flashed his badge to the gentleman assisting him in the event he had qualms with Sam's presence.

Prickler's over-tanned, orange-shaded skin glowed against his pristine white attire. The man, about ten pounds underweight, was leathered with deep creases from too much sun, tanning beds and cigarettes. The veins in his hands and neck protruded like rivers of blue.

"Step no further," Prickler commanded in a low voice. "These judges are concentrating on cumulating scores. A man like you cannot possibly appreciate the amount of money and time these owners, trainers, riders and everyone involved spend on this." Prickler landed his pointer finger between Sam's deltoids.

Sam directly eyed the finger.

"This isn't a little Western event your kind might be accustomed to. A lot is at stake here. I will be speaking to Ty about your removal from this venue for the rest of the weekend." He turned to the man at his side. "Get Ty Burns on the phone right now."

Sam glanced at his watch. "Sergeant Burns is a little indisposed at the moment." Prickler ignored him. "I merely want to ask a few questions."

Prickler curled a finger for the buff ogre to come closer and remove Sam while the assistant was still dialing his cell.

Sam raised his voice. "It's about the murder."

Prickler's hand transformed into a stop sign. He immediately snapped the phone away from his assistant. Clearly Sam's words had the desired effect.

"Mr. Prickler, don't worry. I'm not here to disrupt. I just have a few questions for you." The crowd was roaring sympathy applause for Penny as she and her injured horse exited the ring. Ben Donahue was following, holding his phone, curling his finger to someone in the seat next to Tina Prickler.

Prickler circled the crowd with his eyes. "You need to keep your voice down. I haven't murdered anyone. The drugging is minor. Substances, both illegal and not, have been part of this institution since the onset. Go ahead and try to charge me. You can't."

Prickler's finger was again tapping Sam's chest. This time making better contact.

The announcer's voice interrupted, calling for entry number 222. That was Anna.

"As for murder, no one has been murdered by my hands. Although, I may think about strangling you. I'll have your badge if you go any further with this."

The repetitive hit of the director's finger on Sam's chest was adding to his irritation, his jaw back to its usual grinding. "Is that a threat? You like strangling as a method to your murder? Wasn't that what you also wanted to do to Wyatt Evans?"

Sam saw the fire bubble in the man's eyes. He noticed another gentleman rise behind Tina. This man was large, out of shape and not at all sharply attired like the rest of the group sitting near the judges. His hair and full beard were scruffy. Dressed in brown Carharts with mud-stained jeans and cumbersome work boots, it was Doug Kinard, glaring at Sam and dropping his phone into his pocket.

Donahue must have Doug at his beck and call.

Flustered by the accusations, Prickler continued railing. "I am pressing charges for what you and the Australian did the other day. I have been ill ever since, plus he owes me. Jaxson Bay and that kid, Wyatt, need to report back to the set or there will be hell to pay."

"Well, Mr. Prickler, there might be hell to pay for the damage you have inflicted upon Wyatt, and anyone else including furry friends."

Sam was finished with Prickler's index finger aiming dead center on his chest. He latched on to it in one maneuver, shocking the director. The security guard lunged forward.

Sam stopped the brute with raised hands. It didn't hurt that his jacket happened to open wide enough to display the contents of his holster. "Let's keep the peace, pal." Everyone froze.

The announcer added to the blow as his voice resonated over the crowd, "222. We are waiting for 222." Then he added, "One more chance or it's elimination for Anna McCoy and *Hobby's Little Belle.*"

Time suspended. Sam felt a nervous chill. Where was Anna?

He looked the director dead in the eyes. "Well, in regard to the Australian, that's between you and him. But the boy is my business." Sam freed his finger with a harsh shove. "I am here to ask about the murder of my friend, Buddy, and a young girl, possibly named Lola."

Prickler chuckled with an evil release of foul breath. "Good luck on that Lola identification," he muttered. Then he pointed overhead to the timer. "Looks like this discussion is over, and I will be headed to the winner's circle to see my granddaughter. Your girl is running out of time."

Precisely then, the crowd uttered different cheers and slurs.

Anna and Belle trotted into the ring, slightly disheveled, but slowly gaining composure. Sam turned his head to them as Anna cantered her courtesy circle for the judges. When she veered on the straight toward the first jump, something shifted her weight, and the crowd shuddered. One of her stirrups fell into the dirt in a silent puff.

Sam's heart sank, but not for the last time that day. A few steps further something malfunctioned again. This time the other stirrup landed in the dirt, but the leather strap remained attached, slapping Belle in the abdomen.

The two were on a stampede toward the first fence. The crowd screamed in horror. Sam searched for Jax, who was planted at the gate very much poised and in control. Jess, on the other hand, had her hands clasped over her mouth in fear.

"Seems like your girl is no longer a contender. Tack error because of rider negligence. There's no way she can win." He chuckled again and slapped Sam's shoulder hard. "Seems you are out of your league. Now, take your family and go home, Samuel Quaid."

Prickler turned to go to his seat with his assistant in tow, but then apparently changed his mind. With devilish eyes he spun on Sam and said, "And you know where the boy is, I am sure. Return *my* Wyatt, because he is *my* business."

Jess pressed her lips closed to hold back a scream. She wanted to holler Anna's name, order the judges to stop the pattern, fearing the worst for them both.

She heard a man behind her say, "Well, this competition is over." Another woman laughed. "Who let them in the arena? Little roan horses can't compete with these high-class jumpers."

Jess cringed, her stomach sickened by a potent stew of anguish. She searched for Sam who was amid a conversation with a group of people behind the judges' stand. There was no way she could get his attention… and no time. Jess lowered her arm, shouting for Jax at the gate. But he was intent and focused on Anna and Belle as they charged the fence.

She felt her phone vibrate. *Sam!* She quickly glanced. He could alert the judges. Jess eyeballed her phone, only adding to her anxiety. It was Lola! Jess shoved the phone back into her pocket to concentrate on the safety of her daughter and Belle.

Anna could barely think about anything except colliding with the fence like the night she had been attacked at the farm. Her brain and body were in full panic mode, which she shared with Belle. The roan was charging, fleeing in a weaving pattern for the first fence while Anna seesawed in the saddle.

Funny, Anna thought. *Belle is responding exactly how I'm commanding.* Dive left, then weave right, as if at the pole bending championship and not show jumping.

Anna closed her eyes. The audience was gasping in almost a uniform breath. The vertical was upon them. They were too close. She was going to plow right into the hard wooden poles and lovely flower display. Someone was going to have stitches.

But Belle was no longer waiting for a cue from Anna. The mare soloed an initiative to rocket straight up like a rearing Roy Rogers on Trigger into the air. Belle was reaching for the top of the dome when she cut a sharp angle and plummeted over in an arc to the left as Anna leaned in the same direction.

Belle stretched and cupped her back legs. Then in a nose-dive to the ground, the mare corkscrewed right, throwing Anna in the same direction. Belle had completely cleared the jump. Staggering to her feet, she was now digging dirt with the full intention of traveling forward toward the second.

Anna was face to shoulder on the landing, clinging to the mare's neck, her mouth practically eating the roan's mane and the taste of sweat combined with her recent lather in horse shampoo.

Anna could barely catch her breath. She veered up and glanced back at the rail, still standing. Luckily, the straight line down the arena merely consisted of two jumps: the vertical and the wall. There was enough distance between the two that Anna could hopefully gain composure and stop this catastrophe before either hit the earth.

She corrected herself in the saddle as best she could with every muscle in her body shaking. She shifted and held her position firmly. Anna pressed her butt into her seat asking Belle to stop. Her eyes focused ahead on the red wall with the fake cement appearance. That wall was approaching quickly as Anna gathered the reins uniformly in her hands.

Perhaps Anna's elbows were too rigid, or her hands too stiff and that irritated Belle. Or it might be the leather strap slapping Belle's belly with each rotation of her canter. The mare violently shook her head, crunching down on the bit. Belle stretched her neck, yanking the reins from Anna. She had no intention of listening or stopping.

Anna was left with no choice but to center her body in an effort to clear another fence. Again she closed her eyes and thought of Jax's words, *"Bareback in the woods."*

Belle proceeded in a frenzy of momentum over the wall.

This time to help Belle, Anna bent forward and lifted her head so the mare could glide over the fence straighter. Her petite hand cinched up some of Belle's mane with the reins. They easily cleared the four-and-one-half foot wall.

Anna was straight on the landing, but she suddenly realized her heels were still digging into Belle's sides. Instead, she arched her shoulders, reached for the sky and pressed her heels to the earth in imaginary stirrups. Belle lifted slightly and balanced between Anna's legs.

Anna decided to do the 180-degree pivot as if taking the next three jumps of the course. Her plan was to bring Belle to a halt, suck up her embarrassment, quit pony club, and return to barrel racing.

She took the twist aiming in the other direction. Belle responded in a flash. Anna advanced ahead before sitting deep when she saw Jax. He was positioned at Gate 4 cheering them on as if they could finish the course.

The Australian horse whisperer—the one she had wished for to save her family... the *magic*. He stood out, visible above the others, his massive shoulders, his kangaroo hat and his strong arms resting on the lip of the gate wall... calmly believing. His chocolate eyes were concentrating on Belle and on Anna, hypnotizing her.

Anna sat up straight, collected the reins and glanced at the stands. She imagined she was in the forest at Tunnel Hill, and the audience was nothing more than trees. The only sound was the wind as the two soared bareback over three obstacles in the woods. Logs simply posed as a cross rail, gate, and a triple bar. She looked at the enormous timer dangling by cables from the dome. Maybe they would fail, but they were going to try.

"Come on, Belle."

The horse must have heard her as she melded in under her seat. In jolting leaps and rhythmic strides, the pair burst forward. On the triple bar, the audience of trees sucked in air with a gasp because Belle nicked the top. They held their breath on the landing. For Anna there was no glancing back, but when the crowd exhaled and cheered, she knew the pole had only wobbled and held its place.

"You got this, girl!"

Anna twisted Belle like a soldier to circle and change leads facing the next set of three. She passed Jax. She briefly peeked at him, and he tipped his hat with a wink inspiring her onward.

In unison, they executed the plank, the upright poles and the difficult parallel. Belle was listening to Anna's every command and click.

Only three more to go. They were the hardest. Her mount was usually exhausted, but this little mare was feeding off the frenzy, no longer panicked or worried about the strap whipping her belly.

"Final ones, girl. I could not ask for anything more."

Belle was puffing like a locomotive on the tight turn in a full out gallop. Anna could almost touch her flaring red nostrils. The mare and Anna were drenched in sweat. The challenges ahead included the water event and her least favorite—the oxer.

"You are the best, girl. The best!"

The mare pricked her ears as if she knew the oxer approached. But she was full steam ahead. Releasing a mighty grunt when Anna gripped her sides, they soared the water, millimeters from touching the edge, which would be a fault for sure. Three strides more. Belle was drenched with exhaustion. Anna clicked, releasing her tension by counting, "One, two, three... and engage."

The mare soared as if in slow motion. Her panting was the only sound. The audience had risen to their feet, all silent, some clutching their neighbors, others clasping their mouths. Belle tucked her legs as tight as she could, and even the judges tilted on the edge of their seats.

The landing was hard, jarring Anna. She was as weak as Belle. The force catapulted her forward like the first jump. Anna found herself clinging to her horse. Belle's neck was so sweaty that Anna could barely hold on. Belle stumbled to remain on all fours, and Anna was sure they were not going to make the timer.

Belle had given her all. The failure was on Anna. Her skinny legs bearhugged Belle's girth. Once more she saw Jax at the gate with his chin lifted, aiming up.

Anna imagined him saying, *"Believe,"* but his mouth never moved.

There was only one possible attempt to resuscitate her body. In one momentous effort, Anna raised her hand in the air, reaching straight toward the dome. Like magic, a force winched her up and centered her body atop Belle. The roan stabilized and stretched across the timer.

The crowd's roars swelled in exhilaration, releasing waves of thunderous clapping and yelling.

Jess was flabbergasted. She had not breathed in minutes. She nabbed the first man to her left, clutched him and started jumping up and down in jubilation. "She did it! They did it! That's my Anna!"

Anna and Belle passed the finish line with no faults and no stirrups. The announcer was repeating the fact so outlandishly that it seemed his hoarse voice echoed for miles.

Jess couldn't remember Maria's time, but by the expressions of Tina and Sir Prickler who were still sitting, the Qualifier was going to be close.

Jess gathered her senses and eyed the man she was clinging to. He was little with dark hair. Jess smiled. "That's my daughter."

He returned a brief smile, his head bobbing up and down. Not until a second individual wrapped her other arm did Jess realize something was terribly wrong.

"Jessica McCoy?" the man asked, barely audible. The crowd was not waning. Instead they voiced fanatical screams over Anna and Belle in the arena.

The person now at Jess's other side was a woman. She repositioned closer and said, "I'm Lola. And you're coming with me."

Jess tried to wrench away, but the sharp poke pressing her rib cage told her not to resist. That was definitely a gun.

CHAPTER 33

Sam zeroed in on Sir Prickler and his once daughter-in-law, both pouting in their seats. They were re-examining Anna and Belle's run of the course on Maria's phone, waiting for the crowd to simmer down and the judges to determine the winner.

Sam couldn't remember Maria's time, but the man standing in the first bleacher could be heard yelling over top of the crowd to his wife, "That course was a split second shorter than the first go, not to mention amazing."

Sam was clapping, watching Belle and Anna canter a cool-down in a final circle. Jax entered the ring to retrieve Anna's stirrups. Anna rode up to him, bending in the saddle, delivering him an enormous hug. He stroked Belle with such kindness the horse's head melted into him. Sam felt the pang again, the one that wanted him to be the magic and not Jax.

Jax studied the stirrups, then searched for Sam in the crowd. Their eyes connected. Sam sensed Jax's concern—that the stirrups had been tampered with. Jax headed to the ring steward with her clipboard. She was moving to the area below the judges' stand.

Prickler could no longer wait. He stepped forward into the judges' space around the table, trying to speak. He darted between them to break the huddle. His secretary fanned himself with his own clipboard, seeing the judges shocked at Prickler's presence in their area.

A security official promptly removed the director, and the same muscle man that had denied Sam access now bulldozed Prickler. Sam had assumed the beast was one of Prickler's bodyguards, but surprisingly Sam was wrong.

"Take your hands off me!" Prickler shouted. "This is absurd. Do you know who I am? How could a quarter horse out-jump a prodigy of *Ernest Earner?* A Grand Prix champion! This ride could not possibly count. The rider was negligent. The pair of them should be eliminated. I will be notifying the Alliance."

Sam moved his focus across the ring to Jess, positive she would be ecstatic. He scanned the area where she had been standing and saw nothing. Then he realized she must have been on her way to the underground stables. He was about to turn and head there himself when his eyes ascended to an exit alleyway directly across. He caught sight of a man and a woman parading Jess out. They seemed to have her wedged between them, arms interlocked, giving Sam a gut feeling Jess was attempting to resist.

Sam stiffened. He surveyed the arena. How could he swiftly reach the other side? No sense dialing an officer because he was out of his jurisdiction. For certain, he would never make good enough time through the peanut gallery, cutting across and down. They would escape. Likewise, dashing the entire length of the oval coliseum would make it impossible to reach them. For a moment, Sam raked his hair and thought he would leap directly into the arena. He could then dart across. But climbing back out onto the bleachers, approximately twenty feet high, would not be an option. Then he got an idea.

Sam decided to hurdle over the rail to Gate 4, then race inside the tunnel where Jax had been standing and up the stairwell. The surest route. He promptly executed his plan, skirting through the standing and chanting crowd.

For one second he sized up the jump, then vaulted to the ground below praying for a good landing. Miraculously, he landed on his feet, although jolting his body. His side was searing in pain. *Too old for this.* Once on the ground, no one appeared to notice him except Jax. Sam was about to take off, but the Australian stopped him. He was handing the stirrups to the steward.

"Everything okay, mate?"

"Someone has Jess. Please keep Anna and Belle in your sights."

Jax responded with a nod, then Sam eyed Wyatt. "You stay put, with them."

Wyatt appeared to have seen a ghost, his face ashen. The boy could only bob his head. "I saw them. I saw them take Miss Jess."

Sam pointed at him again. "You stay put."

As Sam sprinted into the stairwell, he could hear the muffled crowd, still whistling, screaming in a standing ovation.

The announcer was attempting to make them sit and quiet. *"Let's give the judges a moment. Soon it will be time to broadcast our winner and reserve,"* his deep throaty voice was heralding.

Sam gauged the several levels of steps rising to the top. He was alone in the fully enclosed cement stairwell. The public on the other side of the wall was glued to the excitement.

Voices resonated from several flights above. But they were growing louder in what sounded like a scuffle. Someone was headed right toward him. Sam took off in flight, soaring two stairs at a time. His steps echoed as he was in hot pursuit.

Suddenly, a head arched over the rail two flights above. Sam stopped, secured his position, and braced himself. As suspected, within seconds of locking eyes with the dark-haired avenger, a pistol was aimed over the edge pointed directly at him.

"Don't follow us, or we'll hurt her." The voice was that of a woman.

Sam dodged low. A shot was fired. The bullet clanged and ricocheted off the rail, then seared past him with a high-pitched whistle echoing to the top of the dome ceiling. He could hear Jess scream, "No, stop!" There was more fighting. Sam could imagine that Jess was trying to free herself. Thinking of her, he continued with a vengeance.

The two kidnappers forced Jess to spin in the opposite direction and climb the steps. Sam cautiously scaled the wall and followed. His long legs were doing double time, gaining on them. When he was a mere flight below, the woman shooter leaned over the rail again. She fired two shots. This time armed with his gun, Sam fired back, forcing her to take cover.

Sam had ducked, but not low enough. A burning pain sliced his shoulder, sending a blistering feeling through his veins. A bullet had skimmed his upper bicep.

The force slammed him into the wall. He hovered momentarily, then heard the clang of a metal bar being compressed to open a door, followed by silence. The three clearly left the open area for another level or room.

Noise from the crowd in the arena softened as Sam slid up the wall, moving quicker as he neared the door. The wound in his shoulder left a trail of blood where he pressed.

When he reached the door, he hit the bar hard to open it, only to find a dark room. Another bullet soared above his head. He cut back and let the door slam shut. The three were obviously corralled in a room. A dead-end situation.

Sam leaned against the wall breathing heavy, scouting his next move when he heard a faint voice from behind.

He pivoted in a flash, aiming his Ruger in the direction down the stairs. Sam was set off-guard when his sights caught a familiar boy with red hair dancing wildly in curls.

"Wyatt?" Sam lowered his gun.

The boy appeared in shock, even greyer than before. Not only had Sam aimed his gun dead center at the child, but Wyatt was now horrified, pointing at the wall. "You... you're bleeding, Mr. Sam."

The arm of Sam's shirt was stained in blood. "Wyatt," Sam rushed him. "I told you to stay put." Gripping his spindly shoulders, he delivered him a shake. "You didn't listen."

Wyatt's saucer eyes filled with tears. "I... I... thought you needed help saving Miss Jess," he said innocently. "She's all Anna and I have..."

Sam was in no mood to sympathize. "This is not a game. What the hell? Nobody listens to me." He released the boy and pointed down the stairs. "You need to go back to the arena with Jax. Now."

"But Miss—" he sniffled.

Sam interrupted, "I love her too, but you're in danger. Don't make the situation worse." Sam didn't even think about the words. There was no cuddling for this situation. He could only dwell on the boy's safety and saving Jess.

Wyatt pedaled backwards, almost falling. Then he turned and rushed the stairs in the nick of time.

An arm extended out the door, equipped with a gun. Wildly, the shooter fired at Sam in the hallway. *Thank God Wyatt bolted in time.*

The gun fired three times, again ricocheting, splicing off a metal door, and breaking a large glass picture off to Sam's left with a crash.

Unexpectedly, the gun clicked. It was shot in succession three more times. Nothing more than click... click... click.

Sam lunged at the woman. As the two rustled in the doorway, another person vaulted over them. It was not Jess, but the man who was burrowed in the room with her. He bound over Sam and the woman and escaped.

Sam's heart was pounding for Jess's safety. He had to find her. *What's her condition?* His mind was running rampant as he tangled on the floor. He was wrapped in the legs of the remaining kidnapper, and she was attempting to kick herself away in a crawl.

Sam had a flashback of the bathroom incident from Ginger Jake's. *Could it be the same woman?* This person was kicking Sam's already painful shoulders with a pair of high black boots. *Déjà vu.*

After twenty years in the FBI, Sam knew how to eliminate pain from his brain. He stumbled to his feet about to grab the woman by her mid-section and elevate her to standing. That was, until he eyed a shadow in the doorway. Sam gazed up to discover the sizable guard from the judges' stand planted spread eagle. He was facing Sam, blocking the hallway like the Hoover Dam.

The man's arms fisted on his waist. "Thought I told you to leave?" the brute remarked.

Sam wasn't prepared, as the guard's powerful knuckles hit him dead center between his eyes. He dropped to the floor, held a kneeling position briefly, then completely blacked out.

Jess had managed to slip from her nemesis's clutches once in the dark room. The other person was preoccupied shooting and warding off Sam. The woman was firing out the door, so Jess was able to disappear. She bumped into a slew of oval tables and metal folding chairs until she could crawl to a safe spot. Then she heard Sam's grunt, causing her to gravitate toward the light in the open doorway.

Jess watched in horror as the outline of Sam's body tumbled to his knees and then hit the floor flat. Once Sam was down, Jess saw the silhouette of a massive man standing over his body. She quivered. Fortunately, the man's concern appeared to be the woman who had helped accost Jess. He nabbed her arm and they both fled, leaving the door propped open by Sam's lifeless body.

Jess waited seconds to be sure they were gone, then rushed to Sam. As soon as she reached his body, he was gaining consciousness with a slight moan. She helped him turn over, and he shimmied against the door, sitting back, rubbing his forehead.

"My God, are you all right?"

Jess was touching his good shoulder. He said nothing, simply staring at her, coming to his senses.

She slid to sit in front of him, brushing against his thigh as she examined the bruise forming on his forehead. The cut on his lip reopened and dotted with blood.

Jess gasped when she noticed his blood-soaked shirt. "Sam, you're really hurt. I have to call for help."

"Jess." Her name was all he could manage. Sam blocked her hand from searching her pocket. Then he layered his fingers overtop hers resting on his arm.

"Just let me catch my air. We have to... get... Wyatt."

"Wyatt? Why? Did someone try to hurt him?"

"Wyatt was here. I forced him to go back to Jax." Sam squeezed his eyes shut, then open. He appeared to blame himself, realizing his harshness may have been the mistake. "I have to know he's safe. Are you okay?" He stroked her hand.

She nodded. Sam attempted to stand.

Jess clenched his arm. "You need more time."

He refused to obey so Jess straddled his legs and planted herself firm to help him up. Once standing, he pulled her close, unexpectedly. She thought it was to catch his balance, but when his lips feathered her forehead, she wasn't prepared. Jess hoped he didn't feel the vibration of her heart.

Sam was gaining his wits. He leaned back. "Jess, I'm sorry for..." He raised his head, and drew her close again in a hug.

"The woman said her name was Lola right before they jumped me at the arena. Was it really Lola?"

The echo of the name transformed his demeanor.

"Seems everyone is a Lola." He gripped her wrist to steady the wobble in his legs and led her toward the stairs. His focus was on one person now—Wyatt.

As soon as he felt confident, Sam picked up the pace, continuing to use Jess's hand as a crutch and his other for dialing Jax.

Jax was waiting for them by the stalls. No Wyatt in sight.

Simultaneously, Anna skipped down the aisle toward them, returning from the paparazzi which now was being held back by security at Gate 4. They were trying to obtain a glimpse of Anna and the infamous horse whisperer who had taught her the skills to ride a show jumping course without stirrups and still take the win.

Belle was tethered in Anna's one hand, a triple-layered blue ribbon in the other. "Jax, they want you and Mom in a picture. Can you come to the arena... and—"

When Anna's ebony eyes fixed on Sam, his shoulder was covered in red.

Jess tried to block the view. "Come on, lady. Let's go bathe this girl. I will explain. There's no time for gloating just yet."

As the two shifted toward the wash rack, another man came into view. Ty Burns was storming toward Sam and Jax.

Clearly irate, Ty beelined to Sam. "You set me up, didn't you? There was no Lola at Ginger Jake's!"

"Ty, we meet again. Did you have a beer on me?" A looming agitation was mounting in Sam, but he still managed to poke fun.

When the officer caught a side glance of Sam's shirt, he felt a little faint. Stepping back he said, "You look like shit. What the hell happened to you?"

A medical tech was rushing down from the arena, carrying a first-aid box. Someone had called her, and Sam assumed it was Jess. Sam tried to ward her away, but the tech ordered him to a chair in front of Dundee's stall. "Just sit. You two can battle this out from here."

Ty hovered over Sam, crunching his deep wrinkles tighter. "That doesn't look too good."

"Someone tried to kidnap Jess, Ty. I want round-the-clock protection on her and these horses at this facility. Do you understand?"

"Are you going to stop setting me up?"

"This is no joke. Did you ask anyone for their ID?"

"I had no reason to."

"Do your homework. Plenty of grooms and barn hands from the stables hang out at Ginger Jake's. If my suspicion is correct, you might have found a lot of Lolas."

Ty scratched his head.

"I'll explain later. But if I'm right, Lola Diaz is only a code. I suspect the girl's body you found is an illegal working for whoever is behind this operation. She was most likely attempting to go rogue and bring down the entire house." Sam winced at the medical tech cleaning the wound on his shoulders.

She whispered, "Suck it up, buttercup." He smiled. "You should really be seen by a doctor."

Sam ignored her and continued talking. "This is way beyond illegal substances. There are sinister criminal activities taking place, and we can take the entire empire down." Sam was concerned he was losing his influence. "Ty, you can take all the credit."

Ty said nothing, only shook his head in refusal.

"Ty, I need you to provide protection. And I need you to do something else."

Ty looked up. "What is the something else?"

"I need you to find Wyatt Evans. He is a red-haired little..."

"You mean this boy?" Ty reached in his pocket and flashed Sam the picture. "The boy Sir Prickler is searching for? As I said earlier today, he insists I will find the boy at Tunnel Hill. The man claims you're harboring him. That true?"

"Would I ask you to help find Wyatt if I already had him? Ty, Wyatt Evans is in danger." Sam clenched his jaw. "Do you know what it's like to be a child on the run? Being abused? Having no one?"

Ty looked like he was about to say something that Sam was positive was going to be a *No, but have a nice day.* Then his opponent focused on the picture.

"Yes, Sam. I do know what that feels like."

Apparently Sam had hit a nerve.

Ty thumbed the boy in the picture and said, "I will help you."

Without warning, Sam saw Anna running alone down the aisleway toward him. She was frantic, forcing Sam to pull away from the medic.

"Sam! Sam! Where's Wyatt?" She was planted in front of him, tears cascading down her cheeks. "Mom said he's missing."

Sam rubbed his forehead. "Honey…"

"Did you yell at him? Wyatt has no one. You have to find him, or I will never speak to you again."

So much for being the magic.

Jax remained at the show facility with the three horses: Belle, Dundee, and Cowboy. He intended to camp out with them until the championship.

"I've slept on a bed of straw many a night for the sake of my team," he assured Sam.

In addition, Ty provided armed guards as promised.

Before leaving, Jax pulled Sam aside. "Mate, there's something not right about Doug Kinard, the Humane Officer."

"Funny, that's what Sandra says, too."

"He was here, with the group by the horse's stall. The massive beautiful chestnut that Penny Donahue rode. Kinard was speaking with the newspaper guy after their vet's diagnosis regarding the horse's condition. The vet advised an immediate x-ray. He seemed adamant the horse would most likely be three-legged for the rest of his life."

"Too bad," Sam added.

"That's the crazy part. That stall was reserved for the championship on Sunday by Ben Donahue just tonight. Only two horses can go to the championship: the winner of the Qualifier—which is Anna—and a backup which would be reserve." Jax reached for the rake to clean Dundee's stall. "That would be Sir Prickler's horse as Reserve, not Donahue's, eh?"

Sam nodded, as perplexed as Jax. "Odd. Perhaps Ben Donahue was preparing for a horse to scratch or disappear?"

"I'm upset by any animals in pain. This gelding certainly should not perform Sunday, even if he was in the reserve spot. The horse needs rest and proper care."

It was late when Sam, Jess and Anna returned to Tunnel Hill after the win and all the drama. Sam had so many thoughts streamlining his mind that Anna not speaking to him was okay for the moment. He understood her frustration. Anna was sniffling in the back seat until she drifted off to sleep. Once home, she marched straight to her room.

Sam had made one point clear; he was sleeping in the main log house tonight. For their safety, he would be sleeping on the couch in the great room. And he would be armed. To his surprise, Jess did not object. In fact, she appeared relieved.

Sam took a quick shower in the springhouse and gathered some necessities and items to review the case. Then he returned to the main house. He should have been exhausted. His shoulder and side were throbbing. But worrying about Wyatt drove him to the kitchen for a cup of coffee.

At 3:00 A.M. he was alone spinning the Lazy Susan with one hand, sedentary, staring at the items on the table—the ripped note with partial lines, the Horse Haven file, *The Child Spy* box and some notes of his own. All were laid out in front him.

Sam's shirt was unbuttoned and untucked from his jeans. He drifted in deep thought, hypnotized by the Lazy Susan's circular motion. He returned to reality when he heard a faint clearing of Jess's throat. She had slipped in behind him, and Sam wondered how long she had been in the room.

"Life is bittersweet, isn't it?" She'd started talking without even acknowledging him.

Sam stiffened in the chair. He stopped the motion of the Lazy Susan. His eyes penetrated her.

"First, Anna wins a nearly impossible jumping competition, and we should all be ecstatic," she said. "Then Wyatt, a boy we barely know, goes missing, and our hearts are breaking. I can't sleep."

Jess proceeded to the counter and poured herself a cup of coffee. Then she froze, the cup suspended in her hand, her back facing Sam. He waited while following the outline of her body in her pink nightshirt, her shapely smooth legs and bare feet. Her hair was wet like his, leaving a dampness on the collar. By the movement of her shoulders and the empty cup, she was crying.

"Jess." His heart ached. Sam said no more. He cautiously approached, standing behind her. His body brushed hers. Sam could smell the sweet aroma of her skin and freshly washed hair. He rested his hands on both sides of the counter as close as he possibly could without touching her. Then he bent in and whispered at her ear, "I will fix this. I promise."

Jess turned to face him. "Please, please."

He wrapped her in his arms, and she melted under his chin. Sam kissed her forehead, then slid down her cheek, and parted her salty lips that were wet with tears.

Sam was so enthralled in the taste of her that he slightly lifted her body onto her tiptoes. He pressed her against his bare chest and released a soft moan. He was filled with her sweetness. He had longed to hold Jess's body against him for months. Then he lowered her. She glided down, her head nestled in his neck, and her hand resting on the skin of his broad chest.

"I never want to let you go, Jess." As he spoke, she reached under his open shirt. She fingered down his side to the edge of his jeans. Then her hand collided with his leather holster.

Sam's phone vibrating on the counter intervened.

He clenched his jaw and inhaled. Sam had no choice but to answer. Too much was at stake. He kept her in his arms while picking up the phone.

The person did not wait for a hello. "Sam Quaid, I have someone who wants to say hello."

Jess shuddered. She could hear the meek voice of Wyatt. She attempted to speak, but Sam raised his finger to gently silence her.

"Wyatt, it's Sam. Are you okay, pal?"

Sam could hear rustling in the background. Perhaps horses? Then definitely a train whistle. *Blowing at three in the morning?*

"He will not be okay if you don't stop your investigation. End it, now," a man's voice demanded.

"Okay, okay..." Sam conceded. "If you hurt the boy in any way, I vow, I will track you down until the day I die." Despite his rough words, Sam tenderly touched Jess's tear.

"You stop this investigation. And you scratch *Hobby's Little Belle* from the championship on Sunday. Then the boy can be yours."

"Wyatt has nothing to do with this investigation."

"You have no ground to stand on, Mr. Quaid. I have the boy. I can take care of the horse, too. The Australian is in my sights."

Sam heard Wyatt's cries.

"Take your hands off him," Sam barked into the phone. "Wyatt, I'm coming for you. So help me God..." But the line was already dead.

CHAPTER 34

Immediately after Wyatt's kidnapper hung up, Sam made two phone calls. The first was to Sandra, who was in a bottomless sleep.

"Sam, it's 3:30 in the morning. This is grounds for an even bigger raise." Her voice was groggy. "What could possibly be a concern at this hour?"

"Someone kidnapped Wyatt."

Sandra gasped. "No, not that dear little boy!" Her voice suddenly clear as a bell, Sam pictured her whipping off the black eye covering she told him she always wore to sleep.

"Look, the ransom demand said they would give instructions tomorrow night as to his location, as long as we scratch Belle and Anna from the championship. But I want to try to find Wyatt first. Background noise indicated horses and a railway. Find out where a train runs at 3:00 A.M. that's close to a barn or *equestrian center*." Sam stressed the latter. "In fact, let me make your job a little easier. I am guessing maybe the Auction House. I believe there is a loading station there at Block 5."

Sandra was already in motion. "Consider it done, boss. Poor boy, probably scared to death. By the way, later this morning you are scheduled to hear from Carol at the children's home. And don't forget about the two young men in interrogation."

Sandra only needed ten minutes to get the location for Sam. She was her normal rambling self on the return call. "A friend of a friend of my Aunt Susie works at the Block 5 station. She said you're right on target with your hunch. The train just pulled in for the night. This is the monthly Saturday auction. Afterward some horses head to their demise. They get loaded up on a train, crammed in like sardines to a slaughterhouse. I'd like a chance to remove the battery on that train. And one more thing."

Sam latched onto the open space to say, "Great work, but trains don't run on batteries. I need to call Ty Burns, so make it quick."

"Ty? I thought you hated... whatever, boss. I know you suspect that Sir Prickler. He's one of the wealthiest directors in Hollywood. Everyone and thing around him makes money, so no one speaks out against him. That's why Tri-County is waltzing on tiptoes around the movie set. It's bringing a lot of revenue and attention to the area. Did I say his movies are good? But after all this tabloid news, I don't much like him anymore."

"Tabloid news?" Sam asked.

"Prickler is rumored to have an island in the Caribbean. Reports of human trafficking, but nothing has ever been proven. He owns ranches in New Mexico and Montana, and a 100-acre estate right here where his daughter-in-law and granddaughter have horses to their heart's content. His money always places them in the winner's circle. There've been local reports of child labor and illegals. No secret some of the grooms complain about his facility's mistreatment of them, not to mention the horses. However, that could be at the hands of his managers. Sir Prickler, I am sure, lives in Hollywood most of the time. Could all be rumors, but one more odd note, boss. Mr. Prickler supposedly had a horse on rest at Clancy's rescue, and it disappeared."

"Where did you receive that little piece of info? Tabloid news? Prickler owns his own estate in the tri-county area, and besides I think he's the culprit behind the Rescue incident."

"Well, this info came right from Janice at Judge Massey's. You know her?"

"Sandra, is this really important?"

"She said Mr. Prickler is filing a claim against Clancy. It landed right on her desk."

After Sandra hung up, Sam was puzzled but he had no time to contemplate. He made his second call. Apparently he was the only protection left for Jess and Anna, and he was not about to leave the loves of his life at Tunnel Hill alone in harm's way. Hopefully, Ty Burns would live up to his promise.

After a quick conversation, Ty agreed to personally go out to Block 5 with a fleet of officers. When he called Sam back an hour later with an update, he was out of breath.

"Sam, we combed every inch of the auction house and found nothing. Not one man, woman or *boy*." He emphasized the last word. "Plenty of horses though. I guess all for auction later this evening. Sad, very sad."

Ty inhaled, as if something rang a bell in his head.

"You know, I had a call a few months back. I hate to say this. A Lola Diaz... didn't speak very good English, something about horse drugging and theft, even mistreatment of the handlers. I told her if she could write the information down and drop it off at the station, I would investigate. I did look into the auction the following sale, but everything seemed legit... especially because it's run by Doug Kinard, the Humane Officer."

"That might not mean anything. A good cover for dirty work," Sam suggested.

"Come on, do you really think he harms animals? Perfect person for such a job to maintain a protected environment in a sad situation. I told the woman to call P.E.T.A."

"All right," Sam muttered almost disbelieving and wishing he could go see for himself. He flushed with guilt. At one point he had advised Lola to go to P.E.T.A. also.

Sam had handled this case poorly. He struggled over to the couch in the center of the great room. Jess had fallen asleep under a throw. He sculpted her body with his eyes and mind. She lay curled in a restful sleep finally after the last three days.

He slipped a piece of gum in his mouth to loosen his jaw. Then he scanned the puzzle he held in his hand.

This Lola Diaz was searching for help, making a diagram. Maybe as Ty suggested she couldn't speak fluent English. Maybe, that was the way she intended to explain to Sam, by a simple puzzle on paper.

Ty Burns, Doug Kinard, *Ernest*, the dormosedan sedative, even Sam. The person... whoever she was... wanted Sam to have this puzzle. And the person who accosted him in the restroom didn't want him to have it. It was that simple.

Sam walked across the room to stand over Jess. He softly lifted the brightly patterned Navaho blanket over her shoulder. He went to the massive fireplace and stirred the ashes. It was only the first September weekend, but they needed a warming fire because of the record-breaking low that had moved in across the valley. Perhaps a sign winter could be a frigid one.

He was convinced Sir Prickler was his man. All arrows pointed in that direction. He just needed to connect the evidence. Like the lines in the puzzle in his pocket. Until Sam had spoken to Sandra... now there was a new twist.

Sam was not in the house when Jess awoke mid-morning. She found herself on the couch in the great room, surprised to see Officer Martin. Martin was guarding over her from the highback chair, eating a waffle drenched in molasses and butter. In between bites, he informed her Sam was at the station.

"Good thing your sister didn't go home, yet. She sure can cook. Be hard for a man to stay slim around here."

Jess smiled and sat up. She reflected on the past evening, remembering the tumultuous kiss with Sam. *Was I dreaming?* Then she recalled the holster at Sam's waist and Wyatt's voice on the other side of the phone. That wasn't a dream.

They had thought Sam's returning to Seven Springs would be a walk-in-the-park move after serving in the FBI. But both the case that brought him here and this investigation were proving quite the opposite.

Jess briefly closed her eyes, holding her breath. She reimagined his lips encircling hers, his hand encasing her neck and chin, the firmness of his body next to hers.

"Miss Jess." It took Officer Martin several calls to snag her attention. "Tonight is the big event. And don't you worry. I'll be here on guard."

When Sam entered the office, he was sucking on a toothpick.

Sandra was already at her desk. "You're late." She was eating a muffin from her mother's café, but that didn't stop her rambling. "This is one for the record books, me before you. Has anyone told you that you look exhausted?"

Sam wanted to say, *I need sleep, please*, but the woman continued.

"No time for that. Tonight is the big ordeal! So excited." She handed him a stack of papers with a bag on top. "Now the note in the plastic bag is something Dallas said he forgot to show you with his file. He wants to send it out for a fingerprint comparison since there seems to be several fake Lola Diazes. So don't touch it."

Sandra slapped Sam's fingers with her pen. He smiled and his dimple appeared.

"Even though this paper was in the dead woman's possession, it did not burn up." Sandra shook the baggy then took a breath. "Go ahead and ask me why." She didn't give Sam a moment to respond before adding, "I will tell you why. Dallas said the victim had it in a platinum cigarette holder. Can you believe that? Anyway, he dropped it off and will pick it back up after lunch."

She sneaked a slurp of coffee.

"Now I didn't make you coffee because Carol has been waiting patiently over at the café to talk to you about Wyatt."

Sam had tuned Sandra out. He didn't have to analyze the paper. One look and he recognized it as the rest of the torn note from the Ginger Jake's incident, the one in his pocket.

"Sam, are you listening?" Sandra's voice was raised. She took the files back. "You can look at this later. Carol, now."

Sam cocked his head. "Carol?"

"Carol is waiting... at the café." Sandra shooed him with her hand, and he slowly backed away.

He removed the toothpick from his mouth and pointed at her. "Don't lose that note."

"Sam, really? Who amongst us has been guilty of that lately? And don't be long. You have two boys still waiting in the back."

Sam slid into the booth across from Carol. She was wearing her children's home badge. "You're working too, on a Saturday?" he asked.

"Sad to say, our work is never done. You thought it would be easy here in Seven Springs." Carol was eating her last bite of croissant.

A familiar waitress set a hot coffee in front of him and winked. Sam nodded.

"I paid a visit to Wyatt Evans's mom. Seems we have met before. She had another boy."

"Did he work for Prickler?"

"No, no connection to him. There are rumors about that man, but I think he's just what his name insinuates."

Sam smiled.

"The brother overdosed last year. She's nothing we would call a mother, Sam. She's been a walking timebomb for having her parental rights revoked. But that won't be necessary. One of my associates has been following Wyatt for years. He is a sweet boy."

Sam watched as she shuffled through papers.

"I was looking through all this stuff while I waited for you." Sam noticed a program from the Alliance Championship resting on top. "Here it is."

Carol slid a court order in front of him.

Sam skimmed the paper. "She relinquished custody?"

"Yup, she signed off. I will proceed to have him moved to the children's home. Do you think you can find him?"

"I pray I can." He fingered the Alliance brochure.

"Hey, I saw Anna last night. She was amazing on that little horse. I was just talking to the waitress about it. That Australian friend of yours is magic."

Sam smiled again. "She was something." He opened the brochure. "He is, too. I guess." Sam had not seen the glossy handout and was curious to read the inside as the waitress poured another round.

Sam scanned the document.

Horse	Rider
Ernest Living	Maria Prickler
Hobby's Little Belle	Anna McCoy
Splendor	Sierra Derk
Gutless Wonder	Gail Plessent
Ernest Hem-n-Way	Penny Donahue

"What will Jessica and Anna do with their portion of the $100,000 purse if she wins?" Carol was blowing on her fresh coffee about to take a sip.

Sam was mesmerized. "*Ernest Hem-n-Way?*" he muttered out loud.

"Hey yes, isn't that a cool name? Ironically, the horse is owned by the newspaper mongrel."

"What?" Sam eyed Carol.

She smiled and looked perplexed about why he didn't understand. "Didn't you know Ben owns that gelding? He bought two Ernest offspring after Sir Prickler purchased one for Maria. I heard the other is a stud. Probably hopes with this win, he'll make a mint. Also, probably didn't figure on a contender like Belle. Either way, if Penny or Maria wins, he's in the black." Carol shook her head. "I think it's great that Anna kicked ass! But I sure would have liked the children's home to receive a portion of the winnings. Ben has always been a donator."

Sam didn't take a sip but tossed a twenty on the table. "Tell her thanks and that should cover yours, too."

Sam dashed back to the station and focused on the paper in the plastic bag. He held up his half and connected the two as one. The name wasn't *Ernest Living* but instead *Ernest Hem-n-way.* A line was drawn from Ben to the horse.

Sandra watched him from her desk. Then she held out two USBs in her hand.

"I have three updates for you, boss. First, these came back from being deciphered. You might want to watch the videos before interrogating the boys in the back. And you better do it quick."

Sam popped one in the computer. "Quick?"

"That's the second update. Judge Massey has a court order to remove the two goons you are about to interrogate from under your care. His paddy wagon is on the way."

"What? He's definitely being pressured from someone." Sam whipped out a toothpick and chomped on it hard.

"Yup, so you better move. Someone wants them out of your possession. And, I might add, probably silenced. So that brings me to the next and final point."

"What's that?" Sam could hardly wait to be bombarded with another assumption from his favorite secretary.

"I thought you wouldn't mind, so I watched the clips. They were from Buddy. I may need a bodyguard now that I know the truth."

Sam snapped the toothpick. He felt every muscle in his body fill with tension. He pressed the enter button on the computer to watch. He had presumed the mastermind's identity before he had all the evidence.

After interrogating the two boys and watching all the clips Buddy left, it seemed Sam had been wrong. Dead wrong.

Sam rang the doorbell. He had not sported a tux in over two years. Admiring himself in the mirror before he left—even though he had a slight black and blue coloration developing under one eye, and he ached all over—he thought he appeared quite handsome. He ironed his hand down the white shirt, smoothing along the buttons, then cleared his throat.

He was grinding on a toothpick when the door opened. He was actually nervous for Sandra to see him clean-shaven and dressed. He wished the woman he loved was on his arm instead, but she had insisted on being Ty's date. Jess was still trying to obtain information about Buddy's death, information that Sam already had squared away.

Sam had waited until Jess was in Ty's car to leave. He had only seen her from a distance, leaving him to imagine how beautiful she was. It was comforting to know Jax would be there upon her arrival.

When Sandra came to the door, Sam's lip twitched. She was stunning in a navy-blue gown with capped sleeves. The dress fit her curves like a Cinderella, with little rhinestones dancing throughout the material. Her eighty-year-old mother was behind her snapping pictures.

Sam's eyes must have popped, and Sandra snapped the toothpick from his mouth. "Well, thank you. I must say you clean up nice, boss. Except that shiner on your eye from last night. But no toothpicks allowed tonight, and don't mind my mom. I never went to prom."

"I'm honored to have you on my arm."

In the car, they discussed the investigation. "I am praying for Wyatt. You know, boss, we had the wrong guy pegged all along. Prickler is no more than a spoiled, over-paid Hollywood celebrity."

"So right you are, Sandra. The horse in the accident at the Rescue was owned by Sir Prickler. One of his valuables from his own estate. Donahue was making sure Prickler didn't dare win that competition. He had Doug Kinard kill that horse, and made it look like an accident, all as a warning. I knew Donahue had something more up his sleeve after Jax informed me he reserved the stall even after Penny's horse was injured."

"Do you think he's going to switch the horse?"

"I have a feeling 'Ernest Hem-n-Way' will be in his stall ready to go tomorrow in the event someone scratches. You seen one chestnut, you seen 'em all."

"Wow, Donahue is obsessed with winning and doesn't take a second to no one. I heard he blasted Penny, his granddaughter, after the run. This is one powerful man exploiting his family and the community that respects him."

"We're going to need all the prayers we can get to bring the criminals to justice tonight. Word to the wise, Sandra. You are one of my top safety priorities. Please, follow my orders."

CHAPTER 35

The valet took Sam's keys while he assisted Sandra out of the car. Ironically, a locomotive whistle echoed from across the river that bordered the Expo Center.

The valet watched as Sam's head tilted in the direction of the train. "The only straight run to go north tonight, sir. Hope you're heading south when you leave."

"What's that?" Sam asked.

"There was a huge accident and explosion on the main road out of the city. Fire police informed us to tell all attendees you'll have to use the winding back way or across the river to head north. Sorry for any inconvenience. It will be shut until early morning."

Sam nodded and checked his phone alerts. His main concern was the auction house and Wyatt. If the valet was correct, the incident was on the road north, and not near the tracks or auction house.

Mink stoles were dropping off shoulders at the check-in as Sam escorted Sandra inside. The elevator took them to the conference room, which had transformed into a ballroom.

Sandra squeezed Sam's arm. "It's hard to believe the horses are three stories below, and we're dressed for a ball above."

"Best of show here, Sandra."

The elevator opened and the sound of dinging glasses and chattering resonated from a large room beyond double doors. Sam momentarily had a flashback from the knockout punch he'd received the night before. The brute hadn't been working for Prickler at all... instead the wrongdoer was Ben Donahue.

When the two stepped into the room, Sandra gasped. The setting was exquisite. Windows the length of the outside wall overlooked the city. Dim crystal lights lined the entire ceiling which was draped in sheer white fabric. The theme was horses, and every table had faux leather tablecloths and fall centerpieces lit with flickering votives.

"Oh Sam, thank you," Sandra gushed in appreciation.

Sam's heart melted. "I couldn't think of anyone else who deserved to sit next to Jax." The hostess handed him a card which resembled a stall door. It read "Stall 23"... their table. He cringed. *Definite set-up.*

Sam could see Jess in quick peeks as they weaved in and out of tables to the front. There was already music and dancing. He caught glimpses as he approached Table 23. She was speaking to Ben Donahue. Sam could barely contain his emotions until finally reaching them.

Sandra must have sensed his ache. "Try to play hard to get, boss."

Jess and Ben both gazed in his direction. Jess cocked her head and delivered a timid smile. She was as Sam expected, drop dead gorgeous, forcing his heart to skip a beat. Her hair was swept up draping in curls from the top of her crown. A single tendril had slipped over her forehead and cheek.

Jess wore a black silk jumpsuit, conforming like skin to her body. It was adorned with a simple rhinestone necklace which cascaded to the exact point where the outfit dipped low at her breast. The back draped even lower, revealing the tender skin Sam longed to touch. He focused on her curves. Then his eyes descended, dissecting every inch until he reached her glittery black stilettos.

Ben did not acknowledge Sam's presence. "Buddy was the best, Jessica. But let the authorities take care of it. As for the championship, sheer luck was the reason for Anna and Belle's win." He shifted his weight. "An undersized quarter horse with no pedigree can't possibly compete against thoroughbreds and crosses. Scratching is my best advice before either one gets hurt. Why embarrass her?"

Soft music was playing and attendees headed to the floor as Sam stepped between them. "Seems Anna and Belle did just fine."

He slipped his arm under Jess's. "And I need to have a word with Jess."

"Sam Quaid, how's that investigation going? The accident at Horse Haven?" Sam knew Ben was edging on a threat.

"Honestly, Ben, I recently acquired new information. Seems I was hanging around the wrong stall."

"Seems. So was that boy... was it Wyatt Evans?"

Sam lurched forward, but Jess slid between them, facing Sam. "If any hair on that boy is touched, there is no telling what I will do." Sam laid an index finger pointing at Ben over Jess's shoulder. "I promise."

Annoyance was written all over Ben's glare. He was about to speak, but at that moment, Jaxson Bay stepped into the room. His aura in the tuxedo commanded the entire crowd of a hundred to turn in his direction as if magic dusted them all.

Jax's massive shoulders and powerful build commanded the room. He approached Table 23 and graciously pulled Sandra's seat out. "You look lovely, darlin'." Sandra blushed three shades.

Perfect timing. Sam led Jess to the floor.

"Sam..." She tried to resist. "What's going on?"

"Please, let me speak." He gently wrapped his arm around her waist and cupped her hand. "It's about Buddy."

She froze and he pulled her toward him. He laid his mouth to her ear, and felt her succumb. "Horse Haven was no accident. A set-up," he whispered intently. "Buddy happened to be at a party when he came upon the scene. The woman, a handler, was killed in the accident—but not by a horse. A trailer, owned by Doug Kinard, brought the horse, very much alive. He shot him on the spot, point blank, dropping the animal in front of the car. Good side up. Dallas had no reason to turn the horse over. The woman had some evidence against Doug Kinard that he was working for Ben Donahue. It was all arranged."

"Why, Sam?" Jess was playing along nicely, pretending to be enraptured in the dance, but Sam could hear the panic in her voice.

"Insurance money and a kingpin displaying his power. The horse was insured for over $100,000. Prickler owned the animal. Donahue was letting him know this was his territory and he could do anything he wanted. Since Prickler couldn't prove he had a horse at Clancy's, not only did he lose an animal... but he couldn't retrieve a penny. Your friend Donahue was showing the almighty director who really was in control."

Jess jerked back and stared into his eyes.

Sam nestled her waist closer. "Listen, you have to trust me. Buddy wanted you to know without directly involving you. He accomplished that through the dog tags. He knew his life was in danger. Everything went hush-hush. He explains the whole incident on a USB drive. Clancy was a scapegoat, but Doug Kinard is involved—fraud, drugs, theft, the works. And yes, abuse of the grooms and handlers, too."

"Sam... Wyatt. What about Wyatt?"

"That's where you come in tonight. I need you to make an announcement when it's time for the winning owner of the Qualifier to speak."

Jess nodded.

Sam kissed her bare shoulder softly. He caught Ty rolling his eyes. Sam shrugged an *I'm sorry* in his direction, as if to say he got the girl. Then he mouthed and pointed at Ty, *"But you will get the credit."*

Sam tightened his embrace around Jess before releasing her. "One more thing. You look absolutely ravishing." He stroked her cheek. "I have never stopped loving you. Never will."

Immediately after that, Jess stood at the podium and announced the scratching of Belle and Anna from Sunday's championship, the crowd shuddered. Sam's phone simultaneously rang.

The man on the other end spoke in a low voice. "Sorry man, I didn't trust you. I had to take the horse, too."

Sam threw a glance at Jax and dialed the lower stable.

"Sir, we have a situation here. Two men down and the horse... the horse is gone."

"Gone?"

"A handler witnessed the horse being loaded onto one of Kinard's 1-800-dead-cow trailers."

"Dead?" Sam held his breath.

"Very much alive, sir."

"For now!" Sam blurted. Jax was already standing next to him. When Sam told Jax what had happened, he felt the heat rise from the Australian's body.

Ty stopped them. "The train with the horses leaves in thirty minutes. You won't make it! The main road is closed."

"I'm not that easy to stop," Jax said. "I have a better way, mate."

Sam eyed Sandra. "Stay here and watch her." He pointed to Jess.

But Jess was already storming in front of Sam behind Jax. "I'm going to find Wyatt."

Sam didn't have time to argue.

One thing Jess never imagined was riding horseback along the Susquehanna River at night through the city of lights, Jax and Sam in tuxedos thundering ahead at a gallop. Jess, still in her sexy satin jumpsuit, was mounted on a horse named Bruiser that one of the stewards offered. Thankfully, Sam had given her his tux jacket because the air was crisp though exhilarating.

The horse auction was located right above the Expo Center at the next block, a distance by road, but a short run along the rails. Tonight was the monthly auction. The unlucky horses would be loaded and delivered to the slaughterhouse. Sam had told Jess he had a 110% gut feeling Wyatt was held hostage with Belle at that location.

The three crested a hill and stopped, surveying the descent to Block 5. The night was clear, and the moon bright. Lights shining on Block 5 and along the railway created a very visible view.

Dundee pranced in repetitive three and four stationary steps while Jax eyed the block below. By the sound of it, the horses were trapped in cars, stamping and kicking at the sides. Their whinnies and screams sounded over the puffs and grinds of the idle train until Doug Kinard seized a vision of them.

He hollered a command to the engineer, "Leave now!" then vaulted on the back car and skirted inside.

The whistle sounded, and the train wheels clanged against the rails in rotation. Jax never looked at Sam, only ahead, contemplating the situation.

"Mate, I'll take the train. I'm jumping on board. Let me set them all free, and then we'll run them back to the Expo. Plenty of stalls right now. Just like a cattle drive on the ranch."

Sam nodded. There was no other chance. "Just be careful. By the time you make the train, she'll be rolling. Belle is most likely on one of the cars."

Jax cued Dundee. The stallion leaped off the crest instantly, snorting through his already flaming pink nostrils, his black mane and tail rocketing in the air.

Sam took Jess's reins. "I'm going in to find Wyatt. You hold position. We'll need you to veer the horses toward the Expo Center." Sam sent Cowboy forward.

But Jess was not about to listen.

She held Bruiser back momentarily, both anxious to go. Then she tailed Sam as he loped directly into the auction house. The arena was cleared of people, except for the bodyguard from the Expo who had managed to knock out Sam in one blow. The ogre was in the office behind a glass window appearing to raid computer files.

Upon seeing Sam, he dashed toward a row of stalls leading to the outside. Sam squeezed Cowboy's flanks, and Jess watched as the brute was about to meet his match.

The powerful gelding gained on the massive man in a matter of steps. Sam plowed Cowboy's muscular shoulder directly into the man, knocking him flat. "You have nothing on this weightlifter!" Jess heard Sam holler before he dismounted and lunged for him.

The man fisted Sam in the shoulder, delivering him a surge of pain. "You are too late, detective. The boy and horse are gone!"

Sam grunted and sucked in air. "You know, I'm done with you." He pivoted to return a knockout punch in one blow.

Jess simultaneously dismounted and began yelling for Wyatt, ripping open stall doors as she called. She reached the outside row facing the railway and was about to search the line of stalls when she saw Jax's silhouette in the lights of the railway.

Jax had stopped ahead on a rocky crag. *Is he going to jump for the flatbed car and hope Dundee can stop in time? What's he thinking?*

The train was gaining, and Jax nudged Dundee to start descending. The stallion reared and resisted, his thick neck bobbing up and down, curled in refusal. Jax did not give. He pressed the horse.

Jess covered her mouth. She could see Jax had no choice but to commit. Dundee opened like an accordion, soaring, hitting the rocks with an uproar.

The locomotive was closing in. Rock crumbled with every downward gallop. Then it was time... the jump had to be now.

Jax squeezed Dundee one last time, and the horse obeyed.

The engine steam was thick, and Jess could barely see the silhouette of Jax and Dundee. Without hesitation, the stallion soared into the air like a magical horse with wings. Hitting the train, his hooves danced in sparks as metal scarred metal.

Dundee lost his footing and landed on his side, luckily, bringing them to a stop, while practically falling off the edge of the other side. They were saved by Dundee's scramble to stand.

Jax catapulted off and headed for the first car.

Jax is on the train!

Jess listened as the locomotive rumbled further away. She heard double clomping hooves from behind. It was Sam, on Cowboy, with Bruiser tethered. "Wyatt's on the train."

Jess mounted, not without noticing Sam's shoulder dampening the white shirt in red. "Are you...?"

"All good. Come on."

Wyatt had managed to free his tied hands and sneak away from the stall where he had been imprisoned. The train car was loaded with stomping horses, and the smell of manure and hay was heavy in the air and ready to roll. The train abruptly started to move forward before the scheduled departure time. Wyatt contemplated a plan to escape.

The safest hiding place would be amidst the forty dancing hooves—especially one set. He had recognized Belle by the white softball spot on her belly when they brought her in with a herd of horses. He had to save her. He could jump on and hide with the horses in their car.

Wyatt's heart pounded as he darted in and out of the first car, then across the flatbed like Indiana Jones. He balanced on each connector, leaping from railcar edge to railcar edge, each time chanting, *"Don't look down!"* The skinny boy made the final car. Spilling with excitement, he was about to balance across the last connector to the other when he heard a man's voice from behind.

"I don't think so, brat." It was the Humane Officer, Doug Kinard, his captor. The man had his neck and belt loop holding his body mid-air. "I think this will be your next and last stop. Right there, on the ground." He pointed and tossed his cigar. "We'll just let this baby pick up speed!"

Wyatt tried to jerk and swivel his body, but he was no match.

"Say, bye-bye."

The ground was moving faster and faster, the horses rustling and screaming in the next car. This was it. Wyatt would never survive the landing. Unexpectedly, the door behind Doug propelled open with a clang, metal against metal. A familiar voice ordered, "Take hold of the rail, little mate."

The Australian cracked his whip which coiled around the captor's neck like a cobra. Doug yelled and released his grip on the boy.

Wyatt stretched for the rail but missed, and for a second he balanced on the steel edge. He was too weak to stabilize for long, flailing for something to grab when he locked the forearm of Jax.

"I got you."

Jax sent Doug a hard kick and let him spindle free from the whip. Doug's hands were holding his own neck when he soared off the train, then collided with the earth.

Wyatt looked up at the Australian. His strong arm was Wyatt's lifeline. The man's physique was larger than life.

"All good, Wyatt. I have to stop this train now. Then we can save our mates. Wait here."

Jax's massive shadow disappeared into the horse car as he headed toward the front locomotive. The horses appeared hypnotized by the kangaroo hat that was walking between their backs. The stamping settled, and their voices neighed.

The next thing Wyatt remembered after the train stopped was Jax's mighty hand, placing him on the back of Dundee. "Come on, let's take this herd home."

Wyatt wrapped his arms around the muscular neck of the steed, preparing to leap off the flat bed. He closed his eyes, inhaled Dundee's aroma, and felt safe for one of the few times in his life. Dundee gently soared downward to the ground as if once again protecting the boy.

The train slowed to a stop. Jess waited in anticipation, her heart flatlining until she heard Jax's voice. "Ready, mates!" Jax called, "I'll guide them your way. It's going to be one hell of a drive!"

Jax slowly released the train cargo door with a screech. About twenty horses trotted and bobbed toward them. The Australian was in his glory swinging his kangaroo whip in circular snaps, cracking the air, clicking and whistling.

Bruiser perked his ears. Jess clapped her hands when she discovered Jax was atop Belle—bareback and bridleless. Then she saw dear Wyatt slapping his thigh behind Jax, mounted on Dundee and helping to push the herd free.

CHAPTER 36

Sam knew Ben Donahue assumed there was no possible way the three would catch the train. He was convinced his puppet Doug Kinard would see to it Belle ended up at the slaughterhouse and Wyatt would disappear. His other pawn, Judge Massey, had arranged the disappearance of the two goons and presumed Clancy Heidel was no threat as long as his wife Margaret was still alive. What Ben wasn't aware of was Jaxson Bay's determination and the USB clips from Buddy.

When Sam pulled up to Ben's estate, Officer Martin was already parked at the edge of the lane, papers in hand. The two exited their cars.

"He hasn't left, sir," Martin said, handing over the arrest warrant.

Still dressed in his blood-stained tuxedo and chewing on a toothpick, Sam shook Martin's hand and accepted the document. "Couldn't ask for a better partner."

Martin grinned ear to ear under the praise.

Sam ached from pain and he was exhausted, but when the door opened his body surged with adrenaline. Ben Donahue was headed out with suitcase in hand, shocked to find them plastered in his doorway.

Sam thrust the warrant forward.

Ben didn't look down at first. Instead he glared at Sam. "You look pathetic, as to be expected from your kind."

"Now it's my turn," Sam remarked. "You might as well go back inside. Your pilot phoned. Your flight has been cancelled."

Ben's sinister grey eyes stared at the warrant. "You have nothing on me. You're barking up the wrong tree. So get out of my way."

"Well, Ben Donahue, you are under arrest for the murder of Buddy Sterling. And that is just for starters."

"What? Why don't you go find that little roan horse, and spend your time doing what small-town police officers do?"

"No worries on that little roan horse, and about twenty-five others," Sam said with a grin. "They are housed safely at the Expo Center under the watchful eye of Jaxson Bay, awaiting new homes. The same goes for Doug Kinard and your friend Judge Massey. They will have a new home too—a prison cell."

Ben ripped the warrant from Sam and began to dial his cell phone.

"Let me guess." Sam removed the toothpick. "Attorney Cousins. Hey, you'll soon be seeing him down at the little station." Another man walked up behind Sam. "Meet my pal, Sergeant Ty Burns. He will do the honors. This case is all his baby."

Ben's face fumed. "Ty, I'll have your head for this."

Sam ignored him and focused on the other officer. Sam opened a notepad then handed Ty official papers. "It's all in there. The business of Ernest Equestrians, LLC, which mistreated grooms, handlers and immigrants. Human trafficking, horse theft and attempted horse theft of one such horse named Belle, insurance fraud, not to mention the selling and use of illegal substances in an equestrian environment. Then of course there's the big stuff... like murder. Plus attempted murder on me and my family."

Sam curled a lip. His lone dimple appeared and he placed the toothpick back in his mouth. "Sergeant Burns will be reading you your rights... while Officer Martin will be holding me back."

Ben squinted, obviously questioning Sam's last remark.

"You see, if you threaten Jaxson Bay, my family, or Wyatt Evans ever again, or a little mare named Belle, I can't begin to say what I will do."

Anna was not a hair nervous as five national winners were about to compete for the $100,000 purse of the Youth Alliance Championship. That's because she was no longer worried about winning. Jax had been right. The ride was about two engaging as one.

The entire Tri-County Pony Club was sitting on the first set of bleachers. Maria Prickler was sulking because of her reserve position. Penny Donahue was crying. The rest were all there cheering Anna on in another packed coliseum.

Penny had no idea about her grandfather's criminal activity. In fact, the girl had apologized to Anna and Wyatt. Anna knew she was a follower from the first time they met. It was Maria who was the instigator. Anna could not help but feel sympathy for Penny's embarrassment. She'd lost not only her horse, but her grandfather who was going to jail for a very long time. Sam made sure of that.

Anna locked eyes with Jax who smiled and nodded, seemingly reading her mind. She was elated that Sam was holding her mom's hand. Plus, she was thrilled that Wyatt was staying with their family as long as he needed.

Anna squeezed Belle's neck. "I have a favor to ask you, girl."

Anna waved Penny to Gate 4. There was plenty of time for her to school Belle.

Jess noticed her and said, "Honey, what are you doing?"

Anna didn't answer. Instead she slid the reins up over Belle's neck, and removed her helmet and jacket.

Penny was wiping her tears as she descended to the holding pen.

"Anna?" her mom questioned again, shooting Jax and Sam a troubled look.

Penny approached, confused.

"You have your boots and jodhpurs on, right?" Anna's voice was quiet but firm. "Penny, you can still make the dream of the winner's circle before you age out." She stepped back from Belle and held out her arm. "Take off your spurs. You won't need them tonight. This little roan quarter horse has a huge motor."

Anna winked to Jax.

Maria started protesting in the bleachers, stomping her feet. "You've got to be kidding!"

The entire pony club was awestruck. "Bravo!" they cheered.

Penny slowly took the reins, drying her tears.

"Come on. Head to the schooling ring. You're an awesome rider, but Belle can be a witch."

Penny removed her spurs as requested, almost in a daze.

Anna winked back again to Jax. Then she turned to face her mother. "It's the right thing to do, Mom. Belle gave her all for me. I could never ask for anything else. The show jumping competition is scored on the horse. It doesn't matter who rides."

Jess teared up. Sam moved alongside to hold Belle's reins for Penny. "Hop on, little lady."

Anna hugged Sam, and he grinned from ear to ear. Then she embraced the mare.

"Come on, Wyatt. Let's go help Penny." She and Wyatt skipped along to the practice pen.

Sam touched Jess's waist. "The two boys I arrested the day Jax and I got chased admitted they'd been hired by Ben Donahue. Your boss owns Ernest Equestrians, LLC. Doug Kinard confessed to Buddy's murder after he witnessed the horse being slaughtered."

Jess looked away and Sam could sense her agony. He pulled her close.

"When it came to Ben's horse business, he was a narcissist. No one was going to keep him out of the winner's circle. When Belle and Anna became a threat to the reserve and winner positions, he panicked. He tried to have them kidnapped... then when he heard Jaxson Bay was visiting the farm, he when into a frenzy to stop them."

He felt Jess shiver in his arms, but knew there was more to share.

"Ben's been mishandling his grooms for years, mostly immigrant workers, not to mention selling illegal drugs. He'll be locked away for a long time, if not forever. As for Sir Prickler, I put in a word about that spoiled man to my friends at the FBI. So, I guess the bad guys are all locked away." Sam's jaw flinched. "Do you think maybe we could… have that wedding?" He opened his hand and revealed the gold ring she had returned to him. "And maybe adopt Buddy's kitty since it's been rehabbing at Tunnel Hill?"

Jess's eyes widened.

"And Wyatt, too?" he added.

Jess gasped. "Wyatt? Sam, do you mean for us to adopt Wyatt?"

"That child has had a horrible life. I would love to see him have a chance. Carol said she could make it happen." Sam pressed the ring into her palm and touched her cheek. He raised her head and lowered his lips to encircle hers in a kiss.

Their lips were still lightly touching when she whispered, "That's a huge step. Let's say you and Wyatt move to the main house… and kitty too. We can go from there. I still have that article to finish."

"It's a start." Sam kissed her. "Write away."

They both looked on to the arena. Jess's head rested on her chin against the top of the gate. "$100,000. Oh well." Jess slumped.

"If they do win, the purse will be split multiple ways. I was going to suggest that Carol at the children's home maybe needs it more."

Jess encircled his neck with her arms. Behind him she spotted Jax who appeared very content because twenty-five head of horses were residing in the underground stalls about to find new homes. The Aussie winked those chocolate eyes that melted her heart every time.

Not much later, Penny and Belle entered the ring to the encouragement of a roaring crowd. Then even a pin could be heard dropping in the fluffy dirt. The two aimed dead center toward the first jump.

Jess heard Anna as she climbed the fence next to Jax, coaching, "Follow her heart, Penny. Follow her heart!"

Acknowledgments

Please understand that this novel is a work of fiction. In other words, though Lancaster County, Harrisburg, and the Expo Center do exist, I made up all of the events and people in this book. Now on to the thank yous!

With heartfelt thanks to my daughter J.J. and my husband Scott who have been inspirations and tolerated my constant working and dreaming.

Demi Stevens for her roadmap and belief in me.

Best-selling author Debbie Herbert for taking the time to mentor me during her busy career at the onset of this unfolding trilogy.

My dear friends Rhonda Rodriguez and Teresa Shaub who pushed me on the journey from the beginning, and to Darlene Smith, grammar guru-in-chief.

An enormous thank you to Kayla L. Chandler for her creative and artistic abilities. Her talents are highly recommended for cards, posters, and advertising at alyakdesigns@gmail.com.

My treasured equestrian friends at Evergreen Farms, Terry and Peg Helder, who shared their talents and expertise, in addition to many a meal over the Lazy Susan on their kitchen table.

My family, salon friends, and equestrian lovers who continue to cheer me on, including JoAnne and Eileen, my beta readers, and Karen Frank for her investigative wisdom.

To Liz Shorb for show jumping knowledge, and Diane Naylor for her constant support, especially teaching me a new word… *abattoir*.

And enormous thanks to renowned horseman Guy McLean, his wife Emily, and his magnificent team, who spurred this trilogy.

LEAVE A REVIEW

Loved *Spurred to Jump?* Please consider leaving a review on Amazon, Goodreads, or other book recommendation sites!

This is one of the best ways you can help other readers find great books, so authors can continue to write more stories you want to read.

Discover more articles and fiction by Alicia, and be the first to learn about new releases by subscribing to the blog:

aliciastephensmartin.wordpress.com

About the Author

Alicia Stephens Martin has been a teacher and the owner of Rubee Z Salon in southcentral Pennsylvania where she lives with her husband. Her daughter, a First Lieutenant in the United States Army, was an avid equestrian, holding many awards.

Alicia holds a Bachelor's degree in Creative Writing and has published a romantic suspense, *Spurred to Justice* (first in this series), *Private Mom*, a romantic comedy, and an interactive children's workbook for the salon called *Let's Go to the Hairstylist.*

Her short fiction and non-fiction stories have been published in *Salon Ovation Magazine* and *PBA Progress*, and her non-fiction piece "Healing in a Pocket" won the prestigious Bob Hoffman writing award. Her articles have also been published in *PA Equestrian*, *East Coast Equestrian*, and *From Whispers to Roars*. At present, she is working on the next novel in this series—*Spurred to Jealousy*—with hopes of publication in Fall 2022.

Connect with the Author

 Alicia.StephensMartin

 ASMartin_Author

ALSO BY ALICIA STEPHENS MARTIN

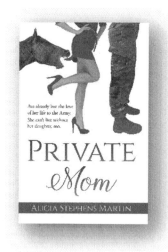

Made in the USA
Monee, IL
17 February 2022

91324637R00153